CONTENTS

ACKNOWLEDGEMENTS

My thanks to earlier editors of annotated *Hound*s, especially W. S. Baring-Gould and W. W. Robson; to Anthony Howlett's *Some Observations on the Dartmoor of Sherlock Holmes* and Philip Weller's *The Dartmoor Locations of the Hound of the Baskervilles*; to Derek Towers who directed my BBC television documentary on *The Hound* (1996), the script of which was the starting point for my Introduction; to those who wrote – in print and in person – after its transmission; and my very special thanks to Richard Lancelyn Green, who generously provided important background materials and commented on my final draft.

THE HOUND OF THE BASKERVILLES

SIR ARTHUR CONAN DOYLE was born in Edinburgh in 1859 and died in 1930. Into these years he crowded a variety of activity and creative work that earned him an international reputation and inspired the French to give him the epithet of 'the good giant'. He was educated at Stonyhurst and later studied medicine at Edinburgh University, where he became the surgeon's clerk to Professor Joseph Bell whose diagnostic methods provided the model for the science of deduction perfected by Sherlock Holmes.

He set up as a doctor at Southsea and it was while waiting for patients that he began to write. His growing success as an author enabled him to give up his practice and to turn his attention to other subjects. He was a passionate advocate of many causes, ranging from divorce law reform and a Channel tunnel to the issuing of steel helmets to soldiers and inflatable life jackets to sailors. He also campaigned to prove the innocence of individuals, and was instrumental in the introduction of the Court of Criminal Appeal. He was a volunteer physician in the Boer War and later in life became a convert to spiritualism.

As well as his Sherlock Holmes stories, Conan Doyle wrote a number of other works, including historical romances, such as *The Exploits of Brigadier Gerard* (1896) and *Rodney Stone* (1896). In the science fiction tale *The Lost World* (1912), he created another famous character, Professor Challenger, who appears in several later stories.

Sherlock Holmes first appeared in *A Study in Scarlet* in 1887. The Holmes stories soon attracted such a following that Conan Doyle felt the character overshadowed his other work. In 'The Final Problem' (1893) Conan Doyle killed him off, but was obliged by public demand to restore the detective to life. Despite his ambivalence towards Holmes, he remains the character for which Conan Doyle is best known.

CHRISTOPHER FRAYLING is Rector of London's Royal College of Art and Professor of Cultural History there. He is well known as a historian, a critic and an award-winning broadcaster on radio and television. He has published many books and articles on aspects of cultural history, including *Spaghetti Westerns* (1980), *Vampyres: Lord Byron to Count Dracula* (1991), *The Face of Tutankhamun* (1982), *Nightmare: The Birth of Horror* (1996) and *Sergio Leone: Something To Do with Death* (2000). He has contributed articles on film, popular culture and the visual arts to many newspapers and magazines, including the *New Statesman*, *Modern Painters*, *Sight & Sound*, *Time Out*, *Granta* and the *Burlington Magazine*. He is chairman of the Design Council and of the Royal Mint Advisory Committee, and the longest-serving Trustee of the Victoria and Albert Museum. He was knighted for services to art and design education in 2001 and was awarded the Royal Society of Arts' Bicentennial Medal the following year.

ARTHUR CONAN DOYLE

The Hound of the Baskervilles

Another Adventure of Sherlock Holmes

Edited with an Introduction and Notes by
CHRISTOPHER FRAYLING

PENGUIN BOOKS

PENGUIN BOOKS

Published by the Penguin Group
Penguin Books Ltd, 80 Strand, London WC2R ORL, England
Penguin Putnam Inc., 375 Hudson Street, New York, New York 10014, USA
Penguin Books Australia Ltd, 250 Camberwell Road, Camberwell, Victoria 3124, Australia
Penguin Books Canada Ltd, 10 Alcorn Avenue, Toronto, Ontario, Canada M4V 3B2
Penguin Books India (P) Ltd, 11 Community Centre, Panchsheel Park, New Delhi – 110 017, India
Penguin Books (NZ) Ltd, Cnr Rosedale and Airborne Roads, Albany, Auckland, New Zealand
Penguin Books (South Africa) (Pty) Ltd, 24 Sturdee Avenue, Rosebank 2196, South Africa

Penguin Books Ltd, Registered Offices: 80 Strand, London WC2R ORL, England

www.penguin.com

The Hound of the Baskervilles first published 1902
Published in Penguin Classics 2001
Reprinted 2003

13

Set in 10/12.5 pt Monotype Baskerville
Typeset by Rowland Phototypesetting Ltd, Bury St Edmunds, Suffolk
Printed in Great Britain by Clays Ltd, St Ives plc

INTRODUCTION

I have always associated *The Hound of the Baskervilles* in my mind's eye with Sir Edwin Landseer's painting *Dignity and Impudence* (1839), which was on exhibition in the National Gallery during Conan Doyle's lifetime and which now hangs – periodically – in the Tate Britain at Millbank. The painting shows a large, supercilious-looking, unperturbed bloodhound on the left of the picture, next to a tiny, eager-looking, white Scottish terrier who looks as though he is about to start barking at any moment, both framed by the entrance to a wooden kennel in a parody of seventeenth-century Dutch domestic paintings. Landseer deliberately gave the two dogs almost human qualities. An engraving of Landseer's most popular work was on the library wall of the small prep school in Sussex where I first read *The Hound* (in a bound run of the *Strand* magazine) at the age of ten. Although Landseer's bloodhound was actually called Grafton and the terrier Scratch – the dogs belonged to the man who commissioned the picture – in my imagination they were for ever Sherlock Holmes and Dr Watson, precursors in canine form of the immortal partnership. They were also more than a little grotesque and scary.

In the very first Holmes book, *A Study in Scarlet* (1887), Dr Watson watches the detective examining the scene of the crime and is 'irresistibly reminded of a pure-blooded, well-trained foxhound, as it dashes backward and forward through the covert, whining in its eagerness, until it comes across the lost scent'. Holmes himself later adds, 'I am one of the hounds and not the wolf.' Throughout the subsequent Sherlock Holmes stories, Watson likes to compare Holmes on a case with a hunting dog on the scent: the detective combines the excited single-mindedness of a hound, with periods back home of depresssed or lethargic dreaminess. Watson's own well-intentioned but usually misguided impetuousness is very like Scratch's. He is forever bounding up to Holmes, expecting a pat on the head – only to be disappointed. History has unfortunately not recorded Conan Doyle's verdict on *Dignity and Impudence*. But he liked well-crafted paintings, gundogs and Queen Victoria, so Landseer might well have appealed to his taste. Although he called the first Holmes book *A Study in Scarlet* – 'a little art jargon', as he put it, and a reference to the arty side of the detective's personality, as well as to the studies or nocturnes of Whistler which had been the subject of a much-publicized lawsuit – Conan Doyle's attitude to modern art was dismissive as his private journal was later to reveal: 'A wave of [artistic] insanity is breaking out in various forms in various places. If it stops where it is, it will only be a curious phenomenon . . . One should put one's shoulder to the door and keep out the insanity all one can.'

The 'curious phenomenon' was to become much more than that, and Landseer's brand of anthropomorphism is very out of fashion now, except in the worlds of Walt Disney, George Lucas and some children's book illustrators. But in *The Hound of the Baskervilles*, the dog is without doubt the star of the show. The sleuth-hound on his trail is absent from six out of the fifteen chapters – one reason why the book works so well as a unified novel, rather than as a short story with flashbacks – but the hound is always there, a symbol of the mystery which unleashes the plot, the dark secrets of the moor, and of the ancestral curse which must be explained away. One over-zealous critic of the 1930s referred to the beast as 'the proletariat baying at the gates of the bourgeoisie',[1] which is pushing it. A Freudian would doubtless say it was the Id. At the end of Paul Morrissey's trashy, chaotic film version starring Peter Cook and Dudley Moore (1977) – intended as a homage by the Warhol Factory to both Hammer and *Carry On* films – the friendly Irish wolfhound with whom Sir Henry has fallen in love runs away from Baskerville Hall with a garish family oil painting in a gilt frame round its neck: And so, says the caption, 'The Dog Stole the Picture'. The painting is a portrait of the hound, made in Van Gogh style by the late Sir Charles. In Billy Wilder's film, *The Private*

Life of Sherlock Holmes (1970), the creature's reputation has reached even Russia. The Director General of the Imperial Russian Ballet informs Holmes at one point that 'Madame [Petrova, the great ballerina] is a great admirer of yours. She has read every story. Her favourite is *Big Dog from Baskerville*'; to which the detective replies, 'I'm afraid it loses something in translation.'

In the mid-1990s, I made a BBC television documentary which – as well as examining the genesis of *The Hound of the Baskervilles* in the imagination of Conan Doyle – explored the various black dog legends which have been claimed as the folkloric origin of the curse. In one of the sequences set in Conan Doyle's Dartmoor hotel room, we had an engraving of *Dignity and Impudence* hanging in the background. Not as an example of Victorian kitsch – the way Alfred Hitchcock used the same engraving at the melodramatic climax of *Marnie* (1964) – but as a reminder that the folklore shouldn't be taken too seriously. Conan Doyle's friend, the crime writer Max Pemberton, reckoned that the inspiration for the hound came from Black Shuck or Old Shuck of Norfolk – a particularly nasty specimen (*shuck* or *scucca* meaning 'the demon' in Anglo-Saxon) which was reputed to be the size of a calf and was easily recognizable by his saucer-sized eyes weeping green or red fire. Desperate mothers in the neighbourhood would use the phrase 'Black Shuck will get you' to control their unruly children. Herbert Greenhough Smith, the editor of the *Strand* magazine, by contrast, preferred 'the tradition of the fiery hound in a Welsh guide-book' – probably the phantom boar-hound of Hergest Ridge on the Welsh borders, a creature which put in an appearance, complete with clanking chains, whenever there was a death in the local Baskerville-Vaughan family. Others, particularly since the 1930s, have opted for a whole pack of spectral whisht hounds (whisht or wush meaning 'sad and uncanny' in local dialect), which hunted the evil seventeenth-century squire Richard Cabell or Capel to his doom at Buckfastleigh on the edge of Dartmoor, and which made a comeback every Mid-summer's Eve.

The folklore of the British Isles is, in fact, littered with legends of phantom dogs (known as 'black dogs' by professional folklorists, whatever colour they happen to be), and there are still Black Dog lanes and Black Dog inns in villages all over the map. Most of these dogs are fairly benign creatures which warn of impending disaster or haunt a location where something nasty happened to their owner or their owner's family. Many seem to have been supporters of the Stuarts, and especially King Charles I. One of them was a ghostly bloodhound from Moretonhampstead that snuffled about in a ditch opposite a pub, hunting for spilt beer. Theo Brown,[2] a distinguished West Country folklorist affiliated to the University of Exeter who spent much of her adult life making a vast collection of black dog stories, reckoned that: 'The Hound of the Baskervilles does not correspond with any of the black dogs known so far, and it is probably a hotch-potch of several', a reworking of the usual commemorative or haunting function into something considerably more vicious.

The Holmes stories are full of dogs: dogs that bark in the night-time and dogs that don't. The detective – it is revealed in 'The *Gloria Scott*' – was bitten by one when he was at university, a bull terrier, and it took him a full ten days to recover. In *The Sign of the Four*, Holmes says of the half-spaniel, half-lurcher Toby, 'I would rather have [his] help than that of the whole detective force of London.' Which wasn't saying much, it has to be noted, but Toby *was* a remarkable follower of scents. No other dog in the stories, though, has the charisma and the sheer nastiness of the hound of the Baskervilles. This has created problems, well known in the business, for the production designers of film versions of the book. *The Hound of the Baskervilles* is the most filmed, because the best loved, the most popular and the most horrific, of all the Sherlock Holmes stories and in the past the dilemma of how to present the hound itself has been solved in many different ways. The dilemma is not only how to find a dog which can do what the director wants, it is also to live up to the thrilling curtain-line of Ch. 2: 'Mr Holmes, they were the footprints of a gigantic hound!' Also, how to reduce a powerful metaphor to the level of the literal which film demands. Solutions have included average-sized dogs with big masks on their heads for close-ups; large dogs with enhanced teeth; children dressed up as Holmes and Sir Henry confronting apparently gigantic creatures on pint-sized sets (this one was seriously contemplated by Hammer Films in 1959); animated silhouettes; flames scratched on the negative, frame by frame and, latterly, dogs tinted by computer in post-production with luminous phosphorescent haloes. Even before the first major film version, made in Germany as *Der Hund von Baskerville* in 1914, the hound was causing havoc. Impresario Ferdinand Bonn presented his very successful adaptation at the Berliner Theater in 1907, and recalled:

It so happened that I had a big, black dog that my wife was very attached to . . . when Argyll [the villain, who in this version wants to get hold of Bonnie Prince Charlie's treasure, locked up at Schloss Baskerville in the Scottish Highlands] disappears into the cave, the great black Hound springs over the stage in savage leaps, hunting him. The savage leaps were induced by a piece of wurst that my wife, standing in the wings, held up aloft tantalisingly. At first we put on the Hound a false head with electric lamps, but it would have been loudly ridiculed; a little better was a muzzle with electric lamps . . . The howling presented just as great difficulties. After trying with phonographs, automobile horns, steam whistles and so on, we found the simplest and best way. A man howled through a gramophone horn, at a suitable distance.[3]

For some reason, *Der Hund* – with its supernatural atmosphere which turns out to be all too natural – proved especially popular in Germany. In the silent era, the number of adaptations reached *Der Hund von Baskerville VI* and a copy of the 1937 sound version was discovered at the end of the Second World War in Hitler's private film library at Berchtesgaden. The dictator personally preferred Alsatians to hounds. Many of the sequels dispensed with the dog altogether. In one of the very first Holmes adaptations, released in Denmark in August 1909 as *The Grey Dame/Den Graa Dame*, the hound became a spectral lady.

But no film version, however elaborate the special effects, has managed to match Watson's thrilling description in Ch. 14 of the novel:

A hound it was, an enormous coal-black hound, but not such a hound as mortal eyes have ever seen. Fire burst from its open mouth, its eyes glowed with a smouldering glare, its muzzle and hackles and dewlap were outlined in flickering flame. Never in the delirious dream of a disordered brain could anything more savage, more appalling, more hellish, be conceived than that dark form and savage face which broke upon us out of the wall of fog.

The Hound of the Baskervilles works best on the printed page. When it was first published in the *Strand* magazine of August 1901, the first instalment was by far the most eagerly anticipated of all Conan Doyle's writings. The *Strand*, for the one and only time in its history, went into seven printings and there were queues around the block outside its offices. The magazine's circulation rose to an estimated 300,000 (its average was 180,000). Conan Doyle had predicted that his new story would in all probability 'attract a great deal of attention', but he was being uncharacteristically cautious. He had with a sense of relief killed off his detective in the Reichenbach Falls with 'The Final Problem' nearly eight years before, because Holmes 'takes my mind from better things'. Like his friend Arthur Sullivan, he had been convinced that the work he was best at, the work which had made his creation a household name, was in some sense unworthy of an eminent Victorian. And now he was rid of it. When Conan Doyle finally agreed to write a Preface to the collected Holmes stories (he had refused several times), he was to begin it with the words 'so elementary a form of fiction as the detective story hardly deserves the dignity of a Preface'. Arthur Sullivan broke up his Savoy partnership with W. S. Gilbert, and went on to write ponderous and derivative sacred music. Simultaneously, Conan Doyle sent Sherlock Holmes into 'that dreadful cauldron of swishing water and seething foam', to give himself more time to devote to the historical novels which he regarded as literature proper: opinions differ as to the wisdom of these career moves.

There had been a few signs, in the intervening years, that he might be thinking about relenting. In summer 1896, he wrote a short Sherlock Holmes parody for an Edinburgh student magazine. A year later, he started preparing a play but soon abandoned it because, 'I have grave doubts about Holmes on the stage at all – it's drawing attention to my weaker work which has unduly obscured my better.' By July 1898, however, he had agreed to allow the American actor-manager William Gillette to make his own stage adaptation provided there was to be no 'love business' in the piece. The play *Sherlock Holmes*, presented as the work of Conan Doyle and Gillette, was loosely based on the first and last short stories ('A Scandal in Bohemia' for the 'love business', which *was* eventually allowed in, and 'The Final Problem' for Moriarty and his gang). It ran successfully in New York at the Garrick Theater from November 1899 until June 1900 and was about to open at the Lyceum Theatre in London at precisely the same time (9 September 1901) as *The Hound* first appeared. The play also introduced the catch-phrase 'elementary, my dear fellow' into the English vernacular. But the play was based on back-numbers.

On 15 December 1900, the magazine *Tit-Bits* printed Conan Doyle's admission that from the day he completed 'The Final Problem' 'to this I have never for an instant regretted the course I took in killing Sherlock. That does not say, however, that because he is dead I should not write about him again if I wanted to, for there is no limit to the number of papers he left behind . . .' The seeds of the idea for a new Sherlock Holmes novel, albeit one which was indeed supposed to predate the Reichenbach Falls, were sown on Sunday, 28 April 1901 – not in March 1901, as has been thought up to now – when Conan Doyle was enjoying a brief but much-needed golfing holiday with his young journalist friend Bertram Fletcher Robinson (1872–1907) at the Royal Links Hotel in Cromer, an ace clifftop hotel on the north coast of Norfolk with eighty rooms and a golf course attached. He had stayed there before, with his wife and son, in September 1897. Conan Doyle was feeling, as he'd confided to his mother the previous month, 'the strain of a hard year's work last year, and also my soul is naturally and inevitably rather wrenched in two all the time'.

He had been asked to join Queen Victoria's funeral procession at the beginning of February, and the Queen's death gave him melancholy thoughts about the end of an era: 'And England – how stands England?' On 2 October 1900, he had unsuccessfully stood in the so-called 'khaki' General Election as Liberal Unionist candidate for Edinburgh Central: his defeat after an exhausting round of speeches and personal appearances, following a smear campaign which involved putting up posters in Protestant areas accusing him (in his own words) of being 'a Papist conspirator, a Jesuit emissary, and a subverter of the Protestant faith', had convinced him that electioneering was like 'a mud bath'. Conan Doyle had, in fact, been baptized a Catholic and educated by the Jesuits, but had since rejected the family faith. His domestic life was also under considerable strain:

his wife, Louise Hawkins, had for some time been bedridden with tuberculosis of the lungs, and at the same time it was proving more and more challenging for Conan Doyle to maintain a 'chivalrous' and Platonic attitude towards Jean Leckie, the woman he loved. That was why his soul was 'rather wrenched in two'.

He was suffering from insomnia, and from the long-term effects of a fever he had brought back with him from the Boer War. He had, in fact, met Fletcher Robinson – a well-connected war correspondent sent out by the newly founded *Daily Express*, who was later to become the paper's editor – aboard the SS *Briton* in July 1900 when both were returning from Cape Town. Conan Doyle had tried hard to enlist in the British army to fight the Boers, but had been turned down (he was forty, with no army record) and instead had worked as a voluntary medical officer at John Langman's Field Hospital in Bloemfontein, capital of the Orange Free State, for four months – during which time there had been a devastating epidemic of enteric fever. What he had felt, he'd written to his mother before leaving, 'is that perhaps I have the strongest influence over young men, especially young athletic sporting men, of any one in England (bar Kipling). That being so it is really important that I should give them a lead.' Apart from the fever, other aspects of the war were still preying on his mind in spring 1901. He had written and spoken publicly about military reform. He supported the idea of Civilian Rifle Clubs and formed his own, had strong views on the reasons for Britain's intervention and even stronger ones on the behaviour in the field of ordinary British soldiers – subjects which continued to be controversial among investigative journalists such as W. T. Stead, and about which Conan Doyle was soon to write *The War in South Africa, Its Cause and Conduct*, forcefully putting the British case (including the case for Kitchener's invention: the concentration camp). He was at that time a novelist to whom the government of the day was always prepared to listen.

On the afternoon of Sunday, 28 April (the date is confirmed by Conan Doyle's account book) when the breeze from the North Sea was blowing too strongly for them to play a round of clifftop golf, Conan Doyle and Fletcher Robinson passed the time indoors at the Royal Links Hotel. In the course of a long conversation, Robinson –

who seems from the printed evidence to have been much better at telling tales than putting them down on paper, whatever his talents as a journalist – mentioned the legend of a ferocious black dog which haunted the countryside. This was perhaps the local Black Shuck, or perhaps a folk tale gleaned from a Welsh guidebook, or perhaps a version from around Robinson's family home on the edge of Dartmoor. According to an article written by J. E. Hodder Williams for *The Bookman* exactly a year later: 'Robinson is a Devonshire man, and he mentioned in conversation some old country legend which set Doyle's imagination on fire. The two men began building up a chain of events, and in a very few hours the plot of a sensational story was conceived . . .'

Conan Doyle wrote in the heat of the moment to his mother Mary, from the hotel:

A line to you, dear old Mammie, to say that I have had much good out of my 2 days here, where I have slept soundly at last. All goes well in every way. On Tuesday I give a dinner at the Athenaeum Club [which he did, on Tuesday 30th: one of the guests was Winston Churchill – another confirmation of the April date] . . . Fletcher Robinson came here with me and we are going to do a small book together The Hound of the Baskervilles – a real creeper.

Also from the Royal Links, he gave advance notice to Greenhough Smith, the *Strand*'s editor:

I have the idea of a real creeper for the 'Strand'. It would run, I think, to not less than 40,000 words. It is just the sort of thing that would suit you, full of surprises, and breaking naturally into good lengths for serial purposes. It would be called 'The Hound of the Baskervilles'. There is one stipulation. I must do it with my friend Fletcher Robinson and his name must appear with mine. I hope that does not strike you as a serious bar. I can answer for the yarn being all in my own style without dilution, since your readers like that. But he gave me the central idea and the local colour and so I feel his name must appear. I shall want my usual £50 per thousand for all rights if you do business. Let me know at the Reform Club . . . Let me have [the illustrator Sidney] Paget if you take it.

One reason Conan Doyle was instantly fired up by this 'old country legend' was – according to Max Pemberton, who knew him well – that 'it was ever the bizarre and the daring that drew [him] as a filing is drawn to its magnet',[4] an aspect of his personality which had been rather sidelined by his public association with the arch-rationalist Sherlock Holmes and which maybe also explained the long flirtation with spiritualism which Dr Doyle had begun in earnest in the late 1880s. Holmes was indeed an arch-rationalist on the surface, but he also depended on what he variously called 'intuition', 'speculation' and 'imagination' to reach his conclusions, which involved a significant element of guesswork. He, too, was drawn towards unusual details: in the last chapter of *The Hound*, Holmes observes that 'the more *outré* and grotesque an incident is the more carefully it deserves to be examined . . .' But it appears that from the very beginning of Conan Doyle's interest in the legend there was no question of this 'real creeper' being an out-and-out horror story with a supernatural ending. This approach had, in fact, already been tried with at least two stories: Theo Gift's 'Dog or Demon?' (1889) and Catherine Crowe's 'Dutch Officer's Story' (1859) – the latter based on a folk legend about a phantom hound guarding Peel Castle on the Isle of Man. The 'chain of events' in the new version would, in the finale, prove the phantom to have been flesh and blood, an approach which had already been tested by Conan Doyle in his short story 'The King of the Foxes', first published in *The Windsor* magazine in July 1898 and collected in book form two years later. This was the tale of a legendary spectral fox which turns out to be a grey Siberian wolf 'of the variety known as Lupus Giganticus' on the run from a travelling menagerie, but not before causing havoc with the Anscombe Hunt. The narrator is instantly cured of alcoholism by the experience of meeting this unlikely hunt saboteur:

. . . a creature the size of a donkey jumped on to its feet, a huge grey head, with monstrous glistening fangs, and tapering fox jaws, shot out from among the branches, and the hound was thrown several feet in the air, and fell howling among the cover. Then there was a clashing snap like a rat-trap closing and the howls sharpened into a scream . . .

Later in 1898, Conan Doyle had recycled the idea for the *Strand* in another short story, 'The Brazilian Cat': in this version, the 'treacherous and bloodthirsty' creature called Tommy is part of a murder plot. The idea of a story that seems supernatural, but on closer inspection isn't, appealed to him as a thinker and a writer.

Conan Doyle and Fletcher Robinson may also have had in mind a story called 'Followed' from an even more recent issue of the *Strand* magazine (December 1900). It was by the prolific Irish writer Mrs L. T. Meade, assisted on medical details (as she often was) by Dr Robert Eustace, and its setting was a crumbling manor house called Longmore on Salisbury Plain, complete with sinister servant, ancestral curse and a devilish plot to disinherit a young girl. The story hinged on a monstrous black beast – which again *seems* supernatural – in this case a venomous Tasmanian snake by the name of Darkey (*Pseudechis porphyriacus*), whose bite causes certain death in six minutes. The climax of 'Followed' involves the snake chasing the heroine – young English rose Flower Dalrymple – across the Plain to the slaughter stone of Stonehenge, because the creature has been given one of her boots covered in snake-attracting powder: '. . . whatever it was which was now approaching me, it was a reality, no dream. It was making straight in my direction. The next instant every fibre in my body was tingling with terror, for gliding towards me, in great curves, with head raised, was an enormous black snake!' Conan Doyle seems to have been particularly partial at this time to stories about monstrous beasts giving nightmares to the aristocracy of deep England – biology run amok – and his work was often stimulated by recent articles and events, as well as by plot suggestions and anecdotes from friends and relations.

Neither Fletcher Robinson nor Conan Doyle thought of *The Hound of the Baskervilles* as a Sherlock Holmes novel, at this early stage. But by 25 May, a month after the Cromer holiday, *Tit-Bits* – a sister publication to the *Strand* – was confidently announcing that 'presently [Mr Conan Doyle] will give us an important story to appear in "The Strand", in which the great Sherlock Holmes is the principal character . . . It will be published as a serial of from 30,000 to 50,000 words, and the plot is one of the most interesting and striking that have [sic] ever been put before us.' It must have been earlier in the same month that Conan Doyle wrote again to Greenhough Smith:

The price I quoted [in the Royal Links letter] has for years been my serial price not only with you but with other journals. Now it is evident that this is a very special occasion since as far as I can judge the revival of Holmes would attract a great deal of attention. If put up to open competition I could get very particular terms for this story. Suppose I gave the directors the alternative that it should be without Holmes at my old figure or with Holmes at £100 per thou. which would they choose? . . . Holmes is at a premium in America just now.

The directors of the *Strand*, sensible fellows, did not hesitate. They agreed to the upper figure, for English and American rights, which seemed cheap at the price for the resurrection of Sherlock Holmes – a resurrection in which the '£100 per thou.' had undoubtedly played a part. Some time between the end of April and the end of May 1901, Conan Doyle had decided to make this one of the papers his consulting detective had left behind or rather, as the novel's subtitle was to put it, *Another Adventure of Sherlock Holmes*. The arrival of the great detective on the scene, after the 'scheme of events' had already been planned, was to effect the final shape of the novel.

As Hodder Williams continued, in his *Bookman* piece, 'when he came to working out the details [Conan Doyle] found . . . that some masterful central figure was needed, some strong man who would influence the whole course of events, and his natural reflection was "why should I invent such a character when I have him already in the form of Holmes?"' If the 'old country legend' was powerful, the antidote had to be even more powerful. But this did *not* mean that Conan Doyle was about to start writing a new series of short stories for the *Strand*, to follow *The Adventures* and *The Memoirs*.

Whether or not the decision had yet been made to set the legend on Dartmoor, Conan Doyle arranged to go on a brief walking tour of the moor at the end of May. He had set one of his earlier Holmes short stories there: 'Silver Blaze', first published in the *Strand* in 1892, the one with the famous line about the silent dog in the night-time: 'That was the curious incident.' This had turned out to be an occasion, Conan Doyle subsequently admitted in his autobiography, when 'I have got upon dangerous ground where I have taken risks through my own want of knowledge of the correct atmosphere': the story had a horse-racing theme, and a correspondent for the *Sporting and Dramatic News* who went by the pseudonym of 'Rapier' immediately pointed out that the description of the race itself had been wrong in several particulars, and further that if owners and trainers behaved as he described, half of them would be sent to jail while 'the other half [would be] warned off the turf forever'. Conan Doyle replied publicly to these good-natured and justified criticisms: 'I have never been nervous about details, and one must be masterful sometimes.' Never let accuracy of detail get in the way of a dramatic story. Interestingly, the Sherlock Holmes stories set 'upon dangerous ground' outside the detective's home parish of London – the ones where the author ran the most risks about 'details' – were sometimes based on original ideas suggested by someone else: 'The Copper Beeches', set in the Hampshire countryside, was suggested by his mother; *The Hound of the Baskervilles* by Fletcher Robinson. Holmes himself professed to feel 'in exile' whenever he left the metropolis, and was famously convinced (in 'The Copper Beeches') that 'the lowest and vilest alleys in London do not present a more dreadful record of sin than does the smiling and beautiful countryside [because] the pressure of public opinion can do in the town what the law cannot accomplish'.

Conan Doyle certainly wrote fast. His second wife Jean was later to recall, 'I have known him write a Sherlock Holmes story in a room full of people talking. He would write in a train or anywhere . . .'[5] The manuscript of *The Hound of the Baskervilles* was dispersed in 1902, when S. S. McClure (who had purchased the rights to the book and the second serial rights) dispatched it – as individual pages in frames – to bookstores across the United States, to publicize the title in window displays. The pages were accompanied by a slip bearing the name of 'McClure, Phillips'. Of the pages which somehow survived this process (which itself gives some idea of how casual Conan Doyle was about the business of drafting), one complete chapter, 'The Man on the Tor', is now in New York Public Library, while, of the fifteen other single known pages from a variety of chapters, five are in universities and the remainder in private hands. Apart from small drafting details, they reveal two things: that Conan Doyle wrote decisively and with a minimum of revision in his confident, clear handwriting, and that the surviving pages of manuscript were entirely written by him – even part of 'The Curse of the Baskervilles' from Ch. 2. It is *possible* that Conan Doyle allowed his manuscript to be dispersed in this unusual way because some of the undistributed pages were in Fletcher Robinson's hand. But it is much more likely that by the time Conan Doyle started writing, after the Cromer weekend, the yarn was to be all his own 'in my own style without dilution'. And as he was later to confess to his editor at the *Strand*, 'a story always comes to me as an organic thing and I never recast it without the Life going out of it'. In the case of *The Hound*, this meant that one or two drafting errors found their way into the *Strand* version.

When Conan Doyle reached Dartmoor in late May, as we shall see, he had already written nearly half the novel – that is, 25,000 words or thereabouts. During the same month, he played cricket at Lord's for three days on the same side as W.G. Grace and had dinner at the House of Commons on 16 May as a guest of Winston Churchill, where they discussed their South African experiences. It is likely that at least some of these experiences found their way into the novel he was drafting in the daytime. Churchill was about to take up the case of one Albert Cartwright, editor of the *South African News*, who was sentenced on 2 May to a year's imprisonment for 'criminal and seditious libel' against Lord Kitchener, an alleged libel which had appeared in the London *Times* four months earlier. Liberal journalists and Tory backbenchers, Churchill included, were outraged by this verdict, and the case may well have been transformed into the subplot about the bombastic, red-faced, litigious Mr Frankland of Lafter Hall in *The Hound* ('Cartwright' became a 'little chap at the Express office', who is a messenger boy in London and on Dartmoor). Second Lieutenant Thomas Frankland of the Royal Dublin Fusiliers had been closely involved in one of Winston Churchill's more famous adventures of the South African War – a dramatic escape from Boer ambush and a derailed train – which had been described in gung-ho style by Churchill in *London to Ladysmith via Pretoria*, published in 1900, with the train on the cover. Conan Doyle himself had had 'a curious adventure' on 7 May 1900, when riding with John Langman across open country the day after a skirmish with some Boer snipers:

. . . a mounted Kaffir came across us, and told us that a wounded Englishman had been deserted or overlooked, and was out some two or three miles to the west on the veldt. At last, in the middle of a large clear space, we came across him, but he was dead. He was shot in the stomach and through one arm, and had apparently bled to death.

The body on the veldt was a recent memory in Conan Doyle's mind: the body on the moor was what he was now writing about. He certainly seems to have known more about the veldt than he did about the moor. Despite what he put down on paper at this time, wild orchids do not flower on Dartmoor or anywhere else in mid-October, any more than bitterns, even then almost extinct, mate in the autumn; the bogs on the moor were nothing like the quaking slime of Grimpen Mire; Dr Watson's and Stapleton's descriptions of this vast, barren and mysterious place – much vaster than the actual thing – could fit almost any Gothic wasteland. Almost. The novel may also reveal something about Conan Doyle's deep-seated sense of being 'rather wrenched in two' at this time. There is an uncharacteristic, almost gloating, emphasis on brutality to women throughout *The Hound*: Hugo Baskerville's 'wild, profane, and godless' cruelty to the yeoman's daughter in the manuscript description of the curse; Mrs Laura Lyons's life of 'incessant persecution from a husband whom I abhor' and habit of putting her trust in men who abuse her; Mrs Barrymore's exploitation by her brother and, above all, Stapleton's sadistic treatment of Beryl, who ends up with 'the clear red weal of a whip-lash across her neck' and 'her arms . . . all mottled with bruises'. These go well beyond Holmes's occasional lapses into misogyny. Did they relate to Conan Doyle's guilt as a 'renegade' Catholic about being tempted to neglect his wife Louise (as some have suggested)? Or to his need publicly to repress his feelings towards his beloved Jean Leckie? Whatever the reasons, the result transformed the legend he was told by Fletcher Robinson from an ancestral warning into something much more destructive, something which did not recur in his literary output.

*

Conan Doyle visited Dartmoor, with Robinson, at the end of May/ beginning of June 1901. They stayed at Rowe's Duchy Hotel, Princetown, just down the road from Dartmoor prison. The hotel building was said to have been constructed by French prisoners-of-war in Napoleonic times (which must have struck a chord with Conan Doyle, whose first Brigadier Gerard stories had been written in 1894– 5); it had been 'patronized by royalty' when the Prince of Wales dined at Rowe's Duchy during a visit to Dartmoor prison.

From there, Conan Doyle wrote a letter on hotel notepaper to his mother. In his authorized biography of 1949, based on privileged access to family archives, John Dickson Carr claims that 'the postmark was April 2nd, 1901' but this must have been based on a misreading. He also claims that Conan Doyle had never been to Dartmoor before, which is unlikely since as a young doctor he had lived in Plymouth. The actual date of the postmark was much more likely to have been Sunday, 2 June:

Dearest of Mams, Here I am in the highest town in England. Robinson and I are exploring the Moor over our Sherlock Holmes book. I think it will work out splendidly – indeed I have already done nearly half of it. Holmes is at his very best, and it is a highly dramatic idea – which I owe to Robinson. We did 14 miles over the Moor and we are now pleasantly weary. It is a great place, very sad and wild, dotted with dwellings of prehistoric man, strange monoliths and huts and graves. In those old days there was evidently a population of very many thousands here and now you may walk all day and never see one human being. Everywhere there are gutted tin mines. Tomorrow [Sunday] we drive 6 miles to Ipplepen where R's father lives. Then on Monday Tuesday Sherborne for cricket, 2 days at Bath, 2 days at Cheltenham. Home on Sunday the 9th. That is my programme. My work will proceed all the better . . .

Conan Doyle did indeed play cricket for the Incogniti (a team which also included his brother-in-law E.W. Hornung, of *Raffles* fame) against Sherborne School on Monday and Tuesday, 3–4 June, then another match for the Incogniti against Lansdown at Coombe Park, Bath, on Wednesday and Thursday, 5–6 June, followed by yet another match against Cheltenham College on Friday and Saturday, 7–8 June. All of which confirm the actual date as being the beginning of June. On the sixth of that month, there was a payment in his bank book, to Fletcher Robinson – one of many, varying in amount, over the next three years – of £3.0.0.

Fletcher Robinson described their stay at the comfortable old-fashioned inn 'near the famous convict prison of Princetown' in more detail, in an article for the *Associated Sunday Magazines* of America– published in November 1905, fourteen months before his untimely death at the age of thirty-five (according to his death certificate, from typhoid fever). The morning after the writers arrived, apparently, four distinguished men marched into the smoking room and chatted about 'the weather, the fishing in the moor streams and other general subjects': their visiting cards revealed them to have been the prison governor, the deputy governor, the chaplain and the doctor, and a pencil note explained they had come 'to call on Mr Sherlock Holmes'. But they had been too reticent to raise the subject.

Fletcher Robinson continued:

One morning [probably Saturday 1 June] I took Doyle to see the mighty bog . . . which figured so prominently in *The Hound*. He was amused at the story I told him of the moor man who on one occasion saw a hat near the edge of the morass and poked at it with a long pole he carried. 'You leave my hat alone!' came a voice from beneath it. 'Whoi! Be there a man under the 'at?' cried the startled rustic. 'Yes, you fool, and a horse under the man!' From the bog, we tramped eastward to the stone fort of Grimspound, which the savages of the Stone Age in Britain . . . raised with enormous labour to act as a haven of refuge from the marauding tribes to the South. The good preservation in which the Grimspound fort still remains is marvellous [it had been partially restored in the early 1890s] . . . Into one of these [stone huts] Doyle and I walked, and sitting down on the stone which probably served the three thousand year old chief as a bed we talked of the races of the past. It was one of the loneliest spots in Great Britain . . . Suddenly we heard a boot strike against a stone without and rose together. It was only a lonely tourist on a walking excursion, but at the sight of our heads suddenly emerging from the hut he let out a yell and bolted . . . as he did not return I have small doubt Mr Doyle and I added yet another proof of the supernatural to tellers of ghost stories concerning Dartmoor.

This must have been the '14 miles over the Moor' mentioned by Conan Doyle in the letter to his mother: from Princetown to Fox Tor Mire (the 'mighty bog' with nearby tin mine which became Grimpen Mire in the novel), eastward to the stone circle of Grimspound (the hiding-place of Sherlock Holmes) and back to the hotel again; on foot it is actually nearer twenty-one miles than fourteen. From Conan Doyle's brief account, it is not clear whether they walked or not: a day-long ride in the Robinsons' coach and pair, plus hiking for the inaccessible parts of the journey would also – presumably – have made him 'pleasantly weary' at the age of forty-two, even if he was a more than competent cricketer in good physical condition. A photograph of Conan Doyle on his visit to the moor has recently surfaced, which shows him standing beside a pony and trap near the Warren House Inn – about seven miles east of Princetown. Whether this was taken on Saturday, 1 June, or during the six-mile drive to Ipplepen the following day, or even on the Friday, is not known.

Fletcher Robinson's yarn about the moor man, the mire and the hat was not, in fact, original to him: it came almost verbatim from *A Book of Dartmoor*, published the previous year, by the Revd Sabine Baring-Gould, Rector of the remote parish of Lewtrenchard, situated some twelve miles northwest of Princetown. Baring-Gould was a prolific writer: his output included hymns such as 'Onward Christian Soldiers', some now unreadable novels, and numerous books of West Country folklore and topography; it was thanks to him that the song 'Widecombe Fair' first surfaced into print, the song which the Devon Regiment sang as it marched against the Boers. It was also thanks to him that werewolves had enjoyed something of a literary revival: Baring-Gould's *The Book of Were-wolves, being an Account of a Terrible Superstition* (1865) covered ancient, medieval and modern manifestations and included in a chapter on folk legends the information that:

In Devonshire they range the moors in the shape of black dogs, and I know a story of two such creatures appearing in an inn and nightly drinking the cider, until the publican shot a silver button over their heads, when they were instantly transformed into two ill-favoured old ladies of his acquaintance. On

Heathfield, near Tavistock, the wild huntsman rides by full moon with his 'wush hounds' . . .

Conan Doyle may well have read *A Book of Dartmoor*, as had Robinson: its descriptions of the 'fog, dense as cotton wool', the quaking bogs and neolithic stone huts, escaped convicts stumbling around the moor and legends dating from the time of the great Rebellion, closely resemble the equivalents in the novel, as does the overall atmosphere of a primeval wilderness, a never-land of mist, legend and antiquity. *A Book of Dartmoor* was a plea for a certain kind of conservation, and a polemic in support of the efforts of the new Dartmoor Preservation Society to control 'wanton trippers', over-zealous restorers, enclosing farmers, tin-miners and the military authorities who were turning the place into a shooting range: 'The Transvaal war has brought home to us the need we have to become expert marksmen . . . nevertheless, one accepts the situation with a sigh.' Baring-Gould's Dartmoor is not a living, working landscape. The shallow mines at Whiteworks, right next to Fox Tor Mire, were fully operative at that time – but you wouldn't know it from his book. He preferred to present a Dartmoor which has been scarcely occupied since neolithic times, and which should always remain 'uncontaminated by the hand of man', just like Conan Doyle's perception of the moor as 'very sad and wild, dotted with . . . strange monoliths and huts and graves'. Both in their different ways were romancers.

The final piece in the jigsaw of *The Hound*'s plot – the facial resemblance between the villain and the portrait of Hugo Baskerville dated 1647, 'an interesting instance of a throw-back', as Holmes puts it – was to be found in another Baring-Gould book, *Old Country Life*, published in 1890, ten years before *A Book of Dartmoor*. This contained a long chapter on 'Family Portraits', about the physical resemblances which can be traced through genuine and complete collections of family portraits: his thesis was that facial characteristics, despite having disappeared in the generations between, might reappear in the current generation of a family. 'Consider,' concluded the Revd Baring-Gould, 'what misery a strain of tainted blood brings into a family – a strain of blood that causes vicious propensities with it . . .' This was a well-tried literary theme in late Victorian times – *Tess of the D'Urbervilles* is a classic example – and in various other stories Sherlock Holmes professed his related belief, again characteristic of his time, in the importance of heredity where persistent criminals were concerned. Moriarty, for one, was supposed to have an inherited criminal strain in his blood. In 'The Empty House', which appeared eighteen months after *The Hound*'s serialization finished, Holmes explained:

There are some trees . . . which grow to a certain height and then suddenly develop some unsightly eccentricity. You will see it often in humans. I have a theory that the individual represents in his development the whole procession of his ancestors, and that such a sudden turn to good or evil stands for some strange influence which came into the life of his pedigree. The person becomes, as it were, the epitome of the history of his own family.

But Conan Doyle may well have found the portrait theme in *Old Country Life* either directly or at Fletcher Robinson's suggestion.

As Conan Doyle briskly drafted the second half of his novel at the beginning of June 1901, he made Dartmoor – a place of mystery rather than industry – the key symbol of *The Hound of the Baskervilles*, to the extent that P. D. James has justly called the resulting work 'this atavistic study of violence and evil in the mists of Dartmoor'. The moor becomes in the process less a map reference than a nightmare which has defeated the successive attempts of human beings – prehistoric people or modern tin-miners – to civilize and tame it. Likewise Baskerville Hall, and all that it represents – an 'old race', a title and a coat of arms, a family home with servants, a go-ahead modernizing young heir who has spent most of his life up to now 'in the States and in Canada' and who can perhaps provide a future for the poor, benighted countryside – must at all costs be saved (as Edgar Allan Poe's House of Usher could not) from sinking into the tarn. And England – how stands England? If contemporary life itself has become, as Dr Watson writes, 'like that great Grimpen Mire, with little green patches everywhere into which one may sink with no guide to point the track', all the more reason to hope against hope that the civilized rationality of the great detective, the secular priest, will be able to bring salvation and stop the rot: a masterful central figure to influence the whole course of events, at the start of a new century. W. H. Auden, in his celebrated essay *The Guilty Vicarage*, argued that *the* classic detective story involved explaining away some ancestral blemish, and re-establishing the fragile values of civilization. P. D. James has added that *The Hound of the Baskervilles* remains one of the finest examples of the form precisely *because* it pits 'the Great Detective, combining as he does a dominant intellect with bizarre personal eccentricity and the heroic virtues of triumphant individualism' against the atavism and threat of the moor. No wonder T. S. Eliot associated Watson's moor with the modern wasteland. In *East Coker* part II (1944) he wrote:

> In the middle, not only in the middle of the way.
> But all the way, in a dark wood, in a bramble,
> On the edge of a grimpen, where there is no secure foothold,
> And menaced by monsters . . .

And in the less well-known 'Lines to Ralph Hodgson, Esquire' (1936):

> With his musical sound
> And his Baskerville Hound
> Which, just at a word from
> his master,
> Will follow you faster and faster,
> And tear you limb from limb.

Later in his life, T. S. Eliot was invited to attend a meeting of Holmes enthusiasts in Chicago but politely declined, saying he would have greatly enjoyed preparing 'a short travelogue with lantern slides on the topography of the Great Grimpen'.[6] He had always wondered, he added, how the hound had been supplied with so much food without arousing the suspicions of the local butchers!

The image of Dartmoor in *The Hound* – 'like some fantastic landscape in a dream', as Dr Watson put it – was so strong that it still colours public perceptions. The current conservation debate between 'the wilderness lobby' and 'the working landscape lobby' is at some level a debate between what Conan Doyle wrote and what he must have seen; between Baring-Gould's ancient traditions and the modern world which discomforted him. Not to mention the recent, much-publicized sightings of a predatory beast – a larger-than-life wild cat – on Bodmin Moor. Since 1901, nature in that part of the country has tended to imitate art.

Probably on Sunday, 2 June, Conan Doyle and Fletcher Robinson were then driven by horse-drawn coach to Park Hill House, Ipplepen, near Newton Abbot, home since 1881 of the Fletcher Robinson family. Conan Doyle may also have visited Park Hill House before checking in to Rowe's Duchy Hotel. The coachman and groom there was young Henry (or Harry) Baskerville, who had been in service to the landowner Joseph Fletcher Robinson, Bertram's father, since the age of fifteen. Bertie had perhaps introduced Conan Doyle to the name of his groom at Cromer – the story was already to be called *The Hound of the Baskervilles* by 28 April – and was to present a copy of the first book edition to Harry with the inscription 'To Harry Baskerville, with apologies for using the name, Fletcher Robinson'. From the early 1950s onwards, and especially at the time when the Hammer Films version was released in 1959, Baskerville was to claim that Conan Doyle spent several days and nights at Park Hill 'writing and talking' with his employer's son, and, further, that Fletcher Robinson actually *wrote* substantial chunks of *The Hound* – notably the early chapters about the family curse. Another reason he used the name, Harry added, was that his ancestors, the Dartmoor Baskervilles, had once owned the two-storied Heatree House near Manaton, which with its long drive and imposing porch was the original of Baskerville Hall in the novel. Whatever the truth of the matter – and the story did improve with the telling, especially when Hammer Films's publicists ran with it – Adrian Conan Doyle, Arthur's third son, thundered back to the film company from Switzerland, 'Fletcher Robinson played no part whatever in the writing of *The Hound*. He refused my father's offer to collaborate and retired at an early stage of the project (*vide* letters, Conan Doyle's biographical archives).' He later added to the *Daily Express*, 'My father never stayed with Robinson. He stayed at the Duchy Hotel, Princetown. He accepted Robinson's offer of a coach and went riding with him on the moors . . .' The original archives are privately held. But the two *published* documents relevant to the case (the letters to Conan Doyle's mother, of 28 April and 2 June if my dating is correct) do not contradict Harry Baskerville's memory that the two men stayed for some time at Ipplepen: the second one even mentions a coach-ride to 'Ipplepen where R's parents live'.

Given the evidence of *The Hound* manuscripts, though, the most likely scenario is that Fletcher Robinson provided the initial idea of the folk legend, the overall plot and much local colour – as both men acknowledged – and some time between 28 April (when Conan Doyle wrote to his editor, 'I must do it with my friend Fletcher Robinson') and the arrival on Dartmoor, Robinson declined the 'offer to collaborate'. For his contribution, he claimed the right to use the by-line 'Joint Author with Sir Arthur Conan Doyle . . .': Conan Doyle made several payments to him (evidenced by his bank books), and one of Robinson's contemporaries (Archibald Marshall) later recalled that the journalist had been paid a quarter of the proceeds; if Robinson *did* have a share of the royalties, they would have been paid to him direct by Newnes. Robinson also claimed that he 'wrote most of the first instalment for the *Strand*', and that '[Doyle] made the journey [to Dartmoor] in my company shortly after I had told him, and he had accepted from me, the plot which eventuated in *The Hound of the Baskervilles*'.[7] Harry Baskerville always felt that he – and his master's son – had been cruelly written out of history. When Harry became a national institution, at the time of the Festival of Britain, he at last had the opportunity to say so. He may have recognized a thinly veiled caricature of Fletcher Robinson in the novel's presentation of Dr James Mortimer. One of the curiosities of Baskerville's story, and indeed of Adrian Conan Doyle's gloss on it, is that Conan Doyle was not the type to collaborate as an author with anyone. Another is that the first instalment of *The Hound* – from the stunning deductions about Dr Mortimer's walking stick in Baker Street, to the cliff-hanging line about 'the footprints of a gigantic hound!' – is a classic example of the author's skills as a storyteller. And yet there is no doubt at all that Fletcher Robinson fired Conan Doyle's imagination; without him, there would have been no *Hound*. Beyond that undisputed fact, there is no evidence that Robinson wrote any of *The Hound* (as Harry Baskerville claimed), or that Conan Doyle plagiarized the story/hired Robinson as a ghost writer (as has more recently been claimed, building on Harry's reminiscences).

Conan Doyle left Dartmoor on Monday, 3 June to play cricket. By a fortnight later, he was returning the proofs of the second instalment 'The Problem'/'Sir Henry Baskerville' to Greenhough Smith – from Morley's Hotel, Trafalgar Square – and complaining that his copy of the preceding instalment had not been returned: the 'matter is complex', he wrote, and it was hard to hold all the threads of the story in his head. So he was still tightening up his draft and making final corrections. 'I have the third finished and can deliver any moment. I am here (and at Lords [where he was batting for the MCC and Ground]) until Wednesday next.' A week later, he again wrote to Greenhough Smith from Morley's Hotel, saying that he hoped 50,000 words was not the upper limit for the serial, and that if a few thousand more were needed, he trusted he would be paid for them: the letter was sent, probably on 24 June, enclosing the fourth and fifth instalments – from 'The Stapletons of Merripit House' to 'The Light upon the Moor', an instalment which consisted of 'one long chapter'. 'I write under some difficulty through not having any of the proofs, so I cannot refer back.' There were, he had heard from his agent, 'several eager US buyers for the serial rights of "The Hound" ' – presumably second serial rights after the US publication of the *Strand*, which belonged to McClure and which he could sell on. A couple of days later, he was proposing a toast at a dinner for John Langman – together with various Boer War veterans – at the Devonshire Club. On 17 July, he wrote from the Esplanade Hotel, Southsea (near where he had set up his first medical practice on his own, nineteen years before) requesting a late change to the end of the first paragraph of Ch. 4: 'I should like to convey that Sir Henry Baskerville wore a "ruddy tinted tweed suit".' The change was duly made. Some of Conan Doyle's physical descriptions of his characters seem not to have been communicated to the *Strand*'s artist, Sidney Paget, who had never illustrated a full-length Sherlock Holmes story before, for the *Strand* illustrations contain numerous inconsistencies: the butler Barrymore appears in the first instalment as a stocky, elderly man with a bushy beard, then in the third as a younger man with a square-cut beard; his wife also changes from a tall, slim woman in the third instalment into a rotund, heavy-featured one in the fourth; Hugo Baskerville is dressed in eighteenth-century costume, rather than the clothes from 'the time of the Great Rebellion' he should have been wearing. These inconsistencies suggest either that Paget had not seen the texts he was illustrating, or that he was drawing characters as he surmised they might look since he had not yet seen the subsequent instalments which contained their descriptions. This is further evidence of the speed with which Conan Doyle wrote, on a project which was first conceived at the end of April and which began publication just over three months later.

The first of nine monthly instalments of *The Hound of the Baskervilles* was published in the *Strand* magazine – much to the relief of Sir George Newnes, who had announced the fact to his shareholders at the recent AGM – in August 1901: the novel's serialization coincided with that of H. G. Wells's *The First Men in the Moon*, in the same issue. *The Hound* bore an unusual note at the foot of the first page of double-column text: 'This story owes its inception to my friend, Mr Fletcher Robinson, who has helped me both in the general plot and in the local details. – A. C. D.' The first English book edition, an instant best-seller for Newnes published in 1902, changed this footnote into an open letter to Robinson – the wording of which was slightly but significantly different in the American edition :

MY DEAR ROBINSON:

It was to your account of a West-Country legend that this tale owes its inception. For this and for your help in the detail all thanks.

Yours most truly, A. CONAN DOYLE

(This dedicatory letter has appeared in most subsequent British editions.)

MY DEAR ROBINSON:

It was your account of a West Country legend which first suggested the idea of this little tale to my mind.

For this, and for the help which you gave me in its evolution, all thanks.

Yours most truly, A. CONAN DOYLE

(This prefatory letter, the manuscript of which is now in New York Public Library – dated 26 January 1902 – was written for the McClure, Phillips edition of 1902, and has appeared in all subsequent American editions. It is not in Conan Doyle's hand, but that of his secretary Charles Terry.)

So, Conan Doyle was a little unsure about how to credit his contribution before Fletcher Robinson's death in January 1907. He wanted to be fair, but he also wanted to be accurate. After Robinson's death, he seemed to be much clearer in his mind. His Preface of June 1929 to *The Complete Sherlock Holmes Long Stories* states that: '[*The Hound of the Baskervilles*] arose from a remark by that fine fellow whose premature death was a loss to the world, Fletcher Robinson, that there was a spectral dog near his house on Dartmoor. That remark was the inception of the book, but I should add that the plot and every word of the actual narrative was my own.' No longer a collaboration on 'the central idea and the local colour' (as Conan Doyle wrote in April 1901): just a remark. In his autobiography *Memories and Adventures*, Conan Doyle didn't mention Fletcher Robinson at all in connection with *The Hound*. He did, however, refer once to how fortunate he was to have enjoyed 'friendship with Fletcher Robinson'. One reason why Conan Doyle subtly diminished his acknowledgement of Robinson's contribution with each of the dedications may have been the editorial comments and letters which appeared in the American *Bookman* magazine between autumn 1901 and summer 1902: these expressed the conviction 'that the story is almost entirely Mr Robinson's and that Dr Doyle's only important contribution is the permission to use the character of Sherlock Holmes'; further, that the Sherlock Holmes of *The Hound* was 'a totally different personage' from the Holmes of old. *The Hound* was more of a horror novel than a detective story, said the reviewer. Conan Doyle certainly read the *Bookman*'s comments, and may have been offended by them. The exact wording of these various footnotes and dedications has been debated by Holmes scholars almost as intensely as the question of whatever happened to Dr Watson's bulldog pup – mentioned in *A Study in Scarlet*, only to disappear from all subsequent stories. The dedications have even helped to fuel conspiracy theories.

In many ways *The Hound* is indeed as much a neo-Gothic novel as a detective story, which is why it has proved so very popular in its many horror movie-style versions and why it is the most fondly remembered of all the Holmes stories. Horror stories seem to have more instant global appeal than detective novels. And Sherlock Holmes himself, who is on characteristic form in the early chapters ('Do you find it interesting?'/'To a collector of fairy-tales') does become less and less flippant as the story progresses: the weird atmosphere of the moor brings out a melodramatic streak in him. This mirrors the novel's broader theme of the certainties of science and reason confronted by the legends of the superstitious past: even Holmes seems to have his doubts, when he listens to the sounds of the moor at night. It is Watson's reports about the moor and the sharpness of dialogue they contain, rather than Holmes's presence, which propel the narrative; the doctor is a long way away from the buffoon figure of Hollywood films in this novel. This certainly avoids the problem of seeming to expand a short-story concept (with its by then familiar ingredients) into a full-length novel and, unlike Conan Doyle's other Holmes novels, it achieves the unity of a single, tense narrative. There is no need for a lengthy flashback: instead we have Watson, as surrogate reader, reporting on his perceptions and making contact on our behalf with the absent Holmes. But the cost is that Sherlock Holmes is offstage to a surprising extent – perhaps because he has virtually solved the problem by Ch. 4 when Sir Henry's boot goes missing. *The Hound of the Baskervilles* should really have been subtitled *Another Adventure of Dr Watson*.

When Sherlock Holmes does appear – to challenge some of Watson's perceptions and eventually reveal all – he makes some uncharacteristic errors of judgement. He risks his client's life, not once but twice, in his attempts to catch the villain red-handed; and he never does catch the villain – who escapes arrest. Holmes entrusts the case to Watson, another uncharacteristic move: he then has to apologize, at the end of the story, for the cavalier treatment of his client when he *is* on the case:

That Sir Henry should have been exposed to this is, I must confess, a reproach to my management of the case, but we had no means of foreseeing the terrible and paralysing spectacle which the beast presented, nor could we predict the fog which enabled him to burst upon us at short notice. We succeeded in our object at a cost . . .

So it is the terrible spectacle of the beast, and the fog on the moor, which clouded Holmes's judgement. These same elements, combined with the theme of reason versus the supernatural, are among the most distinctive features of the novel and have ensured that it has never been out of print since 1902. To this extent, the *Bookman* critic certainly had a point.

But in many other ways he missed it. The combination, in *The Hound of the Baskervilles*, of much-loved elements with a surprising setting and plot is a winning one. The novel is far from 'totally different'. It begins in the traditional way with breakfast at 221b Baker Street, and continues with a stunning display, through dialogue, of Sherlock Holmes's methods – involving a much-used walking-stick, an inscription, and the teeth-marks of a curly-haired spaniel – which are a prelude to the main mystery. Like so many of the consulting detective's clients, Dr Mortimer has mislaid a piece of his property – thus providing Holmes with all the evidence he needs to reconstruct the client *in absentia*. In doing so, Holmes utters some classic aphorisms of the kind which Dorothy L. Sayers reckoned 'enriched English literature'.[8] And the early part of the novel also confirms T. S. Eliot's perception that 'every critic of the Novel who has a theory about the reality of characters in fiction, would do well to consider Holmes . . .'[9] By the end of the first *Strand* instalment or Ch. 2 and the immortal words 'Mr Holmes, they were the footprints of a gigantic hound!', the reader has taken the bait. As novelist John Fowles has justly written of these words: 'No English writer knew more about sinking that mysterious hook into the reader . . . My guess is that the least read chapter-title in all literature is the one that heads Chapter 3.'[10] Then, with the arrival of Sir Henry Baskerville carrying a sheet of paper with printed words from yesterday's *Times* pasted on to it, and complaining about the loss of a tan boot, the game is well and truly afoot. Exit

Sherlock Holmes, busy because 'one of the most revered names in England is being besmirched by a blackmailer', and the scene changes to Dartmoor.

From then on, the story as described by Dr Watson in his narratives, letters and diary entries – still with an unusually strong emphasis on dialogue – is indeed more important than Sherlock Holmes, although there is a clever and touching scene when the partnership gets together again.

But that is what helps to make *The Hound of the Baskervilles* one of the greatest crime novels ever written . . . if not the greatest. The imagery of the tightening butterfly-net, which runs through the second half of the story, applies equally well to the reader. Successive polls of crime novelists have voted *The Hound* number one. Readers at the time who expected more of their favourite box of chocolates were in for a surprise. They were offered their favourite box of chocolates, then other forms of nourishment took over. The philosopher Umberto Eco, in *The Name of the Rose* (1980), made *The Hound* stand for the whole of detective fiction – and the 'reading' of external evidence to make sense of the world – through the character of the Franciscan Brother William of Baskerville. *The Hound*, though, in my view transcends the genre of detective fiction. As Conan Doyle wrote in November 1901, in his Preface to the Author's Edition: ' "The Hound of the Baskervilles" represents the inevitable relapse after repentance.' Two years later, 'The Empty House' managed resurrection from the dead as well.

FURTHER READING

UNPUBLISHED

Manuscript of Ch. 11 ('The Man on the Tor'), in the Berg Collection at New York Public Library; also single page ('may fall in with . . . purpose I must now') in Rare Books and Manuscripts Division.

PUBLISHED

Anon., articles in *The Bookman* (October 1901; February, April and May 1902)

Baring-Gould, Sabine, *A Book of Dartmoor* (1900)

—*A Book of Devon* (1899)

—*Old Country Life* (1890)

Baring-Gould, William S. (ed.), *The Annotated Sherlock Holmes* (1992)

Bleiler, E. F. (ed.), *The Best Supernatural Tales of Arthur Conan Doyle* (1979)

Campbell, Maurice, 'The Hound of the Baskervilles – Dartmoor or Herefordshire?' (Guy's Hospital *Gazette*, 1953)

Carr, John Dickson, *The Life of Sir Arthur Conan Doyle* (1990)

Dakin, D. Martin, *A Sherlock Holmes Commentary* (1972)

Davies, David Stuart, *Holmes of the Movies* (1976)

Dickinson, Bickford H. C., *Sabine Baring-Gould* (1970)

Down, H. J. W., 'Arthur Conan Doyle – an Appreciation' (*Associated Sunday Magazine*, 16 November 1905)

Doyle, A. Conan (Robson, W. W., ed.), *The Hound of the Baskervilles* (1993)

Eco, Umberto and Sebeok, Thomas A., *The Sign of Three: Dupin, Holmes, Peirce* (1983)

Green, R. Lancelyn, *The Uncollected Sherlock Holmes*, (1983)

—and Gibson, John Michael, *A Bibliography of Arthur Conan Doyle* (1983)

Greenhough Smith, H., 'Some Letters of Conan Doyle' (*Strand Magazine*, LXXX, October 1930)

Greeves, Tom, *Tin Mines of Dartmoor* (1993)

Hall, Trevor H., *Sherlock Holmes and His Creator* (1978)

Higham, Charles, *The Adventures of Conan Doyle* (1976)

Hodder Williams, J. E., 'Arthur Conan Doyle' (*Bookman*, April 1902)

Howlett, Anthony D., 'Some observations on the Dartmoor of Sherlock Holmes' (The Sherlock Holmes Society of London, 1979)

Jones, Kelvin, *The Mythology of the Hound of the Baskervilles* (1986)

Kissane, James and John, 'Sherlock Holmes and the Ritual of Reason' (*Nineteenth-Century Fiction*, 17, 4 March 1963)

Maurice, Arthur Bartlett, 'Seven Novels of Importance' (*Bookman*, June 1902)

McQueen, Ian, *Sherlock Holmes Detected* (1974)

Nesbitt, F., 'A Reply' (*Devon and Cornwall Notes & Queries*, xvii, January 1932 – October 1933)

Purves, Shirley (ed.), *Hound and Horse – a Dartmoor Commonplace Book* (1992, with key articles by Howlett, A. D. and Green, R. L.)

Riley, Dick and McAllister, Pam, *The Bedside Companion to Sherlock Holmes* (1999)

Stashower, Daniel W., *Teller of Tales – the Life of Arthur Conan Doyle* (2000)

Weller, Philip, *The Hound of the Baskervilles – Hunting the Dartmoor Legend* (2001)

CHRONOLOGY

A chronology of Arthur Conan Doyle's life and work is likely to be skeletal. As a highly professional writer, a medical specialist, a public campaigner against injustice, a would-be politician, as well as a sports-man, spiritualist, and well-meaning amateur in fields ranging from skiing to weaponry, he threw himself with generous energy into a variety of lives, any one of which would have satisfied most people. A brief account of his activities can, at best, only suggest the range of an extraordinary life.

1859	Arthur Conan Doyle born at 11 Picardy Place, Edinburgh, on 22 May, second of ten children of Charles Doyle, a civil servant, and Mary Doyle, née Foley. (This year also saw the publication of Darwin's *The Origin of Species*.)
1868–70	Spends two years at Hodder Preparatory School, Lancashire.
1870–75	Spends five years in secondary education at Stonyhurst, the leading Jesuit school, in Lancashire.
1875–6	Attends Jesuit college at Feldkirch, Austria.
1876	Enters Edinburgh University to study medicine. Taught by Joseph Bell, a surgeon at the Edinburgh Infirmary, on whom he later bases some of Sherlock Holmes's powers of detection.
1878	Begins first job, assisting a Dr Richardson in Sheffield. Stays with relatives in Maida Vale, London, his first visit to the capital. Writes novel, *The Narrative of John Smith*, which is lost in the post and never recovered. Works as

assistant in doctor's practice in Ruyton-of-the-eleven-towns, Shropshire and then in Birmingham.

1879   Publication of first story, 'The Mystery of Sasassa Valley', in the Edinburgh weekly *Chambers's Journal* (September).

1880   Serves as ship's doctor on Greenland whaler the *Hope*.

1881   Serves as ship's doctor on West African cargo steamer the *Mayumba*. Graduates from Edinburgh as Bachelor of Medicine.

1882–90   Establishes solo general medical practice in Southsea, a suburb of Portsmouth, after a brief and unsuccessful partnership with Dr George Turnavine Budd in Plymouth (1882).

1884   Publication in the *Cornhill* magazine of 'J. Habakuk Jephson's Statement', widely taken as a true explanation of the mystery of the *Marie Celeste*.

1885   Marries Louise Hawkins. Obtains a doctorate from Edinburgh for dissertation on syphilis.

1886   Writes *A Study in Scarlet*, the first Sherlock Holmes story, which is rejected by the *Cornhill* magazine and the publishers Arrowsmith but is accepted by Ward Lock who hold it over for a year before publishing.

1887   *A Study in Scarlet* is published in *Beeton's Christmas Annual*.

1889   Birth of first child, Mary Louise. *Micah Clarke*, Conan Doyle's first historical novel, is published. At a meeting arranged by the magazine publishers Lippincott, Conan Doyle is commissioned to write what becomes *The Sign of the Four*, the second Sherlock Holmes story.

1890   Publication of *The Firm of Girdlestone*. *The Sign of the Four* published in *Lippincott's* magazine. Leaves for Austria to study ophthalmology in Vienna.

1891   Opens short-lived oculist practice in Marylebone, London, half a mile east of Baker Street. First six Holmes short stories published in the *Strand* magazine. Abandons medical career and moves to Norwood, south-east London, to take up writing full time. Publication of *The White Company*.

1892   Birth of Kingsley Conan Doyle. *The Adventures of Sherlock Holmes* collection of short stories published.

1893   Louise diagnosed with tuberculosis. More Sherlock Holmes short stories published in the *Strand* and later collected as *The Memoirs of Sherlock Holmes*. In one of these, 'The Final Problem', Conan Doyle apparently kills off Holmes at the Reichenbach Falls. His father, Charles Doyle, dies in the same year. *The Refugees* published.

1894   Makes a very successful US lecture tour with his brother Innes. Publication of *Round the Red Lamp*, a collection of medical stories.

1896   Publication of *The Exploits of Brigadier Gerard* and *Rodney Stone*. *The Field Bazaar*, a Conan Doyle Holmes pastiche and the first new Holmes work since the detective's 'death', is published in an Edinburgh University student magazine. Moves to Hindhead, Surrey.

1897   Publication of *Uncle Bernac*. Meets and falls in love with Jean Leckie.

1898   Publication of *The Tragedy of the Korosko* and *Songs of Action*.

1900   Serves as a volunteer doctor in South Africa during the Boer War and produces an account of the struggle in *The Great Boer War*. Stands (unsuccessfully) as Liberal Unionist candidate for Edinburgh constituency.

1901   *The Hound of the Baskervilles*, set before Holmes's 'official' death in 'The Final Problem', begins publication in the *Strand*.

1902   Receives knighthood. *The Hound of the Baskervilles* published in book form.

1903   Publication of *The Adventures of Gerard*. Holmes properly resurrected in 'The Empty House', published in the *Strand*.

1905   *The Return of Sherlock Holmes*, the latest collection of Holmes short stories that began with 'The Empty House', published in book form.

1906   Stands (unsuccessfully) as Unionist candidate for Hawick on the Scottish Borders. Publication of *Sir Nigel*. Death of Louise Conan Doyle.

1907 Marries Jean Leckie. Publication of *Through the Magic Door*.

1908 Publication of *Round the Fire Stories*. Moves to Crowborough, Sussex. A new Holmes short story, 'The Singular Experience of Mr John Scott Eccles', later renamed 'The Adventure of Wisteria Lodge', published in the *Strand*.

1909 Joins with journalist E. D. Morel (model for Ned Malone in *The Lost World*) to campaign against brutality of the Belgian Congo regime, and writes *The Crime of the Congo*. Birth of son Denis.

1910 Birth of Adrian. Holmes play, *The Speckled Band*, opens at the Adelphi, London. Holmes short story 'The Devil's Foot' published in the *Strand*.

1911 Holmes short stories 'The Red Circle' and 'The Disappearance of Lady Frances Carfax' published in the *Strand*. Conan Doyle is converted to Irish Home Rule by Sir Roger Casement.

1912 *The Lost World*, now the most famous of Doyle's non-Holmes stories, begins serialization in the *Strand* and is published in book form in October. Birth of Jean.

1913 Publication of *The Poison Belt*. Holmes short story 'The Dying Detective' published in the *Strand*.

1914 Conan Doyle forms volunteer force on outbreak of the First World War. Holmes story *The Valley of Fear* begins serialization in the *Strand*.

1915 Publication of *The Valley of Fear* in book form.

1916 Conan Doyle makes first of several visits to the front-line areas and produces an account of the British campaign in France. Joins unsuccessful movement to reprieve Irish patriot Sir Roger Casement from execution for treason following the Easter Rising in Dublin (Lord John Roxton in *The Lost World* is partly based on Casement).

1917 'His Last Bow', subtitled 'The War Service of Sherlock Holmes', published in the *Strand*. The recent Holmes short stories collected as *His Last Bow* and published in book form.

1918 Death of eldest son Kingsley from pneumonia after being wounded at the Somme. Conan Doyle publishes his first book on spiritualism, *The New Revelation*; begins new career as an ardent global campaigner for spiritualism.

1919   Death of younger brother Innes from pneumonia.

1921–7   New Holmes short stories published in the *Strand*.

1921   Death of Conan Doyle's mother, Mary Foley.

1924   Autobiography, *Memories and Adventures*, published.

1926   Publication of third Professor Challenger story, *The Land of Mist* (narrative with a spiritualist theme).

1927   Recent short stories collected in book form as *The Casebook of Sherlock Holmes*, the last volume of Holmes stories published.

1929   Appearance of the final Professor Challenger story, 'When the World Screamed', in *The Maracot Deep and Other Stories*.

1930   Arthur Conan Doyle dies on 7 July at home in Crowborough.

A NOTE ON THE TEXT

This edition of *The Hound of the Baskervilles* is based on the first English book edition (George Newnes, March 1902), collated in the notes with the *Strand* magazine serialization (August 1901–April 1902) and the first New York edition (McClure, Phillips & Co., April 1902).

The Hound of the Baskervilles

Another Adventure of Sherlock Holmes

CONTENTS

This story owes its inception to my friend,
Mr Fletcher Robinson, who has helped me both
in the general plot and in the local details.

A.C.D.

I

Mr Sherlock Holmes

Mr Sherlock Holmes,[1] who was usually very late in the mornings, save upon those not infrequent occasions when he stayed up all night,[2] was seated at the breakfast table. I stood upon the hearthrug and picked up the stick which our visitor had left behind him the night before.[3] It was a fine, thick piece of wood, bulbous-headed, of the sort which is known as a 'Penang lawyer'.[4] Just under the head was a broad silver band, nearly an inch across. 'To James Mortimer, MRCS, from his friends of the CCH',[5] was engraved upon it, with the date '1884'. It was just a stick as the old-fashioned family practitioner used to carry – dignified, solid, and reassuring.

'Well, Watson, what do you make of it?'

Holmes was sitting with his back to me, and I had given him no sign of my occupation.

'How did you know what I was doing? I believe you have eyes in the back of your head.'

'I have, at least, a well-polished, silver-plated coffee-pot[6] in front of me,' said he. 'But, tell me, Watson, what do you make of our visitor's stick? Since we have been so unfortunate as to miss him and have no notion of his errand, this accidental souvenir becomes of importance. Let me hear you reconstruct the man by an examination of it.'

'I think,' said I, following so far as I could the methods of my companion, 'that Dr Mortimer is a successful elderly medical man, well-esteemed, since those who know him give him this mark of their appreciation.'

'Good!' said Holmes. 'Excellent!'

'I think also that the probability is in favour of his being a country practitioner who does a great deal of his visiting on foot.'

'Why so?'

'Because this stick, though originally a very handsome one, has been so knocked about that I can hardly imagine a town practitioner carrying it. The thick iron ferrule[7] is worn down, so it is evident that he has done a great amount of walking with it.'

'Perfectly sound!' said Holmes.

'And then again, there is the "friends of the CCH". I should guess that to be the Something Hunt, the local hunt to whose members he has possibly given some surgical assistance, and which has made him a small presentation in return.'

'Really, Watson, you excel yourself,' said Holmes, pushing back his chair and lighting a cigarette. 'I am bound to say that in all accounts which you have been so good as to give[8] of my own small achievements you have habitually underrated your own abilities. It may be that you are not yourself luminous, but you are a conductor of light.[9] Some people without possessing genius have a remarkable power of stimulating. I confess, my dear fellow, that I am very much in your debt.'

He had never said as much before, and I must admit that his words gave me keen pleasure, for I have often been piqued by his indifference to my admiration and to the attempts which I had made to give publicity to his methods. I was proud, too, to think that I had so far mastered his system as to apply it in a way which earned his approval. He now took the stick from my hands and examined it for a few minutes with his naked eyes. Then, with an expression of interest, he laid down his cigarette,[10] and, carrying the cane to the window, he looked over it again with a convex lens.

'Interesting, though elementary,'[11] said he, as he returned to his favourite corner of the settee. 'There are certainly one or two indications upon the stick. It gives us the basis for several deductions.'[12]

'Has anything escaped me?' I asked, with some self-importance. 'I trust that there is nothing of consequence which I have over-looked?'

'I am afraid, my dear Watson, that most of your conclusions were erroneous. When I said that you stimulated me I meant, to be frank, that in noting your fallacies I was occasionally guided towards the truth. Not that you are entirely wrong in this instance. The man is certainly a country practitioner. And he walks a good deal.'

'Then I was right.'

'To that extent.'

'But that was all.'

'No, no, my dear Watson, not all – by no means all. I would suggest, for example, that a presentation to a doctor is more likely to come from a hospital than from a hunt, and that when the initials "CC" are placed before that hospital the words "Charing Cross" very naturally suggest themselves.'

'You may be right.'

'The probability lies in that direction. And if we take this as a working hypothesis we have a fresh basis from which to start our construction of this unknown visitor.'

'Well, then, supposing that "CCH" does stand for "Charing Cross Hospital", what further inferences may we draw?'

'Do none suggest themselves? You know my methods. Apply them!'

'I can only think of the obvious conclusion that the man has practised in town before going to the country.'

'I think that we might venture a little farther than this. Look at it in this light. On what occasion would it be most probable that such a presentation would be made? When would his friends unite to give him a pledge of their good will? Obviously at the moment when Dr Mortimer withdrew from the service of the hospital in order to start in practice for himself. We know there has been a presentation. We believe there has been a change from a town hospital to a country practice. Is it, then, stretching our inference too far to say that the presentation was on the occasion of the change?'

'It certainly seems probable.'

'Now, you will observe that he could not have been on the *staff* of the hospital,[13] since only a man well established in a London practice could hold such a position, and such a one would not drift into the country. What was he, then? If he was in the hospital and yet not on the staff, he could only have been a house-surgeon or a house-physician – little more than a senior student. And he left five years ago – the date is on the stick. So your grave, middle-aged family practitioner vanishes into thin air, my dear Watson, and there emerges a young fellow under thirty, amiable, unambitious, absent-minded, and the possessor of a favourite dog, which I should describe roughly as being larger than a terrier and smaller than a mastiff.'

I laughed incredulously as Sherlock Holmes leaned back in his settee and blew little wavering rings of smoke up to the ceiling.

'As to the latter part, I have no means of checking you,' said I, 'but at least it is not difficult to find out a few particulars about the man's age and professional career.'

From my small medical shelf I took down the Medical Directory and turned up the name. There were several Mortimers, but only one who could be our visitor. I read his record aloud.

Mortimer, James, MRCS, 1882, Grimpen, Dartmoor, Devon. House-surgeon, from 1882 to 1884, at Charing Cross Hospital. Winner of the Jackson Prize for Comparative Pathology, with essay entitled 'Is Disease a Reversion?' Corresponding member of the Swedish Pathological Society. Author of 'Some Freaks of Atavism' (*Lancet*, 1882),[14] 'Do We Progress?' (*Journal of Psychology*, March, 1883). Medical Officer for the parishes of Grimpen, Thorsley, and High Barrow.

'No mention of that local hunt, Watson,' said Holmes, with a mischievous smile, 'but a country doctor, as you very astutely observed. I think that I am fairly justified in my inferences. As to the adjectives, I said, if I remember right, amiable, unambitious, and absent-minded. It is my experience that it is only an amiable man in this world who receives testimonials, only an unambitious one who abandons a London career for the country, and only an absent-minded one who leaves his stick and not his visiting-card after waiting an hour in your room.'

'And the dog?'

'Has been in the habit of carrying this stick behind his master. Being a heavy stick the dog has held it tightly by the middle, and the marks of his teeth are very plainly visible. The dog's jaw, as shown in the space between these marks, is too broad in my opinion for a terrier and not broad enough for a mastiff. It may have been – yes, by Jove it *is* a curly-haired spaniel.'

He had risen and paced the room as he spoke. Now he halted in the recess of the window. There was such a ring of conviction in his voice that I glanced up in surprise.

'My dear fellow, how can you possibly be so sure of that?'

'For the very simple reason that I see the dog himself on our very doorstep, and there is the ring of its owner. Don't move, I beg you, Watson. He is a professional brother of yours, and your presence may be of assistance to me. Now is the dramatic moment of fate, Watson, when you hear a step upon the stair which is walking into your life, and you know not whether for good or ill. What does Dr James Mortimer, the man of science, ask of Sherlock Holmes, the specialist in crime? Come in!'

The appearance of our visitor was a surprise to me since I had expected a typical country practitioner. He was a very tall, thin man, with a long nose like a beak, which shot out between two keen, grey eyes, set closely together and sparkling brightly from behind a pair of gold-rimmed glasses. He was clad in a professional but rather slovenly fashion, for his frock-coat was dingy and his trousers frayed. Though young, his long back was already bowed, and he walked with a forward thrust of his head and a general air of peering benevolence. As he entered his eyes fell upon the stick in Holmes's hand, and he ran towards it with an exclamation of joy.

'I am so very glad,' said he. 'I was not sure whether I had left it here or in the Shipping Office. I would not lose that stick for the world.'

'A presentation, I see,' said Holmes.

'Yes, sir.'

'From Charing Cross Hospital?'

'From one or two friends there on the occasion of my marriage.'

'Dear, dear, that's bad!' said Holmes, shaking his head.

Dr Mortimer blinked through his glasses in mild astonishment.

'Why was it bad?'

'Only that you have disarranged our little deductions. Your marriage, you say?'

'Yes, sir. I married, and so left the hospital, and with it all hopes of a consulting practice. It was necessary to make a home of my own.'

'Come, come, we are not so far wrong after all,' said Holmes. 'And now, Dr James Mortimer –'

'Mister, sir, Mister – a humble MRCS.'

'And a man of precise mind, evidently.'

'A dabbler in science, Mr Holmes, a picker-up of shells on the shores of the great unknown ocean.[15] I presume that it is Mr Sherlock Holmes whom I am addressing and not –'

'No, this is my friend Dr Watson.'

'Glad to meet you, sir. I have heard your name mentioned in connection with that of your friend. You interest me very much, Mr Holmes. I had hardly expected so dolichocephalic a skull or such well-marked supra-orbital development. Would you have any objection to my running my finger along your parietal fissure?[16] A cast of your skull, sir, until the original is available, would be an ornament to any anthropological museum. It is not my intention to be fulsome, but I confess that I covet your skull.'

Sherlock Holmes waved our strange visitor into a chair.

'You are an enthusiast in your line of thought, I perceive, sir, as I am in mine,' said he. 'I observe from your forefinger that you make your own cigarettes.[17] Have no hesitation in lighting one.'

The man drew out paper and tobacco and twirled the one up in the other with surprising dexterity. He had long, quivering fingers as agile and restless as the antennae of an insect.

Holmes was silent, but his little darting glances showed me the interest which he took in our curious companion.

'I presume, sir,' said he at last, 'that it was not merely for the purpose of examining my skull that you have done me the honour to call here last night and again today?'

'No, sir, no; though I am happy to have had the opportunity of doing that as well, I came to you, Mr Holmes, because I recognize that I am myself an unpractical man, and because I am suddenly confronted with a most serious and extraordinary problem. Recognizing, as I do, that you are the second highest expert in Europe –'

'Indeed, sir! May I inquire who has the honour to be the first?' asked Holmes, with some asperity.

'To the man of precisely scientific mind the work of Monsieur Bertillon[18] must always appeal strongly.'

'Then had you not better consult him?'

'I said, sir, to the precisely scientific mind. But as a practical man of affairs it is acknowledged that you stand alone. I trust, sir, that I have not inadvertently –'

'Just a little,' said Holmes. 'I think, Dr Mortimer, you would do wisely if without more ado you would kindly tell me plainly what the exact nature of the problem is in which you demand my assistance.'

2

The Curse of the Baskervilles

'I have in my pocket a manuscript,' said Dr James Mortimer.

'I observed it as you entered the room,' said Holmes.

'It is an old manuscript.'

'Early eighteenth century, unless it is a forgery.'

'How can you say that, sir?'

'You have presented an inch or two of it to my examination all the time that you have been talking. It would be a poor expert who could not give the date of a document within a decade or so. You may possibly have read my little monograph upon the subject. I put that at 1730.'

'The exact date is 1742.' Dr Mortimer drew it from his breast-pocket. 'This family paper was committed to my care by Sir Charles Baskerville, whose sudden and tragic death some three months ago created so much excitement in Devonshire. I may say that I was his personal friend as well as his medical attendant. He was a strong-minded man, sir, shrewd, practical, and as unimaginative as I am myself. Yet he took this document very seriously, and his mind was prepared for just such an end as did eventually overtake him.'

Holmes stretched out his hand for the manuscript and flattened it upon his knee.

'You will observe, Watson, the alternative use of the long *s* and the short.[1] It is one of several indications which enabled me to fix the date.'

I looked over his shoulder at the yellow paper and the faded script. At the head was written: 'Baskerville Hall', and below, in large scrawling figures: '1742'.[2]

'It appears to be a statement of some sort.'

'Yes, it is a statement of a certain legend which runs in the Baskerville family.'

'But I understand that it is something more modern and practical upon which you wish to consult me?'

'Most modern. A most practical, pressing matter, which must be decided within twenty-four hours. But the manuscript is short and is intimately connected with the affair. With your permission I will read it to you.'

Holmes leaned back in his chair, placed his finger-tips together, and closed his eyes, with an air of resignation. Dr Mortimer turned the manuscript to the light, and read in a high, crackling voice the following curious, old-world narrative.

Of the origin of the Hound of the Baskervilles there have been many statements, yet as I come in a direct line from Hugo Baskerville, and as I had the story from my father, who also had it from his, I have set it down with all belief that it occurred even as is here set forth. And I would have you believe, my sons, that the same Justice which punishes sin may also most graciously forgive it, and that no ban is so heavy but that by prayer and repentance it may be removed. Learn then from this story not to fear the fruits of the past, but rather to be circumspect in the future, that those foul passions whereby our family has suffered so grievously may not again be loosed to our undoing.

Know then that in the time of the Great Rebellion (the history of which by the learned Lord Clarendon[3] I most earnestly commend to your attention) this Manor of Baskerville was held by Hugo of that name, nor can it be gainsaid that he was a most wild, profane, and godless man. This, in truth, his neighbours might have pardoned, seeing that saints have never flourished in those parts, but there was in him a certain wanton and cruel humour which made his name a byword through the West. It chanced that this Hugo came to love (if, indeed, so dark a passion may be known under so bright a name) the daughter of a yeoman who held lands near the Baskerville estate. But the young maiden, being discreet and of good repute, would ever avoid him, for she feared his evil name. So it came to pass that one Michaelmas[4] this Hugo, with five or six of his idle and wicked companions, stole down upon the farm and carried off the maiden, her father and brothers being from home, as he well knew. When they had brought her to the Hall the maiden was placed in an upper chamber, while Hugo and his friends sat down to a long carouse as was their nightly custom. Now, the poor lass upstairs was like to have her wits turned at the singing and shouting and terrible oaths which came up to her from below, for they say that the words used by Hugo Baskerville, when he was in wine, were such as might blast the man who said them. At last in the stress of her fear she did that which might have daunted the bravest or most active man, for by the aid of the growth of ivy which covered (and still covers) the south wall, she came down from under the eaves, and so homeward across the moor, there being three leagues betwixt the Hall and her father's farm.

It chanced that some little time later Hugo left his guests to carry food and drink – with other worse things, perchance – to his captive, and so found the cage empty and the bird escaped. Then, as it would seem, he became as one that hath a devil, for rushing down the stairs into the dining-hall, he sprang upon the great table, flagons and trenchers[5] flying before him, and he cried aloud before all the company that he would that very night render his body and soul to the Powers of Evil if he might but overtake the wench. And while the revellers stood aghast at the fury of the man, one more wicked or, it may be, more drunken than the rest, cried out that they should put the hounds upon her. Whereat Hugo ran from the house, crying to his grooms, that they should saddle his mare and unkennel the pack, and giving the hounds a kerchief of the maid's he swung them to the line,[6] and so off full cry in the moonlight over the moor.

Now, for some space the revellers stood agape, unable to understand all that had been done in such haste. But anon their bemused wits awoke to the nature of the deed which was like to be done upon the moorlands. Everything was now in an uproar, some calling for their pistols, some for their horses, and some for another flask of wine. But at length some sense came back to their crazed minds, and the whole of them, thirteen in number, took horse and started in pursuit. The moon shone clear above them, and they rode swiftly abreast, taking that course which the maid must needs have taken if she were to reach her own home.

They had gone a mile or two when they passed one of the night shepherds upon the moorlands, and they cried to him to know if he had seen the hunt. And the man, as the story goes, was so crazed with fear that he could scarce speak, but at last he said that he had indeed seen the unhappy maiden, with the hounds upon her track. 'But I have seen more than that,' said he, 'for Hugo Baskerville passed me upon his black mare, and there ran mute behind him such a hound of hell as God forbid should ever be at my heels.'

So the drunken squires cursed the shepherd and rode onwards. But soon their skins turned cold, for there came a sound of galloping[7] across the moor, and the black mare, dabbled with white froth, went past with trailing bridle and empty saddle. Then the revellers rode close together, for a great fear was on them, but they still followed over the moor, though each, had he been alone, would have been right glad to have turned his horse's head. Riding slowly in this fashion, they came at last upon the hounds. These, though known for their valour and their breed, were whimpering in a cluster at the head of a deep dip or goyal, as we call it, upon the moor, some slinking away and some, with starting hackles and staring eyes, gazing down the narrow valley before them.

The company had come to a halt, more sober men, as you may guess, than when they started. The most of them would by no means advance, but three of them, the boldest, or, it may be the most drunken, rode forward down the goyal. Now it opened into a broad space in which stood two of those great stones, still to be seen there, which were set by certain forgotten peoples in the days of old. The moon was shining bright upon the clearing, and there in the centre lay the unhappy maid where she had fallen, dead of fear and of fatigue. But it was not the sight of her body, nor yet was it that of the body of Hugo Baskerville lying near her, which raised the hair upon the heads of these three dare-devil roisterers, but it was that, standing over Hugo, and plucking at his throat, there stood a foul thing, a great, black beast, shaped like a hound yet larger than any hound that ever mortal eye has rested upon. And even as they looked the thing tore the throat out of Hugo Baskerville, on which, as it turned its blazing eyes and dripping jaws upon them, the three shrieked with fear and rode for dear life, still screaming, across the moor. One, it is said, died that very night of what he had seen, and the other twain were but broken men for the rest of their days.

Such is the tale, my sons, of the coming of the hound which is said to have plagued the family so sorely ever since. If I have set it down it is because that which is clearly known hath less terror than that which is but hinted at and guessed. Nor can it be denied that many of the family have been unhappy in their deaths, which have been sudden, bloody, and mysterious. Yet may we shelter ourselves in the infinite goodness of Providence, which would not for ever punish the innocent beyond that third or fourth generation which is threatened in Holy Writ.[8] To that Providence, my sons, I hereby commend you, and I counsel you by way of caution to forbear from crossing the moor in those dark hours when the powers of evil are exalted.

(This from Hugo Baskerville to his sons Rodger and John, with instructions that they say nothing thereof to their sister Elizabeth.)

When Dr Mortimer had finished reading this singular narrative he pushed his spectacles up on his forehead and stared across at Mr Sherlock Holmes. The latter yawned and tossed the end of his cigarette into the fire.

'Well?' said he.

'Do you find it interesting?'

'To a collector of fairy-tales.'

Dr Mortimer drew a folded newspaper out of his pocket.

'Now, Mr Holmes, we will give you something a little more recent. This is the *Devon County Chronicle* of June 14th[9] of this year. It is a short account of the facts elicited at the death of Sir Charles Baskerville which occurred a few days before that date.'

My friend leaned a little forward and his expression became intent. Our visitor readjusted his glasses and began:

The recent sudden death of Sir Charles Baskerville, whose name has been mentioned as the probable Liberal candidate for Mid-Devon at the next election, has cast a gloom over the county. Though Sir Charles had resided at Baskerville Hall for a comparatively short period his amiability of character and extreme generosity had won the affection and respect of all who had been brought into contact with him. In these days of *nouveaux riches*[10] it is refreshing to find a case where the scion of an old county family which has fallen upon evil days is able to make his own fortune and to bring it back with him to restore the fallen grandeur of his line. Sir Charles, as is well known, made large sums of money in South African speculation. More wise than those who go on until the wheel turns against them, he realized his gains and returned to England with them. It is only two years since he took up his residence at Baskerville Hall, and it is common talk how large were those schemes of reconstruction and improvement which have been interrupted by his death.

Being himself childless, it was his openly expressed desire that the whole countryside should, within his own lifetime, profit by his good fortune, and many will have personal reasons for bewailing his untimely end. His generous donations to local and county charities have been frequently chronicled in these columns.

The circumstances connected with the death of Sir Charles cannot be said to have been entirely cleared up by the inquest, but at least enough has been done to dispose of those rumours to which local superstition has given rise. There is no reason whatever to suspect foul play, or to imagine that death could be from any but natural causes. Sir Charles was a widower, and a man who may be said to have been in some ways of an eccentric habit of mind. In spite of his considerable wealth he was simple in his personal tastes, and his indoor servants at Baskerville Hall consisted of a married couple named Barrymore, the husband acting as butler and the wife as housekeeper. Their evidence, corroborated by that of several friends, tends to show that Sir Charles's health has for some time been impaired, and points especially to some affection of the heart, manifesting itself in changes of colour, breathlessness, and acute attacks of nervous depression. Dr James Mortimer, the friend and medical attendant of the deceased, has given evidence to the same effect.

The facts of the case are simple. Sir Charles Baskerville was in the habit every night before going to bed of walking down the famous Yew Alley of Baskerville Hall. The evidence of the Barrymores shows that this had been his custom. On the 4th of June[11] Sir Charles had declared his intention of starting next day for London, and had ordered Barrymore to prepare his luggage. That night he went out as usual for his nocturnal walk, in the course of which he was in the habit of smoking a cigar. He never returned. At twelve o'clock Barrymore, finding the hall door still open, became alarmed and, lighting a lantern, went in search of his master. The day had been wet, and Sir Charles's footmarks were easily traced down the Alley. Half-way down this walk there is a gate which leads out on to the moor. There were indications that Sir Charles had stood for some little time here. He then proceeded down the Alley, and it was at the far end of it that his body was discovered. One fact which has not been explained is the statement of Barrymore that his master's footprints altered their character from the time he passed the moorgate, and that he appeared from thence onwards to have been walking upon his toes. One Murphy, a gipsy horse-dealer, was on the moor at no great distance at the time, but he appears by his own confession to have been the worse for drink. He declares that he heard cries, but is unable to state from what direction they came. No signs of violence were to be discovered upon Sir Charles's person, and though the doctor's evidence pointed to an almost incredible facial distortion – so great that Dr Mortimer refused at first to believe that it was indeed his friend and patient who lay before him – it was explained that that is a symptom which is not unusual in cases of dyspnoea[12] and death from cardiac exhaustion. This explanation was borne out by the post-mortem examination, which showed long-standing organic disease, and the coroner's jury returned a verdict in accordance with the medical evidence. It is well that this is so, for it is obviously of the utmost importance that Sir Charles's heir should settle at the Hall, and continue the good work which has been so sadly interrupted. Had the prosaic finding of the coroner not finally put an end to the romantic stories which have been whispered in connection with the affair, it might have been difficult to find a tenant for Baskerville Hall.[13] It is understood that the next-of-kin is Mr Henry Baskerville, if he be still alive, the son of Sir Charles Baskerville's younger brother. The young man, when last heard of, was in America, and inquiries are being instituted with a view to informing him of his good fortune.

Dr Mortimer refolded his paper and replaced it in his pocket.

'Those are the public facts, Mr Holmes, in connection with the death of Sir Charles Baskerville.'

'I must thank you,' said Sherlock Holmes, 'for calling my attention to a case which certainly presents some features of interest. I had observed some newspaper comment at the time, but I was exceedingly preoccupied by that little affair of the Vatican cameos, and in my anxiety to oblige the Pope[14] I lost touch with several interesting English cases. This article, you say, contains all the public facts?'

'It does.'

'Then let me have the private ones.' He leaned back, put his finger-tips together, and assumed his most impassive and judicial expression.

'In doing so,' said Dr Mortimer, who had begun to show signs of some strong emotion, 'I am telling that which I have not confided to anyone. My motive for withholding it from the coroner's inquiry is that a man of science shrinks from placing himself in the public position of seeming to endorse a popular superstition. I had the further motive that Baskerville Hall, as the paper says, would certainly remain untenanted if anything were done to increase its already rather grim reputation. For both these reasons I thought that I was justified in telling rather less than I knew, since no practical good could result from it, but with you there is no reason why I should not be perfectly frank.

'The moor is very sparsely inhabited, and those who live near each other are thrown very much together. For this reason I saw a good deal of Sir Charles Baskerville. With the exception of Mr Frankland, of Lafter Hall,[15] and Mr Stapleton, the naturalist, there are no other men of education within many miles. Sir Charles was a retiring man, but the chance of his illness brought us together, and a community of interests in science kept us so. He had brought back much scientific information from South Africa, and many a charming evening we have spent together discussing the comparative anatomy of the Bushman and the Hottentot.[16]

'Within the last few months it became increasingly plain to me that Sir Charles's nervous system was strained to breaking-point. He had taken this legend which I have read you exceedingly to heart – so much so that, although he would walk in his own grounds, nothing would induce him to go out upon the moor at night. Incredible as it may appear to you, Mr Holmes, he was honestly convinced that a dreadful fate overhung his family, and certainly the records which he was able to give of his ancestors were not encouraging. The idea of some ghastly presence constantly haunted him, and on more than one occasion he has asked me whether I had on my medical journeys at night ever seen any strange creature or heard the baying of a hound. The latter question he put to me several times, and always with a voice which vibrated with excitement.

'I can well remember driving up to his house in the evening, some three weeks before the fatal event. He chanced to be at his hall door. I had descended from my gig[17] and was standing in front of him, when I saw his eyes fix themselves over my shoulder, and stare past me with an expression of the most dreadful horror. I whisked round and had just time to catch a glimpse of something which I took to be a large black calf passing at the head of the drive. So excited and alarmed was he that I was compelled to go down to the spot where the animal had been and look around for it. It was gone, however, and the incident appeared to make the worst impression upon his mind. I stayed with him all the evening, and it was on that occasion, to explain the emotion which he had shown, that he confided to my keeping that narrative which I read to you when first I came. I mention this small episode because it assumes some importance in view of the tragedy which followed, but I was convinced at the time that the matter was entirely trivial and that his excitement had no justification.

'It was at my advice that Sir Charles was about to go to London. His heart was, I knew, affected, and the constant anxiety in which he lived, however chimerical the cause of it might be, was evidently having a serious effect upon his health. I thought that a few months among the distractions of town would send him back a new man. Mr Stapleton, a mutual friend, who was much concerned at his state of health, was of the same opinion. At the last instant came this terrible catastrophe.

'On the night of Sir Charles's death Barrymore the butler, who made the discovery, sent Perkins the groom on horseback to me, and as I was sitting up late I was able to reach Baskerville Hall within an hour of the event. I checked and corroborated all the facts which were mentioned at the inquest. I followed the footsteps down the Yew Alley, I saw the spot at the moor-gate where he seems to have waited, I remarked the change in the shape of the prints after that point, I noted that there were no other footsteps save those of Barrymore on the soft gravel, and finally I carefully examined the body, which had not been touched until my arrival. Sir Charles lay on his face, his arms out, his fingers dug into the ground, and his features convulsed with some strong emotion to such an extent that I could hardly have sworn to his identity. There was certainly no physical injury of any kind. But one false state-ment was made by Barrymore at the inquest. He said that there were no traces upon the ground round the body. He did not observe any. But I did – some little distance off, but fresh and clear.'

'Footprints?'

'Footprints.'

'A man's or a woman's?'

Dr Mortimer looked strangely at us for an instant, and his voice sank almost to a whisper as he answered: 'Mr Holmes, they were the footprints of a gigantic hound!'[18]

3

The Problem

I confess that at these words a shudder passed through me. There was a thrill in the doctor's voice which showed that he was himself deeply moved by that which he told us. Holmes leaned forward in his excitement, and his eyes had the hard, dry glitter which shot from them when he was keenly interested.

'You saw this?'

'As clearly as I see you.'

'And you said nothing?'

'What was the use?'

'How was it that no one else saw it?'

'The marks were some twenty yards from the body, and no one gave them a thought. I don't suppose I should have done so had I not known this legend.'

'There are many sheepdogs on the moor?'

'No doubt, but this was no sheepdog.'

'You say it was large?'

'Enormous.'

'But it had not approached the body?'

'No.'

'What sort of night was it?'

'Damp and raw.'

'But not actually raining?'

'No.'

'What is the Alley like?'

'There are two lines of old yew hedge, twelve feet high and impenetrable. The walk in the centre is about eight feet across.'

'Is there anything between the hedges and the walk?'

'Yes, there is a strip of grass about six feet broad on either side.'

'I understand that the yew hedge is penetrated at one point by a gate?'

'Yes, the wicket-gate[1] which leads on to the moor.'

'Is there any other opening?'

'None.'

'So that to reach the Yew Alley one either has to come down it from the house or else to enter it by the moor-gate?'

'There is an exit through a summer-house at the far end.'

'Had Sir Charles reached this?'

'No; he lay about fifty yards from it.'

'Now, tell me, Dr Mortimer – and this is important – the marks which you saw were on the path and not on the grass?'

'No marks could show on the grass.'

'Were they on the same side of the path as the moor-gate?'

'Yes; they were on the edge of the path on the same side as the moor-gate.'

'You interest me exceedingly. Another point: was the wicket-gate closed?'

'Closed and padlocked.'

'How high was it?'

'About four feet high.'

'Then anyone could have got over it?'

'Yes.'

'And what marks did you see by the wicket-gate?'

'None in particular.'

'Good Heaven! Did no one examine?'

'Yes, I examined myself.'

'And found nothing?'

'It was all very confused. Sir Charles had evidently stood there for five or ten minutes.'

'How do you know that?'

'Because the ash had twice dropped from his cigar.'

'Excellent! This is a colleague, Watson, after our own heart. But the marks?'

'He had left his own marks all over that small patch of gravel. I could discern no others.'

Sherlock Holmes struck his hand against his knee with an impatient gesture.

'If I had only been there!' he cried. 'It is evidently a case of extraordinary interest, and one which presented immense opportunities to the scientific expert. That gravel path upon which I might have read so much has been long ere this smudged by the rain and defaced by the clogs of curious peasants.[2] Oh, Dr Mortimer, Dr Mortimer, to think that you should not have called me in! You have indeed much to answer for.'

'I could not call you in, Mr Holmes, without disclosing these facts to the world, and I have already given my reasons for not wishing to do so. Besides, besides –'

'Why do you hesitate?'

'There is a realm in which the most acute and most experienced of detectives is helpless.'

'You mean that the thing is supernatural?'

'I did not positively say so.'

'No, but you evidently think it.'

'Since the tragedy, Mr Holmes, there have come to my ears several incidents which are hard to reconcile with the settled order of Nature.'

'For example?'

'I find that before the terrible event occurred several people had seen a creature upon the moor which corresponds with this Baskerville demon, and which could not possibly be any animal known to science. They all agreed that it was a huge creature, luminous, ghastly and spectral. I have cross-examined these men, one of them a hard-headed countryman, one a farrier,[3] and one a moorland farmer, who all tell the same story of this dreadful apparition, exactly corresponding to the hell-hound of the legend. I assure you that there is a reign of terror in the district, and that it is a hardy man who will cross the moor at night.'

'And you, a trained man of science, believe it to be supernatural?'

'I do not know what to believe.'

Holmes shrugged his shoulders. 'I have hitherto confined my investigations to this world,' said he. 'In a modest way I have combated evil, but to take on the Father of Evil himself would, perhaps, be too ambitious a task. Yet you must admit that the footmark is material.'

'The original hound was material enough to tug a man's throat out, and yet he was diabolical as well.'

'I see that you have quite gone over to the supernaturalists. But now, Dr Mortimer, tell me this. If you hold these views, why have you come to consult me at all? You tell me in the same breath that it is useless to investigate Sir Charles's death, and that you desire me to do it.'

'I did not say that I desire you to do it.'

'Then, how can I assist you?'

'By advising me as to what I should do with Sir Henry Baskerville, who arrives at Waterloo Station'[4] – Dr Mortimer looked at his watch – 'in exactly one hour and a quarter.'

'He being the heir?'

'Yes. On the death of Sir Charles we inquired for this young gentleman, and found that he had been farming in Canada. From the accounts which have reached us he is an excellent fellow in every way. I speak now not as a medical man but as a trustee and executor of Sir Charles's will.'[5]

'There is no other claimant, I presume?'

'None. The only other kinsman whom we have been able to trace was Rodger Baskerville, the youngest of three brothers of whom poor Sir Charles was the elder. The second brother, who died young, is the father of this lad Henry. The third, Rodger, was the black sheep of the family. He came of the old masterful Baskerville strain, and was the very image, they tell me, of the family picture of old Hugo. He made England too hot to hold him, fled to Central America, and died there in 1876 of yellow fever.[6] Henry is the last of the Baskervilles. In one hour and five minutes I meet him at Waterloo Station. I have had a wire that he arrived at Southampton this morning. Now, Mr Holmes, what would you advise me to do with him?'

'Why should he not go to the home of his fathers?'

'It seems natural, does it not? And yet, consider that every Baskerville who goes there meets with an evil fate. I feel sure that if Sir

Charles could have spoken with me before his death he would have warned me against bringing this, the last of the old race, and the heir to great wealth, to that deadly place. And yet it cannot be denied that the prosperity of the whole poor, bleak countryside depends upon his presence.[7] All the good work which has been done by Sir Charles will crash to the ground if there is no tenant of the Hall. I fear lest I should be swayed too much by my own obvious interest in the matter, and that is why I bring the case before you and ask for your advice.'

Holmes considered for a little time. 'Put into plain words, the matter is this,' said he. 'In your opinion there is a diabolical agency which makes Dartmoor an unsafe abode for a Baskerville – that is your opinion?'

'At least I might go the length of saying that there is some evidence that this may be so.'

'Exactly. But surely if your supernatural theory be correct, it could work the young man evil in London as easily as in Devonshire. A devil with merely local powers like a parish vestry[8] would be too inconceivable a thing.'

'You put the matter more flippantly, Mr Holmes,[9] than you would probably do if you were brought into personal contact with these things. Your advice, then, as I understand it, is that the young man will be as safe in Devonshire as in London. He comes in fifty minutes. What would you recommend?'

'I recommend, sir, that you take a cab, call off your spaniel, who is scratching at my front door, and proceed to Waterloo to meet Sir Henry Baskerville.'

'And then?'

'And then you will say nothing to him at all until I have made up my mind about the matter.'

'How long will it take you to make up your mind?'

'Twenty-four hours. At ten o'clock tomorrow, Dr Mortimer, I will be much obliged to you if you will call upon me here, and it will be of help to me in my plans for the future if you will bring Sir Henry Baskerville with you.'

'I will do so, Mr Holmes.'

He scribbled the appointment on his shirt-cuff and hurried off in his strange, peering, absent-minded fashion. Holmes stopped him at the head of the stair.

'Only one more question, Dr Mortimer. You say that before Sir Charles Baskerville's death several people saw this apparition upon the moor?'

'Three people did.'

'Did any see it after?'

'I have not heard of any.'

'Thank you. Good morning.'

Holmes returned to his seat with that quiet look of inward satisfaction which meant that he had a congenial task before him.

'Going out, Watson?'

'Unless I can help you.'

'No, my dear fellow, it is at the hour of action that I turn to you for aid. But this is splendid, really unique from some points of view. When you pass Bradley's,[10] would you ask him to send up a pound of the strongest shag tobacco? Thank you. It would be as well if you could make it convenient not to return before evening. Then I should be very glad to compare impressions as to this most interesting problem which has been submitted to us this morning.'

I knew that seclusion and solitude were very necessary for my friend in those hours of intense mental concentration during which he weighed every particle of evidence, constructed alternative theories, balanced one against the other and made up his mind as to which points were essential and which immaterial. I therefore spent the day at my club, and did not return to Baker Street until evening. It was nearly nine o'clock when I found myself in the sitting-room once more.

My first impression as I opened the door was that a fire had broken out, for the room was so filled with smoke that the light of the lamp upon the table was blurred by it. As I entered, however, my fears were set at rest, for it was the acrid fumes of strong, coarse tobacco which took me by the throat and set me coughing. Through the haze I had a vague vision of Holmes in his dressing-gown coiled up in an armchair with his black clay pipe between his lips. Several rolls of paper lay around him.

'Caught cold, Watson?' said he.

'No, it's this poisonous atmosphere.'

'I suppose it *is* pretty thick, now that you mention it.'

'Thick! It is intolerable.'

'Open the window, then! You have been at your club all day, I perceive.'

'My dear Holmes!'

'Am I right?'

'Certainly, but how –?'

He laughed at my bewildered expression.

'There is a delightful freshness about you, Watson, which makes it a pleasure to exercise any small powers which I possess at your expense. A gentleman goes forth on a showery and miry day. He returns immaculate in the evening with the gloss still on his hat and his boots. He has been a fixture therefore all day. He is not a man with intimate friends. Where, then, could he have been? Is it not obvious?'

'Well, it is rather obvious.'

'The world is full of obvious things which nobody by any chance ever observes. Where do you think that I have been?'

'A fixture also.'

'On the contrary, I have been to Devonshire.'

'In spirit?'

'Exactly. My body has remained in this armchair; and has, I regret to observe, consumed in my absence two large pots of coffee and an incredible amount of tobacco. After you left I sent down to Stanford's[11] for the Ordnance map of this portion of the moor, and my spirit has hovered over it all day. I flatter myself that I could find my way about.'

'A large-scale map, I presume?'

'Very large.' He unrolled one section and held it over his knee. 'Here you have the particular district which concerns us. That is Baskerville Hall in the middle.'

'With a wood round it?'

'Exactly. I fancy the Yew Alley, though not marked under that name, must stretch along this line, with the moor, as you perceive, upon the right of it. This small clump of buildings here is the hamlet of Grimpen,[12] where our friend Dr Mortimer has his headquarters. Within a radius of five miles there are, as you see, only a very few scattered dwellings. Here is Lafter Hall, which was mentioned in the narrative. There is a house indicated here which may be the residence of the naturalist – Stapleton, if I remember right, was his name. Here are two moorland farmhouses, High Tor and Foulmire.[13] Then fourteen miles away the great convict prison of Princetown.[14] Between and around these scattered points extends the desolate, lifeless moor. This, then, is the stage upon which tragedy has been played,[15] and upon which we may help to play it again.'

'It must be a wild place.'

'Yes, the setting is a worthy one. If the devil did desire to have a hand in the affairs of men –'

'Then you are yourself inclining to the supernatural explanation.'

'The devil's agents may be of flesh and blood, may they not? There are two questions waiting for us at the outset. The one is whether any crime has been committed at all; the second is, what is the crime and how was it committed? Of course, if Dr Mortimer's surmise should be correct, and we are dealing with forces outside the ordinary laws of Nature, there is an end of our investigation. But we are bound to exhaust all other hypotheses before falling back upon this one. I think we'll shut that window again, if you don't mind. It is a singular thing, but I find that a concentrated atmosphere[16] helps a concentration of thought. I have not pushed it to the length of getting into a box to think,[17] but that is the logical outcome of my convictions. Have you turned the case over in your mind?'

'Yes, I have thought a good deal of it in the course of the day.'

'What do you make of it?'

'It is very bewildering.'

'It has certainly a character of its own. There are points of distinction about it. That change in the footprints, for example. What do you make of that?'

'Mortimer said that the man had walked on tiptoe down that portion of the alley.'

'He only repeated what some fool had said at the inquest. Why should a man walk on tiptoe down the alley?'

'What then?'

'He was running, Watson – running desperately, running for his life, running until he burst his heart and fell dead upon his face.'

'Running from what?'

'There lies our problem. There are indications that the man was crazed with fear before ever he began to run.'

'How can you say that?'

'I am presuming that the cause of his fears came to him across the moor. If that were so, and it seems most probable, only a man who had lost his wits would have run *from* the house instead of towards it. If the gipsy's evidence may be taken as true, he ran with cries for help in the direction where help was least likely to be. Then again, whom was he waiting for that night, and why was he waiting for him in the Yew Alley rather than in his own house?'

'You think that he was waiting for someone?'

'The man was elderly and infirm. We can understand his taking an evening stroll, but the ground was damp and the night inclement. Is it natural that he should stand for five or ten minutes, as Dr Mortimer, with more practical sense than I should have given him credit for, deduced from the cigar ash?'

'But he went out every evening.'

'I think it unlikely that he waited at the moor-gate every evening. On the contrary, the evidence is that he avoided the moor. That night he waited there. It was the night before he was to take his departure for London. The thing takes shape, Watson. It becomes coherent. Might I ask you to hand me my violin, and we will postpone all further thought upon this business until we have had the advantage of meeting Dr Mortimer and Sir Henry Baskerville in the morning.'

4

Sir Henry Baskerville

Our breakfast-table was cleared early, and Holmes waited in his dressing-gown for the promised interview. Our clients were punctual to their appointment, for the clock had just struck ten when Dr Mortimer was shown up, followed by the young baronet.[1] The latter was a small, alert, dark-eyed man about thirty years of age, very sturdily built, with thick black eyebrows and a strong, pugnacious face. He wore a ruddy-tinted tweed suit, and had the weather-beaten appearance of one who has spent most of his time in the open air, and yet there was something in his steady eye and the quiet assurance of his bearing which indicated the gentleman.

'This is Sir Henry Baskerville,' said Dr Mortimer.

'Why, yes,' said he, 'and the strange thing is, Mr Sherlock Holmes, that if my friend here had not proposed coming round to you this morning I should have come on my own. I understand that you think out little puzzles, and I've had one this morning which wants more thinking out than I am able to give it.'

'Pray take a seat, Sir Henry. Do I understand you to say that you have yourself had some remarkable experience since you arrived in London?'

'Nothing of much importance, Mr Holmes. Only a joke, as like as not. It was this letter, if you can call it a letter, which reached me this morning.'

He laid an envelope upon the table, and we all bent over it. It was of common quality, greyish in colour. The address, 'Sir Henry Baskerville, Northumberland Hotel',[2] was printed in rough characters; the post-mark 'Charing Cross', and the date of posting the preceding evening.

'Who knew that you were going to the Northumberland Hotel?' asked Holmes, glancing keenly across at our visitor.

'No one could have known. We only decided after I met Dr Mortimer.'

'But Dr Mortimer was, no doubt, already stopping there?'

'No, I had been staying with a friend,' said the doctor. 'There was no possible indication that we intended to go to this hotel.'

'Hum! Someone seems to be very deeply interested in your movements.' Out of the envelope he took a half-sheet of foolscap paper folded into four. This he opened and spread flat upon the table. Across the middle of it a single sentence had been formed by the expedient of pasting printed words upon it. It ran: 'As you value your life or your reason keep away from the moor.' The word 'moor' only was printed in ink.

'Now,' said Sir Henry Baskerville, 'perhaps you will tell me, Mr Holmes, what in thunder is the meaning of that, and who it is that takes so much interest in my affairs?'

'What do you make of it, Dr Mortimer? You must allow that there is nothing supernatural about this, at any rate?'

'No, sir, but it might very well come from someone who was convinced that the business is supernatural.'

'What business?' asked Sir Henry, sharply. 'It seems to me that all you gentlemen know a great deal more than I do about my own affairs.'

'You shall share our knowledge before you leave this room, Sir Henry. I promise you that,' said Sherlock Holmes. 'We will confine ourselves for the present, with your permission, to this very interesting document, which must have been put together and posted yesterday evening. Have you yesterday's *Times*,³ Watson?'

'It is here in the corner.'

'Might I trouble you for it – the inside page, please, with the leading articles?' He glanced swiftly over it, running his eyes up and down the columns. 'Capital article this on Free Trade.⁴ Permit me to give you an extract from it. "You may be cajoled into imagining that your own special trade or your own industry will be encouraged by a protective tariff, but it stands to reason that such legislation must in the long run keep away wealth from the country, diminish the value of our imports, and lower the general conditions of life in this land." What do you think of that, Watson?' cried Holmes, in high glee, rubbing his hands together with satisfaction. 'Don't you think that is an admirable sentiment?'

Dr Mortimer looked at Holmes with an air of professional interest, and Sir Henry Baskerville turned a pair of puzzled dark eyes upon me.

'I don't know much about the tariff and things of that kind,' said he; 'but it seems to me we've got a bit off the trail so far as that note is concerned.'

'On the contrary, I think we are particularly hot upon the trail, Sir Henry. Watson here knows more about my methods than you do, but I fear that even he has not quite grasped the significance of this sentence.'

'No, I confess that I see no connection.'

'And yet, my dear Watson, there is so very close a connection that the one is extracted out of the other. "You", "your", "your", "life", "reason", "value", "keep away", "from the". Don't you see now whence these words have been taken?'

'By thunder, you're right! Well, if that isn't smart!' cried Sir Henry.

'If any possible doubt remained it is settled by the fact that "keep away" and "from the" are cut out in one piece.'

'Well now – so it is!'

'Really, Mr Holmes, this exceeds anything which I could have imagined,' said Dr Mortimer, gazing at my friend in amazement. 'I could understand anyone saying that the words were from a news-paper; but that you should name which, and add that it came from the leading article, is really one of the most remarkable things which I have ever known. How did you do it?'

'I presume, doctor, that you could tell the skull of a Negro from that of an Esquimaux?'[5]

'Most certainly.'

'But how?'

'Because that is my special hobby. The differences are obvious. The supra-orbital crest, the facial angle, the maxillary curve,[6] the –'

'But this is my special hobby, and the differences are equally obvious. There is as much difference to my eyes between the leaded bourgeois type[7] of a *Times* article and the slovenly print of an evening halfpenny paper as there could be between your Negro and your Esquimaux. The detection of types is one of the most elementary branches of knowledge to the special expert in crime, though I confess that once when I was very young I confused the *Leeds Mercury* with the *Western Morning News*.[8] But a *Times* leader is entirely distinctive, and these words could have been taken from nothing else. As it was done yesterday the strong probability was that we should find the words in yesterday's issue.'

'So far as I can follow you, then, Mr Holmes,' said Sir Henry Baskerville, 'someone cut out this message with a scissors[9] –'

'Nail-scissors,' said Holmes. 'You can see that it was a very short-bladed scissors, since the cutter had to take two snips over "keep away".'

'That is so. Someone, then, cut out the message with a pair of short-bladed scissors, pasted it with paste –'

'Gum,' said Holmes.

'With gum on to the paper. But I want to know why the word "moor" should have been written?'

'Because he could not find it in print. The other words were all simple, and might be found in any issue, but "moor" would be less common.'

'Why, of course, that would explain it. Have you read anything else in this message, Mr Holmes?'

'There are one or two indications, and yet the utmost pains have been taken to remove all clues. The address, you observe, is printed in rough characters. But *The Times* is a paper which is seldom found in any hands but those of the highly educated. We may take it, therefore, that the letter was composed by an educated man who wished to pose as an uneducated one, and his effort to conceal his own writing suggests that that writing might be known, or come to be known by you. Again, you will observe that the words are not gummed on in an accurate line, but that some are much higher than others. "Life", for example, is quite out of its proper place. That may point to carelessness or it may point to agitation and hurry upon the part of the cutter. On the whole I incline to the latter view, since the matter was evidently important, and it is unlikely that the composer of such a letter would be careless. If he were in a hurry it opens up the interesting question why he should be in a hurry, since any letter posted up to early morning would reach Sir Henry before he would leave his hotel. Did the composer fear an interruption – and from whom?'

'We are coming now rather into the region of guesswork,'[10] said Dr Mortimer.

'Say, rather, into the region where we balance probabilities and choose the most likely. It is the scientific use of the imagination, but we have always some material basis on which to start our speculations. Now, you would call it a guess, no doubt, but I am almost certain that this address has been written in an hotel.'

'How in the world can you say that?'

'If you examine it carefully you will see that both the pen and the ink have given the writer trouble. The pen has spluttered twice in a single word, and has run dry three times in a short address, showing that there was very little ink in the bottle. Now, a private pen or ink-bottle is seldom allowed to be in such a state, and the combination of the two must be quite rare. But you know the hotel ink and the hotel pen, where it is rare to get anything else. Yes, I have very little hesitation in saying that could we examine the wastepaper baskets of the hotels round Charing Cross until we found the remains of the mutilated *Times* leader we could lay our hands straight upon the person who sent this singular message. Halloa! Halloa! What's this?'

He was carefully examining the foolscap, upon which the words were pasted, holding it only an inch or two from his eyes.

'Well?'

'Nothing,' said he, throwing it down. 'It is a blank half-sheet of paper, without even a watermark[11] upon it. I think we have drawn as much as we can from this curious letter; and now, Sir Henry, has anything else of interest happened to you since you have been in London?'

'Why, no, Mr Holmes. I think not.'

'You have not observed anyone follow or watch you?'

'I seem to have walked right into the thick of a dime novel,'[12] said our visitor. 'Why in thunder should anyone follow or watch me?'

'We are coming to that. You have nothing else to report to us before we go into this matter?'

'Well, it depends upon what you think worth reporting.'

'I think anything out of the ordinary routine of life well worth reporting.'

Sir Henry smiled. 'I don't know much of British life yet, for I have spent nearly all my time in the States and in Canada. But I hope that to lose one of your boots is not part of the ordinary routine of life over here.'

'You have lost one of your boots?'

'My dear sir,' cried Dr Mortimer, 'it is only mislaid. You will find it when you return to the hotel. What is the use of troubling Mr Holmes with trifles of this kind?'

'Well, he asked me for anything outside the ordinary routine.'

'Exactly,' said Holmes, 'however foolish the incident may seem. You have lost one of your boots, you say?'

'Well, mislaid it, anyhow. I put them both outside my door last night, and there was only one in the morning. I could get no sense out of the chap who cleans them. The worst of it is that I only bought the pair last night in the Strand,[13] and I have never had them on.'

'If you have never worn them, why did you put them out to be cleaned?'

'They were tan boots, and had never been varnished. That was why I put them out.'

'Then I understand that on your arrival in London yesterday you went out at once and bought a pair of boots?'

'I did a good deal of shopping. Dr Mortimer here went round with me. You see, if I am to be squire down there I must dress the part, and it may be that I have got a little careless in my ways out West. Among other things I bought these brown boots – gave six dollars for them – and had one stolen before ever I had them on my feet.'

'It seems a singularly useless thing to steal,' said Sherlock Holmes.

'I confess that I share Dr Mortimer's belief that it will not be long before the missing boot is found.'

'And now, gentlemen,' said the baronet, with decision, 'it seems to me that I have spoken quite enough about the little that I know. It is time that you kept your promise, and gave me a full account of what we are all driving at.'

'Your request is a very reasonable one,' Holmes answered. 'Dr Mortimer, I think you could not do better than to tell your story as you told it to us.'

Thus encouraged, our scientific friend drew his papers from his pocket, and presented the whole case as he had done upon the morning before. Sir Henry Baskerville listened with the deepest attention and with an occasional exclamation of surprise.

'Well, I seem to have come into an inheritance with a vengeance,' said he, when the long narrative was finished. 'Of course, I've heard of the hound ever since I was in the nursery. It's the pet story of the family, though I never thought of taking it seriously before. But as to my uncle's death – well, it all seems boiling up in my head, and I can't get it clear yet. You don't seem quite to have made up your mind whether it's a case for a policeman or a clergyman.'

'Precisely.'

'And now there's this affair of the letter to me at the hotel. I suppose that fits into its place.'

'It seems to show that someone knows more than we do about what goes on upon the moor,' said Dr Mortimer.

'And also,' said Holmes, 'that someone is not ill-disposed towards you, since they warn you of danger.'

'Or it may be that they wish for their own purposes to scare me away.'

'Well, of course, that is possible also. I am very much indebted to you, Dr Mortimer, for introducing me to a problem which presents several interesting alternatives. But the practical point which we now have to decide, Sir Henry, is whether it is or is not advisable for you to go to Baskerville Hall.'

'Why should I not go?'

'There seems to be danger.'

'Do you mean danger from this family fiend or do you mean danger from human beings?'

'Well, that is what we have to find out.'

'Whichever it is, my answer is fixed. There is no devil in hell, Mr Holmes, and there is no man upon earth who can prevent me from going to the home of my own people, and you may take that to be my final answer.' His dark brows knitted and his face flushed to a dusky red as he spoke. It was evident that the fiery temper of the Baskervilles was not extinct in this their last representative. 'Meanwhile,' said he, 'I have hardly had time to think over all that you have told me. It's a big thing for a man to have to understand and to decide at one sitting. I should like to have a quiet hour by myself to make up my mind. Now, look here, Mr Holmes, it's half-past eleven now, and I am going back right away to my hotel. Suppose you and your friend, Dr Watson, come round and lunch with us at two? I'll be able to tell you more clearly then how this thing strikes me.'

'Is that convenient to you, Watson?'

'Perfectly.'

'Then you may expect us. Shall I have a cab called?'

'I'd prefer to walk, for this affair has flurried me rather.'

'I'll join you in a walk, with pleasure,' said his companion.

'Then we meet again at two o'clock. Au revoir, and good morning!'

We heard the steps of our visitors descend the stair and the bang of the front door. In an instant Holmes had changed from the languid dreamer to the man of action.[14]

'Your hat and boots, Watson, quick! Not a moment to lose!' He rushed into his room in his dressing-gown, and was back again in a few seconds in a frock-coat. We hurried together down the stairs and into the street. Dr Mortimer and Baskerville were still visible about two hundred yards ahead of us in the direction of Oxford Street.

'Shall I run on and stop them?'

'Not for the world, my dear Watson. I am perfectly satisfied with your company, if you will tolerate mine. Our friends are wise, for it is certainly a very fine morning for a walk.'

He quickened his pace until we had decreased the distance which divided us by about half. Then, still keeping a hundred yards behind, we followed into Oxford Street and so down Regent Street. Once our friends stopped and stared into a shop window, upon which Holmes did the same. An instant afterwards he gave a little cry of satisfaction, and, following the direction of his eager eyes, I saw that a hansom cab with a man inside which had halted on the other side of the street was now walking slowly onwards again.

'There's our man, Watson![15] Come along! We'll have a good look at him, if we can do no more.'

At that instant I was aware of a bushy black beard and a pair of piercing eyes turned upon us through the side window of the cab. Instantly the trapdoor at the top flew up, something was screamed to the driver, and the cab flew madly off down Regent Street. Holmes looked eagerly round for another, but no empty one was in sight. Then he dashed in wild pursuit amid the stream of the traffic, but the start was too great, and already the cab was out of sight.

'There now!' said Holmes, bitterly, as he emerged panting and white with vexation from the tide of vehicles. 'Was ever such bad luck and such bad management, too? Watson, Watson, if you are an honest man you will record this also and set it against my successes!'

'Who was the man?'

'I have not an idea.'

'A spy?'

'Well, it was evident from what we have heard that Baskerville has been very closely shadowed by someone since he has been in town. How else could it be known so quickly that it was the Northumberland Hotel which he had chosen? If they had followed him the first day, I argued that they would follow him also the second. You may have observed that I twice strolled over to the window while Dr Mortimer was reading his legend.'

'Yes, I remember.'

'I was looking out for loiterers in the street, but I saw none. We are dealing with a clever man, Watson. This matter cuts very deep, and though I have not finally made up my mind whether it is a benevolent or a malevolent agency which is in touch with us, I am conscious always of power and design. When our friends left I at once followed them in the hopes of marking down their invisible attendant. So wily was he that he had not trusted himself upon foot, but he had availed himself of a cab, so that he could loiter behind or dash past them and so escape their notice. His method had the additional advantage that if they were to take a cab he was all ready to follow them. It has, however, one obvious disadvantage.'

'It puts him in the power of the cabman.'

'Exactly.'

'What a pity we did not get the number!'

'My dear Watson, clumsy as I have been, you surely do not seriously imagine that I neglected to get the number? 2704 is our man. But that is no use to us for the moment.'

'I fail to see how you could have done more.'

'On observing the cab I should have instantly turned and walked in the other direction. I should then at my leisure have hired a second cab, and followed the first at a respectful distance, or, better still, have driven to the Northumberland Hotel and waited there. When our unknown had followed Baskerville home we should have had the opportunity of playing his own game upon himself, and seeing where he made for. As it is, by an indiscreet eagerness, which was taken advantage of with extraordinary quickness and energy by our opponent, we have betrayed ourselves and lost our man.'

We had been sauntering slowly down Regent Street during this conversation, and Dr Mortimer, with his companion, had long vanished in front of us.

'There is no object in our following them,' said Holmes. 'The shadow has departed and will not return. We must see what further cards we have in our hands, and play them with decision. Could you swear to that man's face within the cab?'

'I could swear only to the beard.'

'And so could I – from which I gather that in all probability it was a false one. A clever man upon so delicate an errand has no use for a beard save to conceal his features. Come in here, Watson!'

He turned into one of the district messenger offices,[16] where he was warmly greeted by the manager.

'Ah, Wilson, I see you have not forgotten the little case in which I had the good fortune to help you?'

'No, sir, indeed I have not. You saved my good name, and perhaps my life.'

'My dear fellow, you exaggerate. I have some recollection, Wilson, that you had among your boys a lad named Cartwright, who showed some ability during the investigation.'

'Yes, sir, he is still with us.'

'Could you ring him up? Thank you! And I should be glad to have change of this five-pound note.'

A lad of fourteen, with a bright, keen face, had obeyed the summons of the manager. He stood now gazing with great reverence at the famous detective.

'Let me have the Hotel Directory,' said Holmes. 'Thank you! Now, Cartwright, there are the names of twenty-three hotels here, all in the immediate neighbourhood of Charing Cross. Do you see?'

'Yes, sir.'

'You will visit each of these in turn.'

'Yes, sir.'

'You will begin in each case by giving the outside porter one shilling. Here are twenty-three shillings.'

'Yes, sir.'

'You will tell him that you want to see the waste paper of yesterday. You will say that an important telegram has miscarried, and that you are looking for it. You understand?'

'Yes, sir.'

'But what you are really looking for is the centre page of *The Times* with some holes cut in it with scissors. Here is a copy of *The Times*. It is this page. You could easily recognize it, could you not?'

'Yes, sir.'

'In each case the outside porter will send for the hall porter, to whom also you will give a shilling. Here are twenty-three shillings. You will then learn in possibly twenty cases out of the twenty-three that the waste of the day before has been burned or removed. In the three other cases you will be shown a heap of paper, and will look for this page of *The Times* among it. The odds are enormously against your finding it. There are ten shillings over in case of emergencies. Let me have a report by wire at Baker Street before evening. And now, Watson, it only remains for us to find out by wire the identity of the cabman, No. 2704, and then we will drop into one of the Bond Street picture-galleries[17] and fill in the time until we are due at the hotel.'

5

Three Broken Threads[1]

Sherlock Holmes had, in a very remarkable degree, the power of detaching his mind at will. For two hours the strange business in which we had been involved appeared to be forgotten, and he was entirely absorbed in the pictures of the modern Belgian masters.[2] He would talk of nothing but art, of which he had the crudest ideas, from our leaving the gallery until we found ourselves at the Northumberland Hotel.

'Sir Henry Baskerville is upstairs expecting you,' said the clerk. 'He asked me to show you up at once when you came.'

'Have you any objection to my looking at your register?' said Holmes.

'Not in the least.'

The book showed that two names had been added after that of Baskerville. One was Theophilus Johnson and family, of Newcastle;[3] the other Mrs Oldmore and maid, of High Lodge, Alton.[4]

'Surely that must be the same Johnson whom I used to know,' said Holmes to the porter. 'A lawyer, is he not, grey-headed, and walks with a limp?'

'No, sir, this is Mr Johnson the coal-owner, a very active gentleman, not older than yourself.'

'Surely you are mistaken about his trade?'

'No, sir; he used this hotel for many years, and he is very well known to us.'

'Ah, that settles it. Mrs Oldmore, too; I seem to remember the name. Excuse my curiosity, but often in calling upon one friend one finds another.'

'She is an invalid lady, sir. Her husband was once Mayor of Gloucester.[5] She always comes to us when she is in town.'

'Thank you; I am afraid I cannot claim her acquaintance. We have established a most important fact by these questions, Watson,' he continued, in a low voice, as we went upstairs together. 'We know now that the people who are so interested in our friend have not settled down in his own hotel. That means that while they are, as we have seen, very anxious to watch him, they are equally anxious that he should not see them. Now, this is a most suggestive fact.'

'What does it suggest?'

'It suggests – halloa, my dear fellow, what on earth is the matter?'

As we came round the top of the stairs we had run up against Sir Henry Baskerville himself. His face was flushed with anger, and he held an old and dusty boot in one of his hands. So furious was he that he was hardly articulate, and when he did speak it was in a much broader and more Western dialect[6] than any which we had heard from him in the morning.

'Seems to me they are playing me for a sucker in this hotel,' he cried. 'They'll find they've started in to monkey with the wrong man unless they are careful. By thunder, if that chap can't find my missing boot there will be trouble. I can take a joke with the best, Mr Holmes, but they've got a bit over the mark this time.'

'Still looking for your boot?'

'Yes, sir, and mean to find it.'

'But surely, you said that it was a new brown boot?'

'So it was, sir. And now it's an old black one.'

'What! you don't mean to say –?'

'That's just what I do mean to say. I only had three pairs in the world – the new brown, the old black, and the patent leathers, which I am wearing. Last night they took one of my brown ones, and today they have sneaked one of the black. Well, have you got it? Speak out, man, and don't stand staring!'

An agitated German waiter had appeared upon the scene.

'No, sir; I have made inquiry all over the hotel, but I can hear no word of it.'

'Well, either, that boot comes back before sundown, or I'll see the manager and tell him that I go right straight out of this hotel.'

'It shall be found, sir – I promise you that if you will have a little patience it will be found.'

'Mind it is, for it's the last thing of mine that I'll lose in this den of thieves. Well, well, Mr Holmes, you'll excuse my troubling you about such a trifle –'

'I think it's well worth troubling about.'

'Why, you look very serious over it.'

'How do you explain it?'

'I just don't attempt to explain it. It seems the very maddest, queerest thing that ever happened to me.'

'The queerest, perhaps,' said Holmes, thoughtfully.

'What do you make of it yourself?'

'Well, I don't profess to understand it yet. This case of yours is very complex, Sir Henry. When taken in conjunction with your uncle's death I am not sure that of all the five hundred cases of capital importance[7] which I have handled there is one which cuts so deep. But we hold several threads in our hands, and the odds are that one or other of them guides us to the truth. We may waste time in following the wrong one, but sooner or later, we must come upon the right.'

We had a pleasant luncheon in which little was said of the business which had brought us together. It was in the private sitting-room to which we afterwards repaired that Holmes asked Baskerville what were his intentions.

'To go to Baskerville Hall.'

'And when?'

'At the end of the week.'

'On the whole,' said Holmes, 'I think that your decision is a wise one. I have ample evidence that you are being dogged in London, and amid the millions of this great city it is difficult to discover who these people are or what their object can be. If their intentions are evil they might do you a mischief, and we should be powerless to prevent it. You did not know, Dr Mortimer, that you were followed this morning from my house?'

Dr Mortimer started violently. 'Followed! By whom?'

'That, unfortunately, is what I cannot tell you. Have you among your neighbours or acquaintances on Dartmoor any man with a black, full beard?'

'No – or, let me see – why, yes. Barrymore, Sir Charles's butler,[8] is a man with a full, black beard.'

'Ha! Where is Barrymore?'

'He is in charge of the Hall.'

'We had best ascertain if he is really there, or if by any possibility he might be in London.'

'How can you do that?'

'Give me a telegraph form. "Is all ready for Sir Henry?" That will do. Address to Mr Barrymore, Baskerville Hall. Which is the nearest telegraph office? Grimpen. Very good, we will send a second wire to the postmaster, Grimpen: "Telegram to Mr Barrymore, to be delivered into his own hand. If absent, please return wire to Sir Henry Baskerville, Northumberland Hotel." That should let us know before evening whether Barrymore is at his post in Devonshire or not.'

'That's so,' said Baskerville. 'By the way, Dr Mortimer, who is this Barrymore, anyhow?'

'He is the son of the old caretaker, who is dead. They have looked after the Hall for four generations now. So far as I know, he and his wife are as respectable a couple as any in the county.'

'At the same time,' said Baskerville, 'it's clear enough that so long as there are none of the family at the Hall these people have a mighty fine home and nothing to do.'

'That is true.'

'Did Barrymore profit at all by Sir Charles's will?' asked Holmes.

'He and his wife had five hundred pounds each.'

'Ha! Did they know that they would receive this?'

'Yes; Sir Charles was very fond of talking about the provisions of his will.'

'That is very interesting.'

'I hope,' said Dr Mortimer, 'that you do not look with suspicious eyes upon everyone who received a legacy from Sir Charles, for I also had a thousand pounds left to me.'

'Indeed! And anyone else?'

'There were many insignificant sums to individuals and a large number of public charities. The residue all went to Sir Henry.'

'And how much was the residue?'

'Seven hundred and forty thousand pounds.' *motive!*

Holmes raised his eyebrows in surprise. 'I had no idea that so gigantic a sum was involved,' said he.

'Sir Charles had the reputation of being rich, but we did not know how very rich he was until we came to examine his securities.[9] The total value of the estate was close on to a million.'

'Dear me! It is a stake for which a man might well play a desperate game. And one more question, Dr Mortimer. Supposing that anything happened to our young friend here – you will forgive the unpleasant hypothesis! – who would inherit the estate?'

'Since Rodger Baskerville, Sir Charles's younger brother, died unmarried, the estate would descend to the Desmonds, who are distant cousins. James Desmond is an elderly clergyman in Westmorland.'[10]

'Thank you. These details are all of great interest. Have you met Mr James Desmond?'

'Yes; he once came down to visit Sir Charles. He is a man of venerable appearance and of saintly life. I remember that he refused to accept any settlement from Sir Charles, though he pressed it upon him.'

'And this man of simple tastes would be the heir to Sir Charles's thousands?'

'He would be the heir to the estate, because that is entailed. He would also be the heir to the money unless it were willed otherwise by the present owner, who can, of course, do what he likes with it.'

'And have you made your will, Sir Henry?'

'No, Mr Holmes, I have not. I've had no time, for it was only yesterday that I learned how matters stood. But in any case I feel that the money should go with the title and estate. That was my poor uncle's idea. How is the owner going to restore the glories of the Baskervilles if he has not money enough to keep up the property? House, land, and dollars must go together.'

'Quite so. Well, Sir Henry, I am of one mind with you as to the advisability of your going down to Devonshire without delay. There is only one provision which I must make. You certainly must not go alone.'

'Dr Mortimer returns with me.'

'But Dr Mortimer has his practice to attend to, and his house is miles away from yours. With all the good will in the world, he may be unable to help you. No, Sir Henry, you must take with you someone, a trusty man, who will be always by your side.'

'Is it possible that you could come yourself, Mr Holmes?'

'If matters came to a crisis I should endeavour to be present in person; but you can understand that, with my extensive consulting practice and with the constant appeals which reach me from many quarters, it is impossible for me to be absent from London for an indefinite time. At the present instant one of the most revered names in England[11] is being besmirched by a blackmailer, and only I can stop a disastrous scandal. You will see how impossible it is for me to go to Dartmoor.'

Shows his arrogance.
He lies.

'Whom would you recommend, then?'

Holmes laid his hand upon my arm.

'If my friend would undertake it there is no man who is better worth having at your side when you are in a tight place. No one can say so more confidently than I.'

Starts as a praise
No trust

The proposition took me completely by surprise, but before I had time to answer Baskerville seized me by the hand and wrung it heartily.

'Well, now, that is real kind of you, Dr Watson,' said he. 'You see how it is with me, and you know just as much about the matter as I do. If you will come down to Baskerville Hall and see me through I'll never forget it.'

The promise of adventure had always a fascination for me, and I was complimented by the words of Holmes and by the eagerness with which the baronet hailed me as a companion.

'I will come with pleasure,' said I. 'I do not know how I could employ my time better.'

'And you will report very carefully to me,' said Holmes. 'When a crisis comes, as it will do, I will direct how you shall act. I suppose that by Saturday all might be ready?'

'Would that suit Dr Watson?'

'Perfectly.'

'Then on Saturday, unless you hear to the contrary, we shall meet at the 10.30 train from Paddington.'[12]

We had risen to depart when Baskerville gave a cry of triumph, and diving into one of the corners of the room he drew a brown boot from under a cabinet.

'My missing boot!' he cried.

'May all our difficulties vanish as easily!' said Sherlock Holmes.

'But it is a very singular thing,' Dr Mortimer remarked. 'I searched this room carefully before lunch.'

'And so did I,' said Baskerville. 'Every inch of it.'

'There was certainly no boot in it then.'

'In that case the waiter must have placed it there while we were lunching.'

The German was sent for, but professed to know nothing of the matter, nor could any inquiry clear it up. Another item had been added to that constant and apparently purposeless series of small mysteries which had succeeded each other so rapidly. Setting aside the whole grim story of Sir Charles's death, we had a line of inexplicable incidents all within the limits of two days, which included the receipt of the printed letter, the black-bearded spy in the hansom, the loss of the new brown boot, the loss of the old black boot, and now the return of the new brown boot. Holmes sat in silence in the cab as we drove back to Baker Street, and I knew from his drawn brows and keen face that his mind, like my own, was busy in endeavouring to frame some scheme[13] into which all these strange and apparently disconnected episodes could be fitted. All afternoon and late into the evening he sat lost in tobacco and thought.

Just before dinner two telegrams were handed in. The first ran:

Have just heard that Barrymore is at the Hall – BASKERVILLE.

The second:

Visited twenty-three hotels as directed, but sorry to report unable to trace cut sheet of *Times* – CARTWRIGHT.

'There go two of my threads, Watson. There is nothing more stimulating than a case where everything goes against you. We must cast round for another scent.'

'We have still the cabman who drove the spy.'

'Exactly. I have wired to get his name and address from the Official Registry. I should not be surprised if this were an answer to my question.'

The ring at the bell proved to be something even more satisfactory than an answer, however, for the door opened and a rough-looking fellow entered who was evidently the man himself.

'I got a message from the head office that a gent at this address had been inquiring for 2704,' said he. 'I've driven my cab this seven years and never a word of complaint. I came here straight from the Yard to ask you to your face what you had against me.'

'I have nothing in the world against you, my good man,' said Holmes. 'On the contrary, I have half a sovereign for you if you will give me a clear answer to my questions.'

'Well, I've had a good day and no mistake,' said the cabman, with a grin. 'What was it you wanted to ask, sir?'

'First of all your name and address, in case I want you again.'

'John Clayton, 3, Turpey Street, the Borough.¹⁴ My cab is out of Shipley's Yard, near Waterloo Station.'

Sherlock Holmes made a note of it.

'Now, Clayton, tell me all about the fare who came and watched this house at ten o'clock this morning and afterwards followed the two gentlemen down Regent Street.'

The man looked surprised and a little embarrassed.

'Why, there's no good my telling you things, for you seem to know as much as I do already,' said he. 'The truth is that the gentleman told me that he was a detective, and that I was to say nothing about him to anyone.'

'My good fellow, this is a very serious business, and you may find yourself in a pretty bad position if you try to hide anything from me. You say that your fare told you that he was a detective?'

'Yes, he did.'

'When did he say this?'

'When he left me.'

'Did he say anything more?'

'He mentioned his name.'

Holmes cast a swift glance of triumph at me.

'Oh, he mentioned his name, did he? That was imprudent. What was the name that he mentioned?'

'His name,' said the cabman, 'was Mr Sherlock Holmes.'

Never have I seen my friend more completely taken aback than by the cabman's reply. For an instant he sat in silent amazement. Then he burst into a hearty laugh:

'A touch, Watson – an undeniable touch!'[15] said he. 'I feel a foil as quick and supple as my own. He got home upon me very prettily that time. So his name was Sherlock Holmes, was it?'

'Yes, sir, that was the gentleman's name.'

'Excellent! Tell me where you picked him up, and all that occurred.'

'He hailed me at half-past nine in Trafalgar Square. He said that he was a detective, and he offered me two guineas if I would do exactly what he wanted all day and ask no questions. I was glad enough to agree. First we drove down to the Northumberland Hotel, and waited there until two gentlemen came out and took a cab from the rank. We followed their cab until it pulled up somewhere near here.'

'This very door,' said Holmes.

'Well, I couldn't be sure of that, but I dare say my fare knew all about it. We pulled up half-way down the street and waited an hour and a half. Then the two gentlemen passed us, walking, and we followed down Baker Street and along –'

'I know,' said Holmes.

'Until we got three-quarters down Regent Street. Then my gentleman threw up the trap, and he cried that I should drive right away to Waterloo Station as hard as I could go. I whipped up the mare, and we were there under the ten minutes. Then he paid up his two guineas, like a good one, and away he went into the station. Only just as he was leaving he turned round and said: "It might interest you to know that you have been driving Mr Sherlock Holmes." That's how I came to know the name.'

'I see. And you saw no more of him?'

'Not after he went into the station.'

'And how would you describe Mr Sherlock Holmes?'

The cabman scratched his head. 'Well, he wasn't altogether such an easy gentleman to describe. I'd put him at forty years of age, and he was of a middle height, two or three inches shorter than you, sir.[16] He was dressed like a toff,[17] and he had a black beard, cut square at the end, and a pale face. I don't know as I could say more than that.'

'Colour of his eyes?'

'No, I can't say that.'

'Nothing more that you can remember?'

'No, sir; nothing.'

'Well, then, here is your half-sovereign. There's another one waiting for you if you can bring any more information. Good night!'

'Good night, sir, and thank you!'

John Clayton departed chuckling, and Holmes turned to me with a shrug of the shoulders and a rueful smile.

'Snap goes our third thread, and we end where we began,' said he. 'The cunning rascal! He knew our number, knew that Sir Henry Baskerville had consulted me, spotted who I was in Regent Street, conjectured that I had got the number of the cab and would lay my hands on the driver, and so sent back this audacious message. I tell you, Watson, this time we have got a foeman who is worthy of our steel.[18] I've been checkmated in London.[19] I can only wish you better luck in Devonshire. But I'm not easy in my mind about it.'

'About what?'

'About sending you. It's an ugly business, Watson, an ugly, dangerous business, and the more I see of it the less I like it. Yes, my dear fellow, you may laugh, but I give you my word that I shall be very glad to have you back safe and sound in Baker Street once more.'

6

Baskerville Hall

Sir Henry Baskerville and Dr Mortimer were ready upon the appointed day, and we started as arranged for Devonshire. Mr Sherlock Holmes drove with me to the station, and gave me his last parting injunction and advice.

'I will not bias your mind by suggesting theories or suspicions, Watson,' said he; 'I wish you simply to report facts in the fullest possible manner to me, and you can leave me to do the theorizing.'

'What sort of facts?' I asked.

'Anything which may seem to have a bearing, however indirect, upon the case, and especially the relations between young Baskerville and his neighbours, or any fresh particulars concerning the death of Sir Charles. I have made some inquiries myself in the last few days, but the results have, I fear, been negative. One thing only appears to be certain, and that is that Mr James Desmond, who is the next heir, is an elderly gentleman of a very amiable disposition, so that this persecution does not arise from him. I really think that we may eliminate him entirely from our calculations. There remain the people who will actually surround Sir Henry Baskerville upon the moor.'

'Would it not be well in the first place to get rid of this Barrymore couple?'[1]

'By no means. You could not make a greater mistake. If they are innocent it would be a cruel injustice, and if they are guilty we should be giving up all chance of bringing it home to them. No, no, we will preserve them upon our list of suspects. Then there is a groom at the Hall, if I remember right. There are two moorland farmers. There is our friend Dr Mortimer, whom I believe to be entirely honest, and there is his wife, of whom we know nothing.[2] There is this naturalist Stapleton, and there is his sister, who is said to be a young lady of attractions. There is Mr Frankland, of Lafter Hall, who is also an unknown factor, and there are one or two other neighbours. These are the folk who must be your very special study.'

'I will do my best.'

'You have arms, I suppose?'

'Yes, I thought it as well to take them.'

'Most certainly. Keep your revolver near you night and day, and never relax your precautions.'

Our friends had already secured a first-class carriage, and were waiting for us upon the platform.

'No, we have no news of any kind,' said Dr Mortimer, in answer to my friend's questions. 'I can swear to one thing, and that is that we have not been shadowed during the last two days. We have never gone out without keeping a sharp watch, and no one could have escaped our notice.'

'You have always kept together, I presume?'

'Except yesterday afternoon. I usually give up one day to pure amusement when I come to town, so I spent it at the Museum of the College of Surgeons.'[3]

'And I went to look at the folk in the park,' said Baskerville. 'But we had no trouble of any kind.'

'It was imprudent, all the same,' said Holmes, shaking his head and looking very grave. 'I beg, Sir Henry, that you will not go about alone. Some great misfortune will befall you if you do. Did you get your other boot?'

'No, sir, it is gone for ever.'

'Indeed. That is very interesting. Well, good-bye,' he added, as the train began to glide down the platform. 'Bear in mind, Sir Henry, one of the phrases in that queer old legend which Dr Mortimer has read to us, and avoid the moor in those hours of darkness when the powers of evil are exalted.'

I looked back at the platform when we had left it far behind, and saw the tall, austere figure of Holmes standing motionless and gazing after us.

The journey was a swift and pleasant one, and I spent it in making the more intimate acquaintance of my two companions, and in playing with Dr Mortimer's spaniel. In a very few hours the brown earth had become ruddy, the brick had changed to granite, and red cows grazed in well-hedged fields where the lush grasses and more luxuriant vegetation spoke of a richer, if a damper climate. Young Baskerville stared eagerly out of the window, and cried aloud with delight as he recognized the familiar features of the Devon scenery.

'I've been over a good part of the world since I left it, Dr Watson,' said he; 'but I have never seen a place to compare with it.'

'I never saw a Devonshire man who did not swear by his county,' I remarked.

'It depends upon the breed of men quite as much as on the county,' said Dr Mortimer. 'A glance at our friend here reveals the rounded head of the Celt, which carries inside it the Celtic enthusiasm and power of attachment. Poor Sir Charles's head was of a very rare type, half Gaelic, half Ivernian[4] in its characteristics. But you were very young when you last saw Baskerville Hall, were you not?'

'I was a boy in my teens at the time of my father's death, and had never seen the Hall, for he lived in a little cottage on the south coast. Thence I went straight to a friend in America. I tell you it is all as new to me as it is to Dr Watson, and I'm as keen as possible to see the moor.'

'Are you? Then your wish is easily granted, for there is your first sight of the moor,' said Dr Mortimer, pointing out of the carriage window.

Over the green squares of the fields and the low curve of a wood there rose in the distance a grey, melancholy hill, with a strange jagged summit, dim and vague in the distance, like some fantastic landscape in a dream.[5] Baskerville sat for a long time, his eyes fixed upon it, and I read upon his eager face how much it meant to him, this first sight of that strange spot where the men of his blood had held sway so long and left their mark so deep. There he sat, with his tweed suit and his American accent, in the corner of a prosaic railway-carriage, and yet as I looked at his dark and expressive face I felt more than ever how true a descendant he was[6] of that long line of high-blooded, fiery, and masterful men. There were pride, valour and strength in his thick brows, his sensitive nostrils, and his large hazel eyes. If on that forbidding moor a difficult and dangerous quest should lie before us, this was at least a comrade for whom one might venture to take a risk with the certainty that he would bravely share it.

The train pulled up at a small wayside station,[7] and we all descended. Outside, beyond the low, white fence, a wagonette with a pair of cobs[8] was waiting. Our coming was evidently a great event, for station-master and porters clustered round us to carry out our luggage. It was a sweet, simple country spot, but I was surprised to observe that by the gate there stood two soldierly men in dark uniforms, who leaned upon their short rifles and glanced keenly at us as we passed. The coachman, a hard-faced, gnarled little fellow,[9] saluted Sir Henry Baskerville, and in a few minutes we were flying swiftly down the broad white road. Rolling pasture lands curved upwards on either side of us, and old gabled houses peeped out from amid the thick green foliage, but behind the peaceful and sunlit countryside there rose ever, dark against the evening sky, the long, gloomy curve of the moor, broken by the jagged and sinister hills.

The wagonette swung round into a side road, and we curved upwards through deep lanes worn by centuries of wheels, high banks on either side, heavy with dripping moss and fleshy hart's-tongue ferns.[10] Bronzing bracken and mottled bramble gleamed in the light of the sinking sun. Still steadily rising, we passed over a narrow granite bridge, and skirted a noisy stream, which gushed swiftly down, foaming and roaring amid the grey boulders. Both road and stream wound up through a valley dense with scrub oak and fir. At every turning Baskerville gave an exclamation of delight,[11] looking eagerly about him and asking countless questions. To his eyes all seemed beautiful, but to me a tinge of melancholy lay upon the countryside, which bore so clearly the mark of the waning year. Yellow leaves carpeted the lanes and fluttered down upon us as we passed. The rattle of our wheels died away as we drove through drifts of rotting vegetation – sad gifts, as it seemed to me, for Nature to throw before the carriage of the returning heir of the Baskervilles.

'Halloa!' cried Dr Mortimer, 'what is this?'

A steep curve of heath-clad land, an outlying spur of the moor, lay in front of us. On the summit, hard and clear like an equestrian statue upon its pedestal, was a mounted soldier, dark and stern, his rifle poised ready over his forearm. He was watching the road along which we travelled.

'What is this, Perkins?' asked Dr Mortimer.

Our driver half turned in his seat.

'There's a convict escaped from Princetown, sir.[12] He's been out three days now, and the warders watch every road and every station, but they've had no sight of him yet. The farmers about here don't like it, sir, and that's a fact.'

'Well, I understand that they get five pounds if they can give information.'

'Yes, sir, but the chance of five pounds is but a poor thing compared to the chance of having your throat cut. You see, it isn't like any ordinary convict. This is a man that would stick at nothing.'

'Who is he, then?'

'It is Selden, the Notting Hill murderer.'[13]

I remembered the case well, for it was one in which Holmes had taken an interest on account of the peculiar ferocity of the crime and the wanton brutality which had marked all the actions of the assassin. The commutation of his death sentence had been due to some doubts as to his complete sanity, so atrocious was his conduct. Our wagonette had topped a rise and in front of us rose the huge expanse of the moor, mottled with gnarled and craggy cairns[14] and tors. A cold wind swept down from it and set us shivering. Somewhere there, on that desolate plain, was lurking this fiendish man, hiding in a burrow like a wild beast, his heart full of malignancy against the whole race which had cast him out. It needed but this to complete the grim suggestiveness of the barren waste, the chilling wind, and the darkling sky.[15] Even Baskerville fell silent and pulled his overcoat more closely around him.

We had left the fertile country[16] behind and beneath us. We looked back on it now, the slanting rays of a low sun turning the streams to threads of gold and glowing on the red earth new turned by the plough and the broad tangle of the woodlands. The road in front of us grew bleaker and wilder over huge russet and olive slopes, sprinkled with giant boulders. Now and then we passed a moorland cottage, walled and roofed with stone, with no creeper to break its harsh outline. Suddenly we looked down into a cup-like depression, patched with stunted oaks and firs which had been twisted and bent by the fury of years of storm. Two high, narrow towers rose over the trees. The driver pointed with his whip.

'Baskerville Hall,'[17] said he.

Its master had risen, and was staring with flushed cheeks and shining eyes. A few minutes later we had reached the lodge gates, a maze of fantastic tracery in wrought iron, with weather-bitten pillars on either side, blotched with lichens, and surmounted by the boars' heads of the Baskervilles.[18] The lodge was a ruin of black granite and bared ribs of rafters, but facing it was a new building, half constructed, the first fruit of Sir Charles's South African gold.

Through the gateway we passed into the avenue, where the wheels were again hushed amid the leaves, and the old trees shot their branches in a sombre tunnel over our heads. Baskerville shuddered as he looked up the long, dark drive to where the house glimmered like a ghost at the farther end.

'Was it here?' he asked, in a low voice.

'No, no, the Yew Alley is on the other side.'

The young heir glanced round with a gloomy face.

'It's no wonder my uncle felt as if trouble were coming on him in such a place as this,' said he. 'It's enough to scare any man. I'll have a row of electric lamps up here inside of six months, and you won't know it again with a thousand-candle-power Swan and Edison[19] right here in front of the hall door.'

The avenue opened into a broad expanse of turf, and the house lay before us. In the fading light I could see that the centre was a heavy block of building from which a porch projected. The whole front was draped in ivy, with a patch clipped bare here and there where a window or a coat-of-arms broke through the dark veil. From this central block rose the twin towers, ancient, crenellated, and pierced with many loopholes. To right and left of the turrets were more modern wings of black granite. A dull light shone through heavy mullioned windows, and from the high chimneys which rose from the steep, high-angled roof there sprang a single black column of smoke.

'Welcome, Sir Henry![20] Welcome to Baskerville Hall!'

A tall man had stepped from the shadow of the porch to open the door of the wagonette. The figure of a woman was silhouetted against the yellow light of the hall. She came out and helped the man to hand down our bags.

'You don't mind my driving straight home, Sir Henry?' said Dr Mortimer. 'My wife is expecting me.'

'Surely you will stay and have some dinner?'

'No, I must go. I shall probably find some work awaiting me. I would stay to show you over the house, but Barrymore will be a better guide than I. Good-bye, and never hesitate night or day to send for me if I can be of service.'

The wheels died away down the drive while Sir Henry and I turned into the hall, and the door clanged heavily behind us. It was a fine apartment in which we found ourselves, large, lofty, and heavily raftered with huge balks of age-blackened oak. In the great old-fashioned fireplace behind the high iron dogs a log-fire crackled and snapped. Sir Henry and I held out our hands to it, for we were numb from our long drive. Then we gazed round us at the high, thin window of old stained glass, the oak panelling, the stags' heads, the coats-of-arms upon the walls, all dim and sombre in the subdued light of the central lamp.

'It's just as I imagined it,' said Sir Henry. 'Is it not the very picture of an old family home? To think that this should be the same hall in which for five hundred years my people have lived! It strikes me solemn to think of it.'

I saw his dark face lit up with a boyish enthusiasm as he gazed about him. The light beat upon him where he stood, but long shadows trailed down the walls and hung like a black canopy above him. Barrymore had returned from taking our luggage to our rooms. He stood in front of us now with the subdued manner of a well-trained servant. He was a remarkable-looking man, tall, handsome, with a square black beard and pale distinguished features.

'Would you wish dinner to be served at once, sir?'

'Is it ready?'

'In a very few minutes, sir. You will find hot water in your rooms. My wife and I will be happy, Sir Henry, to stay with you until you have made your fresh arrangements, but you will understand that under the new conditions this house will require a considerable staff.'

'What new conditions?'

'I only meant, sir, that Sir Charles led a very retired life, and we were able to look after his wants. You would, naturally, wish to have more company, and so you will need changes in your household.'

'Do you mean that your wife and you wish to leave?'

'Only when it is quite convenient to you, sir.'

'But your family have been with us for several generations, have they not? I should be sorry to begin my life here by breaking an old family connection.'

I seemed to discern some signs of emotion upon the butler's white face.

'I feel that also, sir, and so does my wife. But to tell the truth, sir, we were both very much attached to Sir Charles, and his death gave us a shock and made these surroundings very painful to us. I fear that we shall never again be easy in our minds at Baskerville Hall.'

'But what do you intend to do?'

'I have no doubt, sir, that we shall succeed in establishing ourselves in some business. Sir Charles's generosity has given us the means to do so. And now, sir, perhaps I had best show you to your rooms.'

A square balustraded gallery ran round the top of the old hall, approached by a double stair. From this central point two long corridors extended the whole length of the building, from which all the bedrooms opened. My own was in the same wing as Baskerville's and almost next door to it. These rooms appeared to be much more modern than the central part of the house, and the bright paper and numerous candles did something to remove the sombre impression which our arrival had left upon my mind.

But the dining-room which opened out of the hall was a place of shadow and gloom. It was a long chamber with a step separating the dais where the family sat from the lower portion reserved for their dependents. At one end a minstrels' gallery overlooked it. Black beams shot across above our heads, with a smoke-darkened ceiling beyond them. With rows of flaring torches to light it up, and the colour and rude hilarity of an old-time banquet, it might have softened; but now, when two black-clothed gentlemen sat in the little circle of light thrown by a shaded lamp, one's voice became hushed and one's spirit subdued. A dim line of ancestors, in every variety of dress, from the Elizabethan knight to the buck of the Regency, stared down upon us and daunted us by their silent company. We talked little, and I for one was glad when the meal was over and we were able to retire into the modern billiard-room and smoke a cigarette.

'My word, it isn't a very cheerful place,' said Sir Henry. 'I suppose one can tone down to it, but I feel a bit out of the picture at present. I don't wonder that my uncle got a little jumpy if he lived all alone in such a house as this. However, if it suits you, we will retire early tonight, and perhaps things may seem more cheerful in the morning.'

I drew aside my curtains before I went to bed and looked out from my window. It opened upon the grassy space which lay in front of the hall door. Beyond, two copses of trees moaned and swung in a rising wind. A half moon broke through the rifts of racing clouds. In its cold light I saw beyond the trees a broken fringe of rocks and the long, low curve of the melancholy moor. I closed the curtain, feeling that my last impression was in keeping with the rest.

And yet it was not quite the last. I found myself weary and yet wakeful, tossing restlessly from side to side, seeking for the sleep which would not come. Far away a chiming clock struck out the quarters of the hours, but otherwise a deathly silence lay upon the old house. And then suddenly, in the very dead of the night, there came a sound to my ears, clear, resonant, and unmistakable. It was the sob of a woman, the muffled, strangling gasp of one who is torn by an uncontrollable sorrow. I sat up in bed and listened intently. The noise could not have been far away, and was certainly in the house. For half an hour I waited with every nerve on the alert, but there came no other sound save the chiming clock and the rustle of the ivy on the wall.

7

The Stapletons of Merripit House

The fresh beauty of the following morning did something to efface from our minds the grim and grey impression which had been left upon both of us by our first experience at Baskerville Hall. As Sir Henry and I sat at breakfast the sunlight flooded in through the high mullioned windows, throwing watery patches of colour from the coats-of-arms which covered them. The dark panelling glowed like bronze in the golden rays, and it was hard to realize that this was indeed the chamber which had struck such a gloom into our souls upon the evening before.

'I guess it is ourselves and not the house that we have to blame!' said the baronet. 'We were tired with our journey and chilled by our drive, so we took a grey view of the place. Now we are fresh and well, so it is all cheerful once more.'

'And yet it was not entirely a question of imagination,' I answered. 'Did you, for example, happen to hear someone, a woman I think, sobbing in the night?'

'That is curious, for I did when I was half asleep fancy that I heard something of the sort. I waited quite a time, but there was no more of it, so I concluded that it was all a dream.'

'I heard it distinctly, and I am sure that it was really the sob of a woman.'

'We must ask about this right away.'

He rang the bell and asked Barrymore whether he could account for our experience. It seemed to me that the pallid features of the butler turned a shade paler still as he listened to his master's question.

'There are only two women in the house, Sir Henry,' he answered.

'One is the scullery-maid, who sleeps in the other wing. The other is my wife, and I can answer for it that the sound could not have come from her.'

And yet he lied as he said it, for it chanced that after breakfast I met Mrs Barrymore in the long corridor with the sun full upon her face. She was a large, impassive, heavy-featured woman with a stern, set expression of mouth. But her tell-tale eyes were red and glanced at me from between swollen lids. It was she, then, who wept in the night, and if she did so her husband must know it. Yet he had taken the obvious risk of discovery in declaring that it was not so. Why had he done this? And why did she weep so bitterly? Already round this pale-faced, handsome, black-bearded man there was gathering an atmosphere of mystery and of gloom. It was he who had been the first to discover the body of Sir Charles, and we had only his word for all the circumstances which led up to the old man's death. Was it possible that it was Barrymore, after all, whom we had seen in the cab in Regent Street? The beard might well have been the same. The cabman had described a somewhat shorter man, but such an impression might easily have been erroneous. How could I settle the point for ever? Obviously the first thing to do was to see the Grimpen postmaster, and find whether the test telegram had really been placed in Barrymore's own hands. Be the answer what it might, I should at least have something to report to Sherlock Holmes.

Sir Henry had numerous papers to examine after breakfast, so that the time was propitious for my excursion. It was a pleasant walk of four miles along the edge of the moor, leading me at last to a small grey hamlet, in which two larger buildings, which proved to be the inn and the house of Dr Mortimer, stood high above the rest. The postmaster, who was also the village grocer, had a clear recollection of the telegram.

'Certainly, sir,' said he, 'I had the telegram delivered to Mr Barrymore exactly as directed.'

'Who delivered it?'

'My boy here. James, you delivered that telegram to Mr Barrymore at the Hall last week, did you not?'

'Yes, Father, I delivered it.'

'Into his own hands?' I asked.

'Well, he was up in the loft at the time, so that I could not put it into his own hands, but I gave it into Mrs Barrymore's hands, and she promised to deliver it at once.'

'Did you see Mr Barrymore?'

'No, sir; I tell you he was in the loft.'

'If you didn't see him, how do you know he was in the loft?'

'Well, surely his own wife ought to know where he is,' said the postmaster testily. 'Didn't he get the telegram? If there is any mistake it is for Mr Barrymore himself to complain.'

It seemed hopeless to pursue the inquiry any further, but it was clear that in spite of Holmes's ruse we had no proof that Barrymore had not been in London all the time. Suppose that it were so – suppose that the same man had been the last who had seen Sir Charles alive, and the first to dog the new heir[1] when he returned to England. What then? Was he the agent of others, or had he some sinister design of his own? What interest could he have in persecuting the Baskerville family? I thought of the strange warning clipped out of the leading article of *The Times*. Was that his work or was it possibly the doing of someone who was bent upon counteracting his schemes? The only conceivable motive was that which had been suggested by Sir Henry, that if the family could be scared away a comfortable and permanent home would be secured for the Barrymores. But surely such an explanation as that would be quite inadequate to account for the deep and subtle scheming which seemed to be weaving an invisible net round the young baronet. Holmes himself had said that no more complex case had come to him in all the long series of his sensational investigations. I prayed, as I walked back along the grey, lonely road, that my friend might soon be freed from his preoccupations and able to come down to take this heavy burden of responsibility from my shoulders.

Suddenly my thoughts were interrupted by the sound of running feet behind me and by a voice which called me by name. I turned, expecting to see Dr Mortimer but to my surprise it was a stranger who was pursuing me. He was a small, slim, clean-shaven, prim-faced man,[2] flaxen-haired and lean-jawed, between thirty and forty years of age, dressed in a grey suit and wearing a straw hat. A tin box for botanical specimens hung over his shoulder, and he carried a green butterfly-net in one of his hands.

'You will, I am sure, excuse my presumption, Dr Watson,' said he, as he came panting up to where I stood. 'Here on the moor we are homely folk, and do not wait for formal introductions. You may possibly have heard my name from our mutual friend,[3] Mortimer. I am Stapleton, of Merripit House.'[4]

'Your net and box would have told me as much,' said I, 'for I knew that Mr Stapleton was a naturalist. But how did you know me?'

'I have been calling on Mortimer, and he pointed you out to me from the window of his surgery as you passed. As our road lay the same way, I thought that I would overtake you and introduce myself. I trust that Sir Henry is none the worse for his journey?'

'He is very well, thank you.'

'We were all rather afraid that after the sad death of Sir Charles the new baronet might refuse to live here. It is asking much of a wealthy man to come down and bury himself in a place of this kind, but I need not tell you that it means a very great deal to the countryside. Sir Henry has, I suppose, no superstitious fears in the matter?'

'I do not think that it is likely.'

'Of course you know the legend of the fiend dog which haunts the family?'

'I have heard it.'

'It is extraordinary how credulous the peasants are about here! Any number of them are ready to swear that they have seen such a creature upon the moor.' He spoke with a smile, but I seemed to read in his eyes that he took the matter more seriously. 'The story took a great hold upon the imagination of Sir Charles, and I have no doubt that it led to his tragic end.'

'But how?'

'His nerves were so worked up that the appearance of any dog might have had a fatal effect upon his diseased heart. I fancy that he really did see something of the kind upon that last night in the Yew Alley. I feared that some disaster might occur, for I was very fond of the old man, and I knew that his heart was weak.'

'How did you know that?'

'My friend Mortimer told me.'

'You think then, that some dog pursued Sir Charles, and that he died of fright in consequence?'

'Have you any better explanation?'

'I have not come to any conclusion.'

'Has Mr Sherlock Holmes?'

The words took away my breath for an instant, but a glance at the placid face and steadfast eyes of my companion showed no surprise was intended.

'It is useless for us to pretend that we do not know you, Dr Watson,' said he. 'The records of your detective have reached us here,[5] and you could not celebrate him without being known yourself. When Mortimer told me your name he could not deny your identity. If you are here, then it follows that Mr Sherlock Holmes is interesting himself in the matter, and I am naturally curious to know what view he may take.'

'I am afraid that I cannot answer that question.'

'May I ask if he is going to honour us with a visit himself?'

'He cannot leave town at present. He has other cases which engage his attention.'

'What a pity! He might throw some light on that which is so dark to us. But as to your own researches, if there is any possible way in which I can be of service to you, I trust that you will command me. If I had any indication of the nature of your suspicions, or how you propose to investigate the case, I might perhaps even now give you some aid or advice.'

'I assure you that I am simply here upon a visit to my friend Sir Henry, and that I need no help of any kind!'

'Excellent!' said Stapleton. 'You are perfectly right to be wary and discreet. I am justly reproved for what I feel was an unjustifiable intrusion, and I promise you that I will not mention the matter again.'

We had come to a point where a narrow grassy path struck off from the road and wound away across the moor. A steep, boulder-sprinkled hill lay upon the right which had in bygone days been cut into a granite quarry. The face which was turned towards us formed a dark cliff, with ferns and brambles growing in its niches. From over a distant rise there floated a grey plume of smoke.

'A moderate walk along this moor-path brings us to Merripit House,' said he. 'Perhaps you will spare an hour that I may have the pleasure of introducing you to my sister.'

My first thought was that I should be by Sir Henry's side. But then I remembered the pile of papers and bills with which his study table was littered. It was certain that I could not help him with those. And Holmes had expressly said that I should study the neighbours upon the moor. I accepted Stapleton's invitation, and we turned together down the path.

'It is a wonderful place, the moor,' said he, looking round over the undulating downs, long green rollers, with crests of jagged granite foaming up into fantastic surges. 'You never tire of the moor. You cannot think the wonderful secrets which it contains. It is so vast, and so barren, and so mysterious.'

'You know it well, then?'

'I have only been here two years. The residents would call me a new-comer. We came shortly after Sir Charles settled. But my tastes led me to explore every part of the country round, and I should think that there are few men who know it better than I do.'

'Is it so hard to know?'

'Very hard. You see, for example, this great plain to the north here, with the queer hills breaking out of it. Do you observe anything remarkable about that?'

'It would be a rare place for a gallop.'

'You would naturally think so, and the thought has cost folk their lives before now. You notice those bright green spots scattered thickly over it?'

'Yes, they seem more fertile than the rest.'

Stapleton laughed. 'That is the great Grimpen Mire,'[6] said he. 'A false step yonder means death to man or beast. Only yesterday I saw one of the moor ponies wander into it. He never came out. I saw his head for quite a long time craning out of the boghole, but it sucked him down at last. Even in dry seasons it is a danger to cross it, but after these autumn rains it is an awful place. And yet I can find my way to the very heart of it and return alive. By George, there is another of those miserable ponies!'

Something brown was rolling and tossing among the green sedges. Then a long, agonized, writhing neck shot upwards and a dreadful cry echoed over the moor. It turned me cold with horror, but my companion's nerves seemed to be stronger than mine.

'It's gone!' said he. 'The Mire has him. Two in two days, and many more, perhaps, for they get in the way of going there in the dry weather, and never know the difference until the Mire has them in its clutch. It's a bad place, the great Grimpen Mire.'

'And you say you can penetrate it?'

'Yes, there are one or two paths which a very active man can take. I have found them out.'

'But why should you wish to go into so horrible a place?'

'Well, you see the hills beyond? They are really islands cut off on all sides by the impassable Mire, which has crawled round them in the course of years. That is where the rare plants and the butterflies are, if you have the wit to reach them.'

'I shall try my luck some day.'

He looked at me with a surprised face. 'For God's sake put such an idea out of your mind,' said he. 'Your blood would be upon my head. I assure you that there would not be the least chance of your coming back alive. It is only by remembering certain complex landmarks that I am able to do it.'

'Halloa,' I cried. 'What is that?'

A long, low moan, indescribably sad, swept over the moor. It filled the whole air, and yet it was impossible to say whence it came. From a dull murmur it swelled into a deep roar and then sank back into a melancholy, throbbing murmur once again. Stapleton looked at me with a curious expression on his face.

'Queer place, the moor!' said he.

'But what is it?'

'The peasants say it is the Hound of the Baskervilles calling for its prey. I've heard it once or twice before, but never quite so loud.'

I looked round, with a chill of fear in my heart, at the huge swelling plain, mottled with the green patches of rushes. Nothing stirred over the vast expanse save a pair of ravens, which croaked loudly from a tor behind us.

'You are an educated man. You don't believe such nonsense as that?' said I. 'What do you think is the cause of so strange a sound?'

'Bogs make queer noises sometimes. It's the mud settling, or the water rising, or something.'

'No, no, that was a living voice.'

'Well, perhaps it was. Did you ever hear a bittern booming?'

'No, I never did.'

'It's a very rare bird – practically extinct – in England now, but all things are possible upon the moor. Yes, I should not be surprised to learn that what we have heard is the cry of the last of the bitterns.'[7]

'It's the weirdest, strangest thing that ever I heard in my life.'

'Yes, it's rather an uncanny place altogether. Look at the hillside yonder. What do you make of those?'

The whole steep slope was covered with grey circular rings of stone, a score of them at least.

'What are they? Sheep-pens?'

'No, they are the homes of our worthy ancestors. Prehistoric man lived thickly on the moor, and as no one in particular has lived there since, we find all his little arrangements exactly as he left them. These are his wigwams with the roofs off. You can even see his hearth and his couch if you have the curiosity to go inside.'

'But it is quite a town. When was it inhabited?'

'Neolithic man – no date.'[8]

'What did he do?'

'He grazed his cattle on these slopes, and he learned to dig for tin when the bronze sword began to supersede the stone axe. Look at the great trench in the opposite hill. That is his mark. Yes, you will find some very singular points about the moor, Dr Watson. Oh, excuse me an instant. It is surely Cyclopides.'[9]

A small fly or moth had fluttered across our path, and in an instant Stapleton was rushing with extraordinary energy and speed in pursuit of it. To my dismay the creature flew straight for the great Mire, but my acquaintance never paused for an instant, bounding from tuft to tuft behind it, his green net waving in the air. His grey clothes and jerky, zigzag, irregular progress made him not unlike some huge moth himself. I was standing watching his pursuit with a mixture of admiration for his extraordinary activity and fear lest he should lose his footing in the treacherous Mire, when I heard the sound of steps, and, turning round, found a woman near me upon the path. She had come from the direction in which the plume of smoke indicated the position of Merripit House, but the dip of the moor had hid her until she was quite close.

I could not doubt that this was the Miss Stapleton[10] of whom I had been told, since ladies of any sort must be few upon the moor, and I remembered that I had heard someone describe her as being a beauty. The woman who approached me was certainly that, and of a most uncommon type. There could not have been a greater contrast between brother and sister, for Stapleton was neutral-tinted, with light hair and grey eyes, while she was darker than any brunette whom I have seen in England – slim, elegant, and tall. She had a proud, finely cut face, so regular that it might have seemed impassive were it not for the sensitive mouth and the beautiful dark, eager eyes. With her perfect and elegant dress she was, indeed, a strange apparition upon a lonely moorland path. Her eyes were on her brother as I turned, and then she quickened her pace towards me. I had raised my hat, and was about to make some explanatory remark, when her own words turned all my thoughts into a new channel.

'Go back!' she said. 'Go straight back to London, instantly.'

I could only stare at her in stupid surprise. Her eyes blazed at me, and she tapped the ground impatiently with her foot.

'Why should I go back?' I asked.

'I cannot explain.' She spoke in a low, eager voice, with a curious lisp in her utterance. 'But for God's sake do what I ask you. Go back, and never set foot upon the moor again.'

'But I have only just come.'

'Man, man!' she cried. 'Can you not tell when a warning is for your own good? Go back to London! Start tonight! Get away from this place at all costs! Hush, my brother is coming! Not a word of what I have said. Would you mind getting that orchid for me among the mare's-tails[11] yonder? We are very rich in orchids on the moor, though, of course, you are rather late[12] to see the beauties of the place.'

70

Stapleton had abandoned the chase, and came back to us breathing hard and flushed with his exertions.

'Halloa, Beryl!' said he, and it seemed to me that the tone of his greeting was not altogether a cordial one.

'Well, Jack, you are very hot.'

'Yes, I was chasing a Cyclopides. He is very rare, and seldom found in the late autumn. What a pity that I should have missed him!'

He spoke unconcernedly, but his small light eyes glanced incessantly from the girl to me.

'You have introduced yourselves, I can see.'

'Yes. I was telling Sir Henry that it was rather late for him to see the true beauties of the moor.'

'Why, who do you imagine this is?'

'I imagine that it must be Sir Henry Baskerville.'

'No, no,' said I. 'Only a humble commoner,[13] but his friend. My name is Dr Watson.'

A flush of vexation passed over her expressive face.

'We have been talking at cross purposes,' said she.

'Why, you had not very much time for talk,' her brother remarked, with the same questioning eyes.

'I talked as if Dr Watson were a resident instead of being merely a visitor,' said she. 'It cannot much matter to him whether it is early or late for the orchids. But you will come on, will you not, and see Merripit House?'

A short walk brought us to it, a bleak moorland house, once the farm of some grazier in the old prosperous days, but now put into repair and turned into a modern dwelling. An orchard surrounded it, but the trees, as is usual upon the moor, were stunted and nipped, and the effect of the whole place was mean and melancholy. We were admitted by a strange, wizened, rusty-coated old manservant, who seemed in keeping with the house. Inside, however, there were large rooms furnished with an elegance in which I seemed to recognize the taste of the lady. As I looked from their windows at the interminable granite-flecked moor rolling unbroken to the farthest horizon I could not but marvel at what could have brought this highly educated man and this beautiful woman to live in such a place.

'Queer spot to choose, is it not?' said he, as if in answer to my thought. 'And yet we manage to make ourselves fairly happy, do we not, Beryl?'

'Quite happy,' said she, but there was no ring of conviction in her words.

'I had a school,' said Stapleton. 'It was in the North Country. The work to a man of my temperament was mechanical and uninteresting, but the privilege of living with youth, of helping to mould those young minds and of impressing them with one's own character and ideals, was very dear to me. However, the fates were against us. A serious epidemic broke out in the school, and three of the boys died. It never recovered from the blow, and much of my capital was irretrievably swallowed up. And yet, if it were not for the loss of the charming companionship of the boys, I could rejoice over my own misfortune, for, with my strong tastes for botany and zoology, I find an unlimited field of work here, and my sister is as devoted to Nature as I am. All this, Dr Watson, has been brought upon your head by your expression as you surveyed the moor out of our window.'

'It certainly did cross my mind that it might be a little dull – less for you, perhaps, than for your sister.'

'No, no, I am never dull,' said she quickly.

'We have books, we have our studies, and we have interesting neighbours. Dr Mortimer is a most learned man in his own line. Poor Sir Charles was also an admirable companion. We knew him well, and miss him more than I can tell. Do you think that I should intrude if I were to call this afternoon and make the acquaintance of Sir Henry?'

'I am sure that he would be delighted.'

'Then perhaps you would mention that I propose to do so. We may in our humble way do something to make things more easy for him until he becomes accustomed to his new surroundings. Will you come upstairs, Dr Watson, and inspect my collection of Lepidoptera?[14] I think it is the most complete one in the south-west of England. By the time that you have looked through them lunch will be almost ready.'

But I was eager to get back to my charge. The melancholy of the moor, the death of the unfortunate pony, the weird sound which had been associated with the grim legend of the Baskervilles – all these things tinged my thoughts with sadness. Then on the top of these more or less vague impressions there had come the definite and distinct warning of Miss Stapleton, delivered with such intense earnestness that I could not doubt that some grave and deep reason lay behind it. I resisted all pressure to stay for lunch, and I set off at once upon my return journey, taking the grass-grown path by which we had come.

It seems, however, that there must have been some short cut for those who knew it, for before I had reached the road I was astounded to see Miss Stapleton sitting upon a rock by the side of the track. Her face was beautifully flushed with her exertions, and she held her hand to her side.

'I have run all the way in order to cut you off, Dr Watson,' said she. 'I had not even time to put on my hat. I must not stop, or my brother may miss me. I wanted to say to you how sorry I am about the stupid mistake I made in thinking that you were Sir Henry. Please forget the words I said, which have no application whatever to you.'

'But I can't forget them, Miss Stapleton,' said I. 'I am Sir Henry's friend, and his welfare is a very close concern of mine. Tell me why it was that you were so eager that Sir Henry should return to London.'

'A woman's whim, Dr Watson. When you know me better you will understand that I cannot always give reasons for what I say or do.'

'No, no. I remember the thrill in your voice. I remember the look in your eyes. Please, please, be frank with me, Miss Stapleton, for ever since I have been here I have been conscious of shadows all round me. Life has become like that great Grimpen Mire,[15] with little green patches everywhere into which one may sink and with no guide to point the track. Tell me, then, what it was that you meant, and I will promise to convey your warning to Sir Henry.'

An expression of irresolution passed for an instant over her face, but her eyes had hardened again when she answered me.

'You make too much of it, Dr Watson,' said she. 'My brother and I were very much shocked by the death of Sir Charles. We knew him very intimately, for his favourite walk was over the moor to our house. He was deeply impressed with the curse which hung over his family, and when this tragedy came I naturally felt that there must be some grounds for the fears he had expressed. I was distressed, therefore, when another member of the family came down to live here, and I felt that he should be warned of the danger which he will run. That was all which I intended to convey.'

'But what is the danger?'

'You know the story of the hound?'

'I do not believe in such nonsense.'

'But I do. If you have any influence with Sir Henry, take him away from a place which has always been fatal to his family. The world is wide. Why should he wish to live at the place of danger?'

'Because it *is* the place of danger. That is Sir Henry's nature. I fear that unless you can give me some more definite information than this it would be impossible to get him to move.'

'I cannot say anything definite, for I do not know anything definite.'

'I would ask you one more question, Miss Stapleton. If you meant no more than this when you first spoke to me, why should you not wish your brother to overhear what you said? There is nothing to which he, or anyone else, could object.'

'My brother is very anxious to have the Hall inhabited, for he thinks that it is for the good of the poor folk upon the moor. He would be very angry if he knew that I had said anything which might induce Sir Henry to go away. But I have done my duty now, and I will say no more. I must get back, or he will miss me and suspect that I have seen you. Good-bye!'

She turned and had disappeared in a few minutes among the scattered boulders, while I, with my soul full of vague fears, pursued my way to Baskerville Hall.

8

First Report of Dr Watson[1]

From this point onwards I will follow the course of events by transcribing my own letters to Mr Sherlock Holmes which lie before me on the table. One page is missing, but otherwise they are exactly as written, and show my feelings and suspicions of the moment more accurately than my memory, clear as it is upon these tragic events, can possibly do.

Baskerville Hall, Oct. 13th

My Dear Holmes,

My previous letters and telegrams have kept you pretty well up-to-date as to all that has occurred in this most God-forsaken corner of the world. The longer one stays here the more does the spirit of the moor sink into one's soul, its vastness, and also its grim charm. When you are once out upon its bosom you have left all traces of modern England behind you, but on the other hand you are conscious everywhere of the homes and the work of prehistoric people. On all sides of you as you walk are the houses of these forgotten folk, with their graves and the huge monoliths[2] which are supposed to have marked their temples. As you look at their grey stone huts against the scarred hillsides you leave your own age behind you, and if you were to see a skin-clad, hairy man crawl out from the low door, fitting a flint-tipped arrow on to the string of his bow, you would feel that his presence there was more natural than your own. The strange thing is that they should have lived so thickly on what must always have been most unfruitful soil. I am no antiquarian, but I could imagine that they were some unwarlike and harried race who were forced to accept that which none other would occupy.

All this, however, is foreign to the mission on which you sent me, and will probably be very uninteresting to your severely practical mind. I can still remember your complete indifference as to whether the sun moved round the earth[3] or the earth round the sun. Let me, therefore, return to the facts concerning Sir Henry Baskerville.

If you have not had any report within the last few days it is because up till today there was nothing of importance to relate. Then a very surprising circumstance occurred, which I shall tell you in due course. But, first of all, I must keep you in touch with some of the other factors in the situation.

One of these, concerning which I have said little, is the escaped convict upon the moor. There is strong reason now to believe that he has got right away, which is a considerable relief to the lonely householders of this district. A fortnight has passed since his flight, during which he has not been seen and nothing has been heard of him. It is surely inconceivable that he could have held out upon the moor during all that time. Of course so far as his concealment goes there is no difficulty at all. Any one of these stone huts would give him a hiding-place. But there is nothing to eat unless he were to catch and slaughter one of the moor sheep. We think therefore, that he has gone, and the outlying farmers sleep the better in consequence.

We are four able-bodied men in this household, so that we could take good care of ourselves, but I confess that I have had uneasy moments when I have thought of the Stapletons. They live miles from any help. There are one maid, an old manservant, the sister and the brother, the latter not a very strong man. They would be helpless in the hands of a desperate fellow like this Notting Hill criminal, if he could once effect an entrance. Both Sir Henry and I were concerned at their situation, and it was suggested that Perkins, the groom, should go over to sleep there, but Stapleton would not hear of it.

The fact is that our friend the baronet begins to display a considerable interest in our fair neighbour. It is not to be wondered at, for time hangs heavily in this lonely spot to an active man like him, and she is a very fascinating and beautiful woman. There is something tropical and exotic about her which forms a singular contrast to her cool and unemotional brother. Yet he also gives the idea of hidden fires. He has certainly a very marked influence over her, for I have seen her continually glance at him as she talked as if seeking approbation for what she said. I trust that he is kind to her. There is a dry glitter in his eyes, and a firm set of his thin lips, which go with a positive and possibly a harsh nature. You would find him an interesting study.

He came over to call upon Baskerville on that first day, and the very next morning he took us both to show us the spot where the legend of the wicked Hugo is supposed to have had its origin.[4] It was an excursion of some miles across the moor to a place which is so dismal that it might have suggested the story. We found a short valley between rugged tors which led to an open, grassy space flecked over with the white cotton grass. In the middle of it rose two great stones, worn and sharpened at the upper end, until they looked like the huge, corroding fangs of some monstrous beast. In every way it corresponded with the scene of the old tragedy. Sir Henry was much interested, and asked Stapleton more than once whether he did really believe in the possibility of the interference of the supernatural in the affairs of men. He spoke lightly, but it was evident that he was very much in earnest. Stapleton was guarded in his replies, but it was easy to see that he said less than he might, and that he would not express his whole opinion out of consideration for the feelings of the baronet. He told us of similar cases where families had suffered from some evil influence,[5] and he left us with the impression that he shared the popular view upon the matter.

On our way back we stayed for lunch at Merripit House, and it was there that Sir Henry made the acquaintance of Miss Stapleton. From the first moment that he saw her he appeared to be strongly attracted by her, and I am much mistaken if the feeling was not mutual. He referred to her again and again on our walk home, and since then hardly a day has passed that we have not seen something of the brother and sister. They dine here tonight and there is some talk of our going to them next week. One would imagine that such a match would be very welcome to Stapleton, and yet I have more than once caught a look of the strongest disapprobation in his face when Sir Henry has been paying some attention to his sister. He is much attached to her, no doubt, and would lead a lonely life without her, but it would seem the height of selfishness, if he were to stand in the way of her making so brilliant a marriage. Yet I am certain that he does not wish their intimacy to ripen into love, and I have several times observed that he has taken pains to prevent them from being *tête-à-tête*. By the way, your instructions to me never to allow Sir Henry to go out alone will become very much more onerous if a love affair were to be added to our other difficulties. My popularity would soon suffer if I were to carry out your orders to the letter.

The other day – Thursday, to be more exact – Dr Mortimer lunched with us. He has been excavating a barrow at Long Down, and has got a prehistoric skull which fills him with great joy. Never was there such a single-minded enthusiast as he! The Stapletons came in afterwards, and the good doctor took us all to the Yew Alley, at Sir Henry's request, to show us exactly how everything occurred upon that fatal night. It is a long, dismal walk, the Yew Alley, between two high walls of clipped hedge, with a narrow band of grass upon either side. At the far end is an old, tumble-down summer-house. Half-way down is the moor-gate where the old gentleman left his cigar ash. It is a white wooden gate with a latch. Beyond it lies the wide moor. I remembered your theory of the affair and tried to picture all that had occurred. As the old man stood there he saw something coming across the moor, something which terrified him so that he lost his wits, and ran and ran until he died of sheer horror and exhaustion. There was the long, gloomy tunnel down which he fled. And from what? A sheepdog of the moor? Or a spectral hound, black, silent, and monstrous? Was there a human agency in the matter? Did the pale, watchful Barrymore know more than he cared to say? It was all dim and vague, but always there is the dark shadow of crime behind it.

One other neighbour I have met since I wrote last. This is Mr Frankland,[6] of Lafter Hall, who lives some four miles to the south of us. He is an elderly man, red-faced, white-haired, and choleric. His passion is for the British law, and he has spent a large fortune in litigation. He fights for the mere pleasure of fighting, and is equally ready to take up either side of a question, so that it is no wonder that he has found it a costly amusement. Sometimes he will shut up a right of way and defy the parish to make him open it. At others he will with his own hands tear down some other man's gate and declare that a path has existed there from time immemorial, defying the owner to prosecute him for trespass. He is learned in old manorial and communal rights, and he applies his knowledge sometimes in favour of the villagers of Fernworthy[7] and sometimes against them, so that he is periodically either carried in triumph down the village street or else burned in effigy, according to his latest exploit. He is said to have about seven lawsuits upon his hands at present, which will probably swallow up the remainder of his fortune, and so draw his sting and leave him harmless for the future. Apart from the law he seems a kindly, good-natured person, and I only mention him because you were particular that I should send some description of the people who surround us. He is curiously employed at present, for, being an amateur astronomer, he has an excellent telescope, with which he lies upon the roof of his own house and sweeps the moor all day in the hope of catching a glimpse of the escaped convict. If he would confine his energies to this all would be well, but there are rumours that he intends to prosecute Dr Mortimer for opening a grave without the consent of the next-of-kin, because he dug up the neolithic skull in the barrow on Long Down.[8] He helps to keep our lives from being monotonous, and gives a little comic relief where it is badly needed.

And now, having brought you up to date on the escaped convict,[9] the Stapletons, Dr Mortimer, and Frankland of Lafter Hall, let me end on that which is most important, and tell you more about the Barrymores, and especially about the surprising developments of last night.

First of all about the test telegram, which you sent from London in order to make sure that Barrymore was really here. I have already explained that the testimony of the postmaster shows that the test was worthless and that we have no proof one way or the other. I told Sir Henry how the matter stood, and he at once, in his downright fashion, had Barrymore up and asked him whether he had received the telegram himself. Barrymore said that he had.

'Did the boy deliver it into your own hands?' asked Sir Henry.

Barrymore looked surprised, and considered for a little time.

'No,' said he, 'I was in the box-room at the time, and my wife brought it up to me.'

'Did you answer it yourself?'

'No; I told my wife what to answer, and she went down to write it.'

In the evening he returned to the subject of his own accord.

'I could not quite understand the object of your questions this morning, Sir Henry,' said he. 'I trust that they do not mean that I have done anything to forfeit your confidence?'

Sir Henry had to assure him that it was not so and pacify him by giving him a considerable part of his old wardrobe, the London outfit having now all arrived.

Mrs Barrymore is of interest to me. She is a heavy, solid person, very limited, intensely respectable, and inclined to be puritanical. You could hardly conceive a less emotional subject. Yet I have told you how, on the first night here, I heard her sobbing bitterly, and since then I have more than once observed traces of tears upon her face. Some deep sorrow gnaws ever at her heart. Sometimes I wonder if she has a guilty memory which haunts her, and sometimes I suspect Barrymore of being a domestic tyrant. I have always felt that there was something singular and questionable in this man's character, but the adventure of last night brings all my suspicions to a head.

And yet it may seem a small matter in itself. You are aware that I am not a very sound sleeper, and since I have been on guard in this house my slumbers have been lighter than ever. Last night, about two in the morning, I was aroused by a stealthy step passing my room. I rose, opened my door, and peeped out. A long black shadow was trailing down the corridor. It was thrown by a man who walked softly down the passage with a candle in his hand. He was in shirt and trousers, with no covering to his feet. I could merely see the outline, but his height told me that it was Barrymore. He walked very slowly and circumspectly, and there was something indescribably guilty and furtive in his whole appearance.

I have told you that the corridor is broken by the balcony which runs round the hall, but that it is resumed upon the farther side. I waited until he had passed out of sight, and then I followed him. When I came round the balcony he had reached the end of the farther corridor, and I could see from the glimmer of light through an open door that he had entered one of the rooms. Now, all these rooms are unfurnished and unoccupied, so that his expedition became more mysterious than ever. The light shone steadily, as if he were standing motionless. I crept down the passage as noiselessly as I could and peeped round the corner of the door.

Barrymore was crouching at the window with the candle held against the glass. His profile was half turned towards me, and his face seemed to be rigid with expectation as he stared out into the blackness of the moor. For some minutes he stood watching intently. Then he gave a deep groan, and with an impatient gesture he put out the light. Instantly, I made my way back to my room, and very shortly came the stealthy steps passing once more upon their return journey. Long afterwards when I had fallen into a light sleep I heard a key turn somewhere in a lock, but I could not tell whence the sound came. What it all means I cannot guess, but there is some secret business going on in this house of gloom which sooner or later we shall get to the bottom of. I do not trouble you with my theories, for you asked me to furnish you only with facts. I have had a long talk with Sir Henry this morning, and we have made a plan of campaign founded upon my observations of last night. I will not speak about it just now, but it should make my next report interesting reading.

9

The Light upon the Moor

[*Second report of Dr Watson*]

Baskerville Hall, Oct. 15th

My Dear Holmes,

If I was compelled to leave you without much news during the early days of my mission you must acknowledge that I am making up for lost time, and that events are now crowding thick and fast upon us. In my last report I ended upon my top note with Barrymore at the window, and now I have quite a budget[1] already which will, unless I am much mistaken, considerably surprise you. Things have taken a turn which I could not have anticipated. In some ways they have within the last forty-eight hours become much clearer and in some ways they have become more complicated. But I will tell you all, and you shall judge for yourself.

Before breakfast on the morning following my adventure I went down the corridor and examined the room in which Barrymore had been on the night before. The western window through which he had stared so intently has, I noticed, one peculiarity above all other windows in the house – it commands the nearest outlook on to the moor. There is an opening between two trees which enables one from this point of view to look right down upon it, while from all the other windows it is only a distant glimpse which can be obtained. It follows, therefore, that Barrymore, since only this window would serve his purpose, must have been looking out for something or somebody upon the moor. The night was very dark, so that I can hardly imagine how he could have hoped to see anyone. It had struck me that it was possible that some love intrigue was on foot. That would have accounted for his stealthy movements and also for the uneasiness of his wife. The man is a striking-looking fellow, very well equipped to steal the heart of a country girl, so that this theory seemed to have something to support it. That opening of the door which I had heard after I had returned to my room might mean that he had gone out to keep some clandestine appointment. So I reasoned with myself in the morning, and I tell you the direction of my suspicions, however much the result may have shown that they were unfounded.

But whatever the true explanation of Barrymore's movements might be, I felt that the responsibility of keeping them to myself until I could explain them was more than I could bear. I had an interview with the baronet in his study after breakfast, and I told him all that I had seen. He was less surprised than I had expected.

'I knew that Barrymore walked about nights, and I had a mind to speak to him about it,' said he. 'Two or three times I have heard his steps in the passage, coming and going, just about the hour you name.'

'Perhaps, then, he pays a visit every night to that particular window,' I suggested.

'Perhaps he does. If so, we should be able to shadow him, and see what it is that he is after. I wonder what your friend Holmes would do if he were here?'

'I believe that he would do exactly what you now suggest,' said I. 'He would follow Barrymore and see what he did.'

'Then we shall do it together.'

'But surely he would hear us.'

'The man is rather deaf, and in any case we must take our chance of that. We'll sit up in my room tonight, and wait until he passes.' Sir Henry rubbed his hands with pleasure, and it was evident that he hailed the adventure as a relief to his somewhat quiet life upon the moor.

The baronet has been in communication with the architect who prepared the plans for Sir Charles, and with a contractor from London, so that we may expect great changes to begin here soon. There have been decorators and furnishers up from Plymouth,[2] and it is evident that our friend has large ideas, and means to spare no pains or expense to restore the grandeur of his family. When the house is renovated and refurnished, all that he will need will be a wife to make it complete. Between ourselves, there are pretty clear signs that this will not be wanting if the lady is willing, for I have seldom seen a man more infatuated with a woman than he is with our beautiful neighbour, Miss Stapleton. And yet the course of true love does not run quite as smoothly as one would under the circumstances expect. Today, for example, its surface was broken by a very unexpected ripple, which has caused our friend considerable perplexity and annoyance.

After the conversation which I have quoted about Barrymore, Sir Henry put on his hat and prepared to go out. As a matter of course, I did the same.

'What, are *you* coming, Watson?' he asked, looking at me in a curious way.

'That depends on whether you are going on the moor,' said I.

'Yes, I am.'

'Well, you know what my instructions are. I am sorry to intrude, but you heard how earnestly Holmes insisted that I should not leave you, and especially that you should not go alone upon the moor.'

Sir Henry put his hand upon my shoulder, with a pleasant smile.

'My dear fellow,' said he, 'Holmes, with all his wisdom, did not foresee some things which have happened since I have been on the moor. You understand me? I am sure that you are the last man in the world who would wish to be a spoilsport. I must go out alone.'

It put me in a most awkward position. I was at a loss what to say or what to do, and before I had made up my mind he picked up his cane and was gone.

But when I came to think the matter over, my conscience reproached me bitterly for having on any pretext allowed him to go out of my sight. I imagined what my feelings would be if I had to return to you and to confess that some misfortune had occurred through my disregard for your instructions. I assure you my cheeks flushed at the very thought. It might not even now be too late to overtake him, so I set off at once in the direction of Merripit House.

I hurried along the road at the top of my speed without seeing anything of Sir Henry, until I came to the point where the moor path branches off. There, fearing that perhaps I had come in the wrong direction, after all, I mounted a hill from which I could command a view – the same hill which is cut into the dark quarry. Then I saw him at once. He was on the moor path, about a quarter of a mile off, and a lady was by his side who could only be Miss Stapleton. It was clear that there was already an understanding between them and that they had met by appointment. They were walking slowly along in deep conversation, and I saw her making quick little movements of her hands as if she were very earnest in what she was saying, while he listened intently, and once or twice shook his head in strong dissent. I stood among the rocks watching them, very much puzzled as to what I should do next. To follow them and break into their intimate conversation seemed to be an outrage, and yet my clear duty was never for an instant to let him out of my sight. To act the spy upon a friend was a hateful task. Still, I could see no better course than to observe him from the hill, and to clear my conscience by confessing to him afterwards what I had done. It is true that if any sudden danger had threatened him I was too far away to be of use, and yet I am sure that you will agree with me that the position was very difficult, and that there was nothing more which I could do.

Our friend, Sir Henry, and the lady had halted on the path, and were standing deeply absorbed in their conversation, when I was suddenly aware that I was not the only witness of their interview. A wisp of green floating in the air caught my eye, and another glance showed me that it was carried on a stick by a man who was moving among the broken ground. It was Stapleton with his butterfly net. He was very much closer to the pair than I was, and he appeared to be moving in their direction. At this instant Sir Henry suddenly drew Miss Stapleton to his side. His arm was round her, but it seemed to me that she was straining away from him with her face averted. He stooped his head to hers, and she raised one hand as if in protest. Next moment I saw them spring apart and turn hurriedly round. Stapleton was the cause of the interruption. He was running wildly towards them, his absurd net dangling behind him. He gesticulated and almost danced with excitement in front of the lovers. What the scene meant I could not imagine, but it seemed to me that Stapleton was abusing

Sir Henry, who offered explanations, which became more angry as the other refused to accept them. The lady stood by in haughty silence. Finally Stapleton turned upon his heel and beckoned in a peremptory way to his sister, who, after an irresolute glance at Sir Henry, walked off by the side of her brother. The naturalist's angry gestures showed that the lady was included in his displeasure. The baronet stood for a minute looking after them, and then he walked slowly back the way that he had come, his head hanging, the very picture of dejection.

What all this meant I could not imagine, but I was deeply ashamed to have witnessed so intimate a scene without my friend's knowledge. I ran down the hill, therefore, and met the baronet at the bottom. His face was flushed with anger and his brows were wrinkled, like one who is at his wits' ends what to do.

'Halloa, Watson! Where have you dropped from?' said he. 'You don't mean to say that you came after me in spite of all?'

I explained everything to him: how I had found it impossible to remain behind, how I had followed him, and how I had witnessed all that had occurred. For an instant his eyes blazed at me, but my frankness disarmed his anger, and he broke at last into a rather rueful laugh.

'You would have thought the middle of that prairie a fairly safe place for a man to be private,' said he, 'but, by thunder,[3] the whole countryside seems to have been out to see me do my wooing – and a mighty poor wooing at that! Where had you engaged a seat?'

'I was on that hill.'

'Quite in the back row, eh? But her brother was well up to the front. Did you see him come out on us?'

'Yes, I did.'

'Did he ever strike you as being crazy – this brother of hers?'

'I can't say that he ever did.'

'I dare say not. I always thought him sane enough until today, but you can take it from me that either he or I ought to be in a strait-jacket. What's the matter with me, anyhow? You've lived near me for some weeks, Watson. Tell me straight, now! Is there anything that would prevent me from making a good husband to a woman that I loved?'

'I should say not.'

'He can't object to my worldly position, so it must be myself that he has this down on. What has he against me? I never hurt man or woman in my life that I know of. And yet he would not so much as let me touch the tips of her fingers.'

'Did he say so?'

'That, and a deal more. I tell you, Watson, I've only known her these few weeks, but from the first I just felt that she was made for me, and she, too – she was happy when she was with me, and that I'll swear. There's a light in a woman's eyes that speaks louder than words. But he has never let us get together, and it was only today for the first time that I saw a chance of having a few words with her alone. She was glad to meet me, but when she did it was not love that she would talk about, and she wouldn't let me talk about it either if she could have stopped it. She kept coming back to it that this was a place of danger, and that she would never be happy until I had left it. I told her that since I had seen her I was in no hurry to leave it, and that if she really wanted me to go, the only way to work it was for her to arrange to go with me. With that I offered in as many words to marry her, but before she could answer down came this brother of hers, running at us with a face on him like a madman. He was just white with rage, and those light eyes of his were blazing with fury. What was I doing with the lady? How dared I offer her attentions which were distasteful to her? Did I think that because I was a baronet I could do what I liked? If he had not been her brother I should have known better how to answer him. As it was I told him that my feelings towards his sister were such as I was not ashamed of, and that I hoped that she might honour me by becoming my wife. That seemed to make the matter no better, so then I lost my temper too, and I answered him rather more hotly than I should, perhaps, considering that she was standing by. So it ended by his going off with her, as you saw, and here am I as badly puzzled a man as any in this county. Just tell me what it all means, Watson, and I'll owe you more than ever I can hope to pay.'

I tried one or two explanations, but, indeed, I was completely puzzled myself. Our friend's title, his fortune, his age, his character, and his appearance are all in his favour, and I know nothing against him, unless it be this dark fate which runs in his family. That his advances should be rejected so brusquely without any reference to the lady's own wishes, and that the lady should accept the situation without protest, is very amazing. However, our conjectures were set at rest by a visit from Stapleton himself that very afternoon. He had come to offer apologies for his rudeness of the morning, and after a long private interview with Sir Henry in his study the upshot of their conversation was that the breach is quite healed, and that we are to dine at Merripit House next Friday as a sign of it.

'I don't say now that he isn't a crazy man,' said Sir Henry; 'I can't forget the look in his eyes when he ran at me this morning, but I must allow that no man could make a more handsome apology than he has done.'

'Did he give any explanation of his conduct?'

'His sister is everything in his life, he says. That is natural enough, and I am glad that he should understand her value. They have always been together, and according to his account he has been a very lonely man with only her as a companion, so that the thought of losing her was really terrible to him. He had not understood, he said, that I was becoming attached to her, but when he saw with his own eyes that it was really so, and that she might be taken away from him, it gave him such a shock that for a time he was not responsible for what he said or did. He was very sorry for all that had passed, and he recognized how foolish and how selfish it was that he should imagine that he could hold a beautiful woman like his sister to himself for her whole life. If she had to leave him he had rather it was to a neighbour like myself than to anyone else. But in any case it was a blow to him, and it would take him some time before he could prepare himself to meet it. He would withdraw all opposition upon his part if I would promise for three months to let the matter rest, and to be content with cultivating the lady's friendship during that time without claiming her love. This I promised, and so the matter rests.'

So there is one of our small mysteries cleared up. It is something to have touched bottom anywhere in this bog in which we are floundering. We know now why Stapleton looked with disfavour upon his sister's suitor – even when that suitor was so eligible a one as Sir

Henry. And now I pass on to another thread which I have extricated out of the tangled skein,[4] the mystery of the sobs in the night, of the tear-stained face of Mrs Barrymore, of the secret journey of the butler to the western lattice-window. Congratulate me, my dear Holmes and tell me that I have not disappointed you as an agent – that you do not regret the confidence which you showed in me when you sent me down. All these things have by one night's work been thoroughly cleared.

I have said 'by one night's work', but, in truth, it was by two nights' work, for on the first we drew entirely blank. I sat up with Sir Henry in his room until nearly three o'clock in the morning, but no sound of any sort did we hear except the chiming clock upon the stairs. It was a most melancholy vigil, and ended by each of us falling asleep in our chairs. Fortunately we were not discouraged, and we determined to try again. The next night we lowered the lamp and sat smoking cigarettes, without making the least sound. It was incredible how slowly the hours crawled by, and yet we were helped through it by the same sort of patient interest, which the hunter must feel as he watches the trap into which he hopes the game may wander. One struck, and two, and we had almost for the second time given it up in despair, when in an instant we both sat bolt upright in our chairs, with all our weary senses keenly on the alert once more. We had heard the creak of a step in the passage.

Very stealthily we heard it pass along until it died away in the distance. Then the baronet gently opened his door, and we set out in pursuit. Already our man had gone round the gallery, and the corridor was all in darkness. Softly we stole along until we had come into the other wing. We were just in time to catch a glimpse of the tall, black-bearded figure, his shoulders rounded, as he tiptoed down the passage. Then he passed through the same door as before, and the light of the candle framed it in the darkness and shot one single yellow beam across the gloom of the corridor. We shuffled cautiously towards it, trying every plank before we dared to put our whole weight upon it. We had taken the precaution of leaving our boots behind us, but, even so, the old boards snapped and creaked beneath our tread. Sometimes it seemed impossible that he should fail to hear our approach. However, the man is fortunately rather deaf, and he was entirely preoccupied in that which he was doing. When at last we reached the door and peeped through we found him crouching at the window, candle in hand, his white, intent face pressed against the pane, exactly as I had seen him two nights before.

We had arranged no plan of campaign, but the baronet is a man to whom the most direct way is always the most natural. He walked into the room, and as he did so Barrymore sprang up from the window with a sharp hiss of his breath, and stood, livid and trembling, before us. His dark eyes, glaring out of the white mask of his face, were full of horror and astonishment as he gazed from Sir Henry to me.

'What are you doing here, Barrymore?'

'Nothing, sir.' His agitation was so great that he could hardly speak, and the shadows sprang up and down from the shaking of his candle. 'It was the window, sir. I go round at night to see that they are fastened.'

'On the second floor?'

'Yes, sir, all the windows.'

'Look here, Barrymore,' said Sir Henry, sternly, 'we have made up our minds to have the truth out of you, so it will save you trouble to tell it sooner rather than later. Come, now! No lies! What were you doing at that window?'

The fellow looked at us in a helpless way, and he wrung his hands together like one who is in the last extremity of doubt and misery.

'I was doing no harm, sir. I was holding a candle to the window.'

'And why were you holding a candle to the window?'

'Don't ask me, Sir Henry – don't ask me! I give you my word, sir, that it is not my secret, and that I cannot tell it. If it concerned no one but myself I would not try to keep it from you.'

A sudden idea occurred to me, and I took the candle from the window-sill, where the butler had placed it.

'He must have been holding it as a signal,' said I. 'Let us see if there is any answer.'

I held it as he had done, and stared out into the darkness of the night. Vaguely I could discern the black bank of the trees and the lighter expanse of the moor, for the moon was behind the clouds. And then I gave a cry of exultation, for a tiny pinpoint of yellow light had suddenly transfixed the dark veil, and glowed steadily in the centre of the black square framed by the window.

'There it is!' I cried.

'No, no, sir, it is nothing – nothing at all,' the butler broke in; 'I assure you, sir –'

'Move your light across the window, Watson!' cried the baronet. 'See, the other moves also! Now, you rascal, do you deny that it is a signal? Come, speak up! Who is your confederate out yonder, and what is this conspiracy that is going on?'

The man's face became openly defiant. 'It is my business, and not yours. I will not tell.'

'Then you leave my employment right away.'

'Very good, sir. If I must, I must.'

'And you go in disgrace. By thunder, you may well be ashamed of yourself. Your family has lived with mine for over a hundred years under this roof, and here I find you deep in some dark plot against me.'

'No, no, sir; no, not against you!'

It was a woman's voice, and Mrs Barrymore, paler and more horror-struck than her husband, was standing at the door. Her bulky figure in a shawl and skirt might have been comic were it not for the intensity of feeling upon her face.

'We have to go, Eliza. This is the end of it. You can pack our things,' said the butler.

'Oh, John, John, have I brought you to this? It is my doing, Sir Henry – all mine. He has done nothing except for my sake, and because I asked him.'

'Speak out, then! What does it mean?'

'My unhappy brother is starving on the moor. We cannot let him perish at our very gates. The light is a signal to him that food is ready for him, and his light out yonder is to show the spot to which to bring it.'

'Then your brother is –'

'The escaped convict, sir – Selden, the criminal.'

'That's the truth, sir,' said Barrymore. 'I said that it was not my secret, and that I could not tell it to you. But now you have heard it, and you will see that if there was a plot it was not against you.'

This, then, was the explanation of the stealthy expeditions at night and the light at the window. Sir Henry and I both stared at the woman in amazement. Was it possible that this stolidly respectable person was of the same blood[5] as one of the most notorious criminals in the country?

'Yes, sir, my name was Selden, and he is my younger brother. We humoured him too much when he was a lad, and gave him his own way in everything, until he came to think that the world was made for his pleasure, and that he could do what he liked in it. Then, as he grew older, he met wicked companions, and the devil entered into him, until he broke my mother's heart and dragged our name in the dirt. From crime to crime he sank lower and lower, until it is only the mercy of God which has snatched him from the scaffold; but to me, sir, he was always the little curly-headed boy[6] that I had nursed and played with, as an elder sister would. That was why he broke prison, sir. He knew that I was here, and that we could not refuse to help him. When he dragged himself here one night, weary and starving, with the warders hard at his heels, what could we do? We took him in and fed him and cared for him. Then you returned, sir, and my brother thought he would be safer on the moor than anywhere else until the hue and cry was over, so he lay in hiding there. But every second night we made sure if he was still there by putting a light in the window, and if there was an answer my husband took out some bread and meat to him. Every day we hoped that he was gone, but as long as he was there we could not desert him. That is the whole truth, as I am an honest Christian woman, and you will see that if there is blame in the matter it does not lie with my husband, but with me, for whose sake he has done all that he has.'

The woman's words came with an intense earnestness which carried conviction with them.

'Is this true, Barrymore?'

'Yes, Sir Henry. Every word of it.'

'Well, I cannot blame you for standing by your own wife. Forget what I have said. Go to your room, you two, and we shall talk further about this matter in the morning.'

When they were gone we looked out of the window again. Sir Henry had flung it open, and the cold night wind beat in upon our faces. Far away in the black distance there still glowed that one tiny point of yellow light.

'I wonder he dares,' said Sir Henry.

'It may be so placed as to be only visible from here.'

'Very likely. How far do you think it is?'

'Out by the Cleft Tor,[7] I think.'

'Not more than a mile or two off.'

'Hardly that.'

'Well, it cannot be far if Barrymore had to carry out the food to it. And he is waiting, this villain, beside that candle. By thunder, Watson, I am going out to take that man!'

The same thought had crossed my own mind. It was not as if the Barrymores had taken us into their confidence. Their secret had been forced from them. The man was a danger to the community, an unmitigated scoundrel for whom there was neither pity nor excuse. We were only doing our duty in taking this chance of putting him back where he could do no harm. With his brutal and violent nature, others would have to pay the price if we held our hands. Any night, for example, our neighbours the Stapletons might be attacked by him, and it may have been the thought of this which made Sir Henry so keen upon the adventure.

'I will come,' said I.

'Then get your revolver and put on your boots. The sooner we start the better, as the fellow may put out his light and be off.'

In five minutes we were outside the door, starting upon our expedition. We hurried through the dark shrubbery, amid the dull moaning of the autumn wind and the rustle of the falling leaves. The night-air was heavy with the smell of damp and decay. Now and again the moon peeped out for an instant, but clouds were driving over the face of the sky, and just as we came out on the moor a thin rain began to fall. The light still burned steadily in front.

'Are you armed?' I asked.

'I have a hunting-crop.'[8]

'We must close in on him rapidly, for he is said to be a desperate fellow. We shall take him by surprise and have him at our mercy before he can resist.'

'I say, Watson,' said the baronet, 'what would Holmes say to this? How about that hour of darkness in which the power of evil is exalted?'

As if in answer to his words there rose suddenly out of the vast gloom of the moor that strange cry which I had already heard upon the borders of the great Grimpen Mire. It came with the wind through the silence of the night, a long, deep mutter, then a rising howl, and then the sad moan in which it died away. Again and again it sounded, the whole air throbbing with it, strident, wild, and menacing. The baronet caught my sleeve, and his face glimmered white through the darkness.

'Good heavens, what's that, Watson?'

'I don't know. It's a sound they have on the moor. I heard it once before.'

It died away, and an absolute silence closed in upon us. We stood straining our ears, but nothing came.

'Watson,' said the baronet, 'it was the cry of a hound.'

My blood ran cold in my veins, for there was a break in his voice which told of the sudden horror which had seized him.

'What do they call this sound?' he asked.

'Who?'

'The folk on the countryside.'[9]

'Oh, they are ignorant people. Why should you mind what they call it?'

'Tell me, Watson. What do they say of it?'

I hesitated, but could not escape the question.

'They say it is the cry of the Hound of the Baskervilles.'

He groaned, and was silent for a few moments.

'A hound it was,' he said at last, 'but it seemed to come from miles away, over yonder, I think.'

'It was hard to say whence it came.'

'It rose and fell with the wind. Isn't that the direction of the great Grimpen Mire?'

'Yes, it is.'

'Well, it was up there. Come now, Watson, didn't you think yourself that it was the cry of a hound? I am not a child. You need not fear to speak the truth.'

'Stapleton was with me when I heard it last. He said that it might be the calling of a strange bird.'

'No, no, it was a hound. My God, can there be some truth in all these stories? Is it possible that I am really in danger from so dark a cause? You don't believe it, do you, Watson?'

'No, no.'

'And yet it was one thing to laugh about it in London,[10] and it is another to stand out here in the darkness of the moor and to hear such a cry as that. And my uncle! There was the footprint of the hound beside him as he lay. It all fits together. I don't think that I am a coward, Watson, but that sound seemed to freeze my very blood. Feel my hand!'

It was as cold as a block of marble.

'You'll be all right tomorrow.'

'I don't think I'll get that cry out of my head. What do you advise that we do now?'

'Shall we turn back?'

'No, by thunder; we have come out to get our man, and we will do it. We are after the convict, and a hell-hound, as likely as not, after us. Come on. We'll see it through if all the fiends of the pit were loose upon the moor.'

We stumbled slowly along in the darkness, with the black loom of the craggy hills around us, and the yellow speck of light burning steadily in front. There is nothing so deceptive as the distance of a light upon a pitch-dark night, and sometimes the glimmer seemed to be far away upon the horizon and sometimes it might have been within a few yards of us. But at last we could see whence it came, and then we knew that we were indeed very close. A guttering candle was stuck in a crevice of the rocks which flanked it on each side so as to keep the wind from it, and also to prevent it from being visible, save in the direction of Baskerville Hall. A boulder of granite concealed our approach, and crouching behind it we gazed over it at the signal light. It was strange to see this single candle burning there in the middle of the moor, with no sign of life near it – just the one straight yellow flame and the gleam of the rock on each side of it.

'What shall we do now?' whispered Sir Henry.

'Wait here. He must be near his light. Let us see if we can get a glimpse of him.'

The words were hardly out of my mouth when we both saw him. Over the rocks, in the crevice of which the candle burned, there was thrust out an evil yellow face,[11] a terrible animal face, all seamed and scored with vile passions. Foul with mire, with a bristling beard, and hung with matted hair, it might well have belonged to one of those old savages who dwelt in the burrows on the hillsides. The light beneath him was reflected in his small, cunning eyes, which peered fiercely to right and left through the darkness, like a crafty and savage animal who has heard the steps of the hunters.

Something had evidently aroused his suspicions. It may have been that Barrymore had some private signal which we had neglected to give, or the fellow may have had some other reason for thinking that all was not well, but I could read his fears upon his wicked face. Any instant he might dash out the light and vanish in the darkness. I sprang forward, therefore, and Sir Henry did the same. At the same moment the convict screamed out a curse at us and hurled a rock which splintered up against the boulder which had sheltered us. I caught one glimpse of his short, squat, strongly-built figure as he sprang to his feet and turned to run. At the same moment by a lucky chance the moon broke through the clouds. We rushed over the brow of the hill, and there was our man running with great speed down the other side, springing over the stones in his way with the activity of a mountain goat. A lucky long shot of my revolver might have crippled him, but I had brought it only to defend myself if attacked, and not to shoot an unarmed man who was running away.

We were both fair runners and in good condition, but we soon found that we had no chance of overtaking him. We saw him for a long time in the moonlight, until he was only a small speck moving swiftly among the boulders upon the side of a distant hill. We ran and ran until we were completely blown, but the space between us grew ever wider. Finally we stopped and sat panting on two rocks, while we watched him disappearing in the distance.

And it was at this moment that there occurred a most strange and unexpected thing. We had risen from our rocks and were turning to go home, having abandoned the hopeless chase. The moon was low upon the right, and the jagged pinnacle of a granite tor stood up against the lower curve of its silver disc. There, outlined as black as an ebony statue on that shining background, I saw the figure of a man upon the tor. Do not think that it was a delusion, Holmes. I assure you that I have never in my life seen anything more clearly. As far as I could judge, the figure was that of a tall, thin man. He stood with his legs a little separated, his arms folded, his head bowed, as if he were brooding over that enormous wilderness of peat and granite which lay behind him. He might have been the very spirit of that terrible place. It was not the convict. This man was far from the place where the latter had disappeared. Besides, he was a much taller man. With a cry of surprise I pointed him out to the baronet, but in the instant during which I had turned to grasp his arm the man was gone. There was the sharp pinnacle of granite still cutting the lower edge of the moon, but its peak bore no trace of that silent and motionless figure.

I wished to go in that direction and to search the tor, but it was some distance away. The baronet's nerves were still quivering from that cry, which recalled the dark story of his family, and he was not in the mood for fresh adventures. He had not seen this lonely man upon the tor, and could not feel the thrill which his strange presence and his commanding attitude had given to me. 'A warder, no doubt,' said he. 'The moor has been thick with them since this fellow escaped.' Well, perhaps his explanation may be the right one, but I should like to have some further proof of it. Today we mean to communicate to the Princetown people where they should look for their missing man, but it is hard lines that we have not actually had the triumph of bringing him back as our own prisoner. Such are the adventures of last night, and you must acknowledge, my dear Holmes, that I have done you very well in the matter of a report. Much of what I tell you is no doubt quite irrelevant, but still I feel that it is best that I should let you have all the facts and leave you to select for yourself those which will be of most service to you in helping you to your conclusions. We are certainly making some progress. So far as the Barrymores go, we have found the motive of their actions, and that has cleared up the situation very much. But the moor with its mysteries and its strange inhabitants remains as inscrutable as ever. Perhaps in my next I may be able to throw some light upon this also. Best of all would it be if you could come down to us.[12]

10

Extract from the Diary of Dr Watson[1]

So far I have been able to quote from the reports which I have forwarded during these early days to Sherlock Holmes. Now, however, I have arrived at a point in my narrative where I am compelled to abandon this method and to trust once more to my recollections, aided by the diary which I kept at the time. A few extracts from the latter will carry me on to those scenes which are indelibly fixed in every detail upon my memory. I proceed, then, from the morning which followed our abortive chase of the convict and our other strange experiences upon the moor.

October 16th – A dull and foggy day, with a drizzle of rain. The house is banked in with rolling clouds, which rise now and then to show the dreary curves of the moor, with thin, silver veins upon the sides of the hills, and the distant boulders gleaming where the light strikes upon their wet faces. It is melancholy outside and in. The baronet is in a black reaction after the excitements of the night. I am conscious myself of a weight at my heart and a feeling of impending danger – ever-present, which is the more terrible because I am unable to define it.

And have I not cause for such a feeling? Consider the long sequence of incidents which have all pointed to some sinister influence which is at work around us. There is the death of the last occupant of the Hall, fulfilling so exactly the conditions of the family legend, and there are the repeated reports[2] from peasants of the appearance of a strange creature upon the moor. Twice I have with my own ears heard the sound which resembled the distant baying of a hound. It is incredible, impossible, that it should really be outside the ordinary laws of Nature. A spectral hound which leaves material footmarks and fills the air with its howling is surely not to be thought of. Stapleton may fall in with such a superstition, and Mortimer also; but if I have one quality upon earth it is common sense, and nothing will persuade me to believe in such a thing. To do so would be to descend to the level of these poor peasants who are not content with a mere fiend-dog,[3] but must needs describe him with hell-fire shooting from his mouth and eyes. Holmes would not listen to such fancies, and I am his agent. But facts are facts, and I have twice heard this crying upon the moor. Suppose that there were really some huge hound loose upon it; that would go far to explain everything. But where could such a hound lie concealed, where did it get its food, where did it come from, how was it that no one saw it by day?

It must be confessed that the natural explanation offers almost as many difficulties as the other. And always, apart from the hound, there was the fact of the human agency in London, the man in the cab, and the letter which warned Sir Henry against the moor. This at least was real, but it might have been the work of a protecting friend as easily as an enemy. Where was that friend or enemy now? Had he remained in London, or had he followed us down here? Could he – could he be the stranger whom I had seen upon the Tor?

It is true that I have had only the one glance at him, and yet there are some things to which I am ready to swear. He is no one whom I have seen down here, and I have now met all the neighbours. The figure was far taller than that of Stapleton, far thinner than that of Frankland. Barrymore it might possibly have been, but we had left him behind us, and I am certain that he could not have followed us. A stranger then is still dogging us, just as a stranger had dogged us in London. We have never shaken him off. If I could lay my hands upon that man, then at last we might find ourselves at the end of all our difficulties. To this one purpose I must now devote all my energies.

My first impulse was to tell Sir Henry all my plans. My second and wisest one is to play my own game and speak as little as possible to anyone. He is silent and distrait. His nerves have been strangely shaken by that sound upon the moor. I will say nothing to add to his anxieties, but I will take my own steps to attain my own end.

We had a small scene this morning after breakfast. Barrymore asked leave to speak with Sir Henry, and they were closeted in his study some little time. Sitting in the billiard-room, I more than once heard the sound of voices raised, and I had a pretty good idea what the point was which was under discussion. After a time the baronet opened his door and called for me.

'Barrymore considers that he has a grievance,' he said. 'He thinks that it was unfair on our part to hunt his brother-in-law down when he, of his own free will, had told us the secret.'

The butler was standing, very pale but very collected, before us.

'I may have spoken too warmly, sir,' said he, 'and if I have I am sure that I beg your pardon. At the same time, I was very much surprised when I heard you two gentlemen come back this morning and learned that you had been chasing Selden. The poor fellow has enough to fight against without my putting more upon his track.'

'If you had told us of your own free will it would have been a different thing,' said the baronet. 'You only told us, or rather your wife only told us, when it was forced from you and you could not help yourself.'

'I didn't think you would have taken advantage of it, Sir Henry – indeed I didn't.'

'The man is a public danger. There are lonely houses scattered over the moor, and he is a fellow who would stick at nothing. You only want to get a glimpse of his face to see that. Look at Mr Stapleton's house, for example, with no one but himself to defend it. There's no safety for anyone until he is under lock and key.'

'He'll break into no house, sir. I give you my solemn word upon that. And he will never trouble[4] anyone in this country again. I assure you, Sir Henry, that in a very few days the necessary arrangements will have been made and he will be on his way to South America. For God's sake, sir, I beg of you not to let the police know that he is still on the moor. They have given up the chase there, and he can lie quiet until the ship is ready for him. You can't tell on him, without getting my wife and me into trouble. I beg you, sir, to say nothing to the police.'

'What do you say, Watson?'

I shrugged my shoulders. 'If he were safely out of the country it would relieve the taxpayer of a burden.'

'But how about the chance of his holding someone up before he goes?'

'He would not do anything so mad, sir. We have provided him with all that he can want. To commit a crime would be to show where he was hiding.'

'That is true,' said Sir Henry. 'Well, Barrymore —'

'God bless you, sir, and thank you from my heart! It would have killed my poor wife had he been taken again.'

'I guess we are aiding and abetting a felony, Watson? But, after what we have heard, I don't feel as if I could give the man up, so there is an end of it. All right, Barrymore, you can go.'

With a few broken words of gratitude the man turned, but he hesitated and then came back.

'You've been so kind to us, sir, that I should like to do the best I can for you in return. I know something, Sir Henry, and perhaps I should have said it before, but it was long after the inquest that I found it out. I've never breathed a word about it yet to a mortal man. It's about poor Sir Charles's death.'

The baronet and I were both upon our feet.

'Do you know how he died?'

'No, sir, I don't know that.'

'What, then?'

'I know why he was at the gate at that hour. It was to meet a woman.'

'To meet a woman! He?'

'Yes, sir.'

'And the woman's name?'

'I can't give you the name, sir, but I can give you the initials. Her initials were L.L.'

'How do you know this, Barrymore?'

'Well, Sir Henry, your uncle had a letter that morning. He had usually a great many letters, for he was a public man and well known for his kind heart, so that everyone who was in trouble was glad to turn to him. But that morning, as it chanced, there was only this one letter, so I took the more notice of it. It was from Coombe Tracey,[5] and it was addressed in a woman's hand.'

'Well?'

'Well, sir, I thought no more of the matter, and never would have done had it not been for my wife. Only a few weeks ago she was cleaning out Sir Charles's study – it had never been touched since his death – and she found the ashes of a burned letter in the back of the grate. The greater part of it was charred to pieces, but one little slip, the end of a page, hung together, and the writing could still be read, though it was grey on a black ground. It seemed to us to be a postscript at the end of the letter, and it said: "Please, please, as you are a gentleman, burn this letter, and be at the gate by ten o'clock." Beneath it were signed the initials L.L.'

'Have you got that slip?'

'No, sir, it crumbled all to bits after we moved it.'

'Had Sir Charles received any other letters in the same writing?'

'Well, sir, I took no particular notice of his letters. I should not have noticed this one only it happened to come alone.'

'And you have no idea who L.L. is?'

'No, sir. No more than you have. But I expect if we could lay our hands upon that lady we should know more about Sir Charles's death.'

'I cannot understand, Barrymore, how you came to conceal this important information.'

'Well, sir, it was immediately after that our own trouble came to us. And then again, sir, we were both of us very fond of Sir Charles, as we well might be considering all that he has done for us. To rake this up couldn't help our poor master, and it's well to go carefully when there's a lady in the case. Even the best of us –'

'You thought it might injure his reputation?'

'Well, sir, I thought no good could come of it. But now you have been kind to us, and I feel as if it would be treating you unfairly not to tell you all that I know about the matter.'

'Very good, Barrymore; you can go.'

When the butler had left us, Sir Henry turned to me. 'Well, Watson, what do you think of this new light?'

'It seems to leave the darkness rather blacker than before.'

'So I think. But if we can only trace L.L. it should clear up the whole business. We have gained that much. We know that there is someone who has the facts if we can only find her. What do you think we should do?'

'Let Holmes know all about it at once. It will give him the clue for which he has been seeking. I am much mistaken if it does not bring him down.'

I went at once to my room and drew up my report of the morning's conversation for Holmes.[6] It was evident to me that he had been very busy of late, for the notes which I had from Baker Street were few and short, with no comments upon the information which I had supplied, and hardly any reference to my mission. No doubt his blackmailing case is absorbing all his faculties. And yet this new factor must surely arrest his attention and renew his interest. I wish that he were here.

October 17th – All day today the rain poured down, rustling on the ivy and dripping from the eaves. I thought of the convict out upon the bleak, cold, shelterless moor. Poor fellow! Whatever his crimes, he has suffered something to atone for them. And then I thought of that other one – the face in the cab, the figure against the moon. Was he also out in that deluge – the unseen watcher, the man of darkness? In the evening I put on my waterproof and I walked far upon the sodden moor, full of dark imaginings, the rain beating upon my face and the wind whistling about my ears. God help those who wander into the Great Mire now, for even the firm uplands are becoming a morass. I found the Black Tor[7] upon which I had seen the solitary watcher, and from its craggy summit I looked out myself across the melancholy downs. Rain squalls drifted across their russet face, and the heavy, slate-coloured clouds hung low over the landscape, trailing in grey wreaths down the sides of the fantastic hills. In the distant hollow on the left, half hidden by the mist, the two thin towers of Baskerville Hall rose above the trees. They were the only signs of human life which I could see, save only those prehistoric huts which lay thickly upon the slopes of the hills. Nowhere was there any trace of that lonely man whom I had seen on the same spot two nights before.

As I walked back I was overtaken by Dr Mortimer driving in his dog-cart[8] over a rough moorland track, which led from the outlying farmhouse of Foulmire. He had been very attentive to us, and hardly a day has passed that he has not called at the Hall to see how we were getting on. He insisted upon my climbing into his dog-cart and he gave me a lift homewards. I found him much troubled over the disappearance of his little spaniel. It had wandered on to the moor and had never come back. I gave him such consolation as I might, but I thought of the pony on the Grimpen Mire, and I do not fancy that he will see his little dog again.

'By the way, Mortimer,' said I, as we jolted along the rough road, 'I suppose there are few people living within driving distance of this whom you do not know?'

'Hardly any, I think.'

'Can you, then, tell me the name of any woman whose initials are L.L.?'

He thought for a few minutes. 'No,' said he. 'There are a few gipsies and labouring folk for whom I can't answer, but among the farmers or gentry there is no one whose initials are those. Wait a bit, though,' he added, after a pause. 'There is Laura Lyons – her initials are L.L. – but she lives in Coombe Tracey.'

'Who is she?' I asked.

'She is Frankland's daughter.'

'What? Old Frankland the crank?'

'Exactly. She married an artist named Lyons, who came sketching on the moor. He proved to be a blackguard and deserted her. The fault, from what I hear, may not have been entirely on one side. Her father refused to have anything to do with her, because she had married without his consent, and perhaps for one or two other reasons as well. So, between the old sinner and the young one the girl has had a pretty bad time.'

'How does she live?'

'I fancy old Frankland allows her a pittance, but it cannot be more, for his own affairs are considerably involved. Whatever she may have deserved, one could not allow her to go hopelessly to the bad. Her story got about, and several of the people here did something to enable her to earn an honest living. Stapleton did for one, and Sir Charles for another. I gave a trifle myself. It was to set her up in a typewriting business.'

He wanted to know the object of my inquiries, but I managed to satisfy his curiosity without telling him too much, for there is no reason why we should take anyone into our confidence. Tomorrow morning I shall find my way to Coombe Tracey, and if I can see this Mrs Laura Lyons, of equivocal reputation, a long step will have been made towards clearing one incident in this chain of mysteries. I am certainly developing the wisdom of the serpent, for when Mortimer pressed his questions to an inconvenient extent I asked him casually to what type Frankland's skull belonged, and so heard nothing but craniology for the rest of our drive. I have not lived for years with Sherlock Holmes for nothing.

I have only one other incident to record upon this tempestuous and melancholy day. This was my conversation with Barrymore just now, which gives me one more strong card which I can play in due time.

Mortimer had stayed to dinner, and he and the baronet played écarté[9] afterwards. The butler brought me my coffee into the library, and I took the chance to ask him a few questions.

'Well,' said I, 'has this precious relation of yours departed, or is he still lurking out yonder?'

'I don't know, sir. I hope to Heaven that he has gone, for he has brought nothing but trouble here! I've not heard of him since I left out food for him last, and that was three days ago.'

'Did you see him then?'

'No, sir; but the food was gone when next I went that way.'

'Then he was certainly there?'

'So you would think, sir, unless it was the other man who took it.'

I sat with my coffee-cup half-way to my lips, and stared at Barrymore.

'You know that there is another man, then?'

'Yes, sir; there is another man upon the moor.'

'Have you seen him?'

'No, sir.'

'How do you know of him, then?'

'Selden told me of him, sir, a week ago or more. He's in hiding, too, but he's not a convict, so far as I can make out. I don't like it, Dr Watson – I tell you straight, sir, that I don't like it.' He spoke with a sudden passion of earnestness.

'Now, listen to me, Barrymore! I have no interest in this matter but that of your master. I have come here with no object except to help him. Tell me, frankly, what it is that you don't like.'

Barrymore hesitated for a moment, as if he regretted his outburst, or found it difficult to express his own feelings in words.

'It's all these goings-on, sir,' he cried, at last, waving his hand towards the rain-lashed window which faced the moor. 'There's foul play somewhere, and there's black villainy brewing, to that I'll swear! Very glad I should be, sir, to see Sir Henry on his way back to London again!'

'But what is it that alarms you?'

'Look at Sir Charles's death! That was bad enough, for all that the coroner said. Look at the noises on the moor at night. There's not a man would cross it after sundown if he was paid for it. Look at this stranger hiding out yonder, and watching and waiting! What's he waiting for? What does it mean? It means no good to anyone of the name of Baskerville, and very glad I shall be to be quit of it all on the day that Sir Henry's new servants are ready to take over the Hall.'

'But about this stranger,' said I. 'Can you tell me anything about him? What did Selden say? Did he find out where he hid or what he was doing?'

'He saw him once or twice, but he is a deep one, and gives nothing away. At first he thought that he was the police, but soon he found that he had some lay of his own.[10] A kind of gentleman he was, as far as he could see, but what he was doing he could not make out.'

'And where did he say that he lived?'

'Among the old houses on the hillside – the stone huts where the old folk used to live.'

'But how about his food?'

'Selden found out that he has got a lad who works for him and brings him all he needs. I dare say he goes to Coombe Tracey for what he wants.'

'Very good, Barrymore. We may talk further of this some other time.'

When the butler had gone I walked over to the black window, and I looked through a blurred pane at the driving clouds and at the tossing outline of the windswept trees. It is a wild night indoors, and what must it be in a stone hut upon the moor? What passion of hatred can it be which leads a man to lurk in such a place at such a time? And what deep and earnest purpose can he have which calls for such a trial? There, in that hut upon the moor, seems to lie the very centre of that problem which has vexed me so sorely. I swear that another day shall not have passed before I have done all that man can do to reach the heart of the mystery.

I I

The Man on the Tor[1]

The extract from my private diary which forms the last chapter has
brought my narrative up to the 18th of October, a time when these
strange events began to move swiftly towards their terrible conclusion.
The incidents of the next few days are indelibly graven upon my
recollection, and I can tell them without reference to the notes made
at the time. I start, then, from the day which succeeded that upon
which I had established two facts of great importance, the one that
Mrs Laura Lyons of Coombe Tracey[2] had written to Sir Charles
Baskerville and made an appointment with him at the very place and
hour that he met his death, the other that the lurking man upon the
moor was to be found among the stone huts upon the hillside. With
these two facts in my possession I felt that either my intelligence or
my courage must be deficient if I could not throw some further light
upon these dark places.

I had no opportunity to tell the baronet what I had learned about
Mrs Lyons upon the evening before, for Dr Mortimer remained with
him at cards until it was very late. At breakfast, however, I informed
him about my discovery, and asked him whether he would care to
accompany me to Coombe Tracey. At first he was very eager to come,
but on second thoughts it seemed to both of us that if I went alone the
results might be better. The more formal we made the visit the less
information we might obtain. I left Sir Henry behind, therefore, not
without some prickings of conscience, and drove off upon my new
quest.

When I reached Coombe Tracey I told Perkins to put up the
horses, and I made inquiries for the lady whom I had come to

interrogate. I had no difficulty in finding her rooms, which were central and well appointed. A maid showed me in without ceremony, and as I entered the sitting-room a lady, who was sitting before a Remington typewriter,[3] sprang up with a pleasant smile of welcome. Her face fell,[4] however, when she saw that I was a stranger, and she sat down again and asked me the object of my visit.

The first impression left by Mrs Lyons was one of extreme beauty. Her eyes and hair were of the same rich hazel colour, and her cheeks, though considerably freckled, were flushed with the exquisite bloom of the brunette, the dainty pink which lurks at the heart of the sulphur rose.[5] Admiration was, I repeat, the first impression. But the second was criticism. There was something subtly wrong with the face, some coarseness of expression, some hardness, perhaps, of eye, some loose-ness of lip which marred its perfect beauty. But these, of course, are afterthoughts. At the moment I was simply conscious that I was in the presence of a very handsome woman, and that she was asking me the reasons for my visit. I had not quite understood until that instant how delicate my mission was.

'I have the pleasure,' said I, 'of knowing your father.'

It was a clumsy introduction, and the lady made me feel it.

'There is nothing in common between my father and me,' she said. 'I owe him nothing, and his friends are not mine. If it were not for the late Sir Charles Baskerville and some other kind hearts I might have starved for all that my father cared.'

'It was about the late Sir Charles Baskerville that I have come here to see you.'

The freckles started out on the lady's face.

'What can I tell you about him?' she asked, and her fingers played nervously over the stops of her typewriter.

'You knew him, did you not?'

'I have already said that I owe a great deal to his kindness. If I am able to support myself it is largely due to the interest which he took in my unhappy situation.'

'Did you correspond with him?'

The lady looked quickly up, with an angry gleam in her hazel eyes.

'What is the object of these questions?' she asked sharply.

'The object is to avoid a public scandal. It is better that I should ask them here than that the matter should pass outside our control.'

She was silent and her face was very pale. At last she looked up with something reckless and defiant in her manner.

'Well, I'll answer,' she said. 'What are your questions?'

'Did you correspond with Sir Charles?'

'I certainly wrote to him once or twice to acknowledge his delicacy and his generosity.'

'Have you the dates of those letters?'

'No.'

'Have you ever met him?'

'Yes, once or twice, when he came into Coombe Tracey. He was a very retiring man, and he preferred to do good by stealth.'

'But if you saw him so seldom and wrote so seldom, how did he know enough about your affairs to be able to help you, as you say that he has done?'

She met my difficulty with the utmost readiness.

'There were several gentlemen who knew my sad history and united to help me. One was Mr Stapleton, a neighbour and intimate friend of Sir Charles. He was exceedingly kind, and it was through him that Sir Charles learned about my affairs.'

I knew already that Sir Charles Baskerville had made Stapleton his almoner upon several occasions, so the lady's statement bore the impress of truth upon it.

'Did you ever write to Sir Charles asking him to meet you?' I continued.

Mrs Lyons flushed with anger again.

'Really, sir, this is a very extraordinary question.'

'I am sorry, madam, but I must repeat it.'

'Then I answer – certainly not.'

'Not on the very day of Sir Charles's death?'

The flush had faded in an instant, and a deathly face was before me. Her dry lips could not speak the 'No' which I saw rather than heard.

'Surely your memory deceives you,' said I. 'I could even quote a passage of your letter.[6] It ran "Please, please, as you are a gentleman burn this letter, and be at the gate by ten o'clock." '

I thought that she had fainted, but she recovered herself by a supreme effort.

'Is there no such thing as a gentleman?' she gasped.

'You do Sir Charles an injustice. He *did* burn the letter. But sometimes a letter may be legible even when burned. You acknowledge now that you wrote it?'[7]

'Yes, I did write it,' she cried, pouring out her soul in a torrent of words. 'I did write it. Why should I deny it? I have no reason to be ashamed of it. I wished him to help me. I believed that if I had an interview I could gain his help, so I asked him to meet me.'

'But why at such an hour?'

'Because I had only just learned that he was going to London next day and might be away for months. There were reasons why I could not get there earlier.'

'But why a rendezvous in the garden instead of a visit to the house?'

'Do you think a woman could go alone at that hour to a bachelor's house?'

'Well, what happened when you did get there?'

'I never went.'

'Mrs Lyons!'

'No, I swear it to you on all I hold sacred. I never went. Something intervened to prevent my going.'

'What was that?'

'That is a private matter. I cannot tell it.'

'You acknowledge then, that you made an appointment with Sir Charles at the very hour and place at which he met his death, but you deny that you kept the appointment?'

'That is the truth.'

Again and again I cross-questioned her, but I could never get past that point.

'Mrs Lyons,' said I, as I rose from this long inconclusive interview, 'you are taking a very great responsibility and putting yourself in a very false position by not making an absolutely clean breast of all that you know. If I have to call in the aid of the police you will find how seriously you are compromised. If your position is innocent, why did you in the first instance deny having written to Sir Charles upon that date?'

'Because I feared that some false conclusion might be drawn from it, and that I might find myself involved in a scandal.'

'And why were you so pressing that Sir Charles should destroy your letter?'

'If you have read the letter you will know.'

'I did not say that I had read all the letter.'

'You quoted some of it.'

'I quoted the postscript. The letter had, as I said, been burned, and it was not all legible. I ask you once again why it was that you were so pressing that Sir Charles should destroy this letter which he received on the day of his death.'

'The matter is a very private one.'

'The more reason why you should avoid a public investigation.'

'I will tell you, then. If you have heard anything of my unhappy history you will know that I made a rash marriage and had reason to regret it.'

'I have heard so much.'

'My life has been one incessant persecution from a husband whom I abhor.[8] The law is upon his side, and every day I am faced by the possibility that he may force me to live with him. At the time that I wrote this letter to Sir Charles I had learned that there was a prospect of my regaining my freedom if certain expenses could be met.[9] It meant everything to me – peace of mind, happiness, self-respect – everything. I knew Sir Charles's generosity, and I thought that if he heard the story from my own lips he would help me.'

'Then how is it that you did not go?'

'Because I received help in the interval from another source.'

'Why, then, did you not write to Sir Charles and explain this?'

'So I should have done had I not seen his death in the paper next morning.'[10]

The woman's story hung coherently together and all my questions were unable to shake it. I could only check it by finding if she had, indeed, instituted divorce proceedings against her husband at or about the time of the tragedy.

It was unlikely that she would dare to say that she had not been to Baskerville Hall if she really had been, for a trap[11] would be necessary to take her there, and could not have returned to Coombe Tracey until the early hours of the morning. Such an excursion could not be kept secret. The probability was, therefore, that she was telling the truth, or, at least, a part of the truth. I came away baffled and disheartened. Once again I had reached that dead wall which seemed to be built across every path by which I tried to get at the object of my mission. And yet the more I thought of the lady's face and of her manner the more I felt that something was being held back from me. Why should she turn so pale? Why should she fight against every admission until it was forced from her? Why should she have been so reticent at the time of the tragedy? Surely the explanation of all this could not be as innocent as she would have me believe. For the moment I could proceed no farther in that direction, but must turn back to that other clue which was to be sought for among the stone huts upon the moor.[12]

And that was a most vague direction. I realized it as I drove back and noted how hill after hill showed traces of the ancient people. Barrymore's only indication had been that the stranger lived in one of these abandoned huts, and many hundreds of them are scattered through the length and breadth of the moor. But I had my own experience for a guide, since it had shown me the man himself standing upon the summit of the Black Tor. That, then, should be the centre of my search. From there I should explore every hut upon the moor until I lighted upon the right one. If this man were inside it I should find out from his own lips, at the point of my revolver if necessary, who he was and why he had dogged us so long. He might slip away from us in the crowd of Regent Street, but it would puzzle him to do so upon the lonely moor. On the other hand, if I should find the hut, and its tenant should not be within it, I must remain there, however long the vigil, until he returned. Holmes had missed him in London. It would indeed be a triumph for me if I could run him to earth where my master had failed.

Luck had been against us again and again in this inquiry, but now at last it came to my aid. And the messenger of good fortune was none other than Mr Frankland, who was standing, grey-whiskered and red-faced,[13] outside the gate of his garden, which opened on to the high-road along which I travelled.

'Good-day, Dr Watson,' cried he, with unwonted good humour, 'you must really give your horses a rest, and come in to have a glass of wine and to congratulate me.'

My feelings towards him were far from being friendly after what I had heard of his treatment of his daughter, but I was anxious to send Perkins and the wagonette home, and the opportunity was a good one. I alighted and sent a message to Sir Henry that I should walk over in time for dinner. Then I followed Frankland into his dining-room.

'It is a great day for me, sir – one of the red-letter days of my life,' he cried, with many chuckles. 'I have brought off a double event. I mean to teach them in these parts that law is law, and that there is a man here who does not fear to invoke it. I have established a right of way through the centre of old Middleton's park, slap across it, sir, within a hundred yards of his own front door. What do you think of that? We'll teach these magnates that they cannot ride rough-shod over the rights of the commoners, confound them! And I've closed the wood where the Fernworthy folk used to picnic. These infernal people seem to think that there are no rights of property, and that they can swarm where they like with their papers and their bottles.[14] Both cases decided, Dr Watson, and both in my favour. I haven't had such a day since I had Sir John Morland[15] for trespass, because he shot in his own warren.'

'How on earth did you do that?'

'Look it up in the books, sir. It will repay reading – Frankland *v.* Morland, Court of Queen's Bench. It cost me £200, but I got my verdict.'

'Did it do you any good?'

'None, sir, none. I am proud to say that I had no interest in the matter. I act entirely from a sense of public duty. I have no doubt, for example, that the Fernworthy people will burn me in effigy tonight. I told the police last time they did it that they should stop these disgraceful exhibitions. The county constabulary is in a scandalous state,[16] sir, and it has not afforded me the protection to which I am entitled. The case of Frankland v. Regina will bring the matter before the attention of the public. I told them that they would have occasion to regret their treatment of me, and already my words have come true.'

'How so?' I asked.

The old man put on a very knowing expression.

'Because I could tell them what they are dying to know; but nothing would induce me to help the rascals in any way.'

I had been casting round for some excuse by which I could get away from his gossip, but now I began to wish to hear more of it. I had seen enough of the contrary nature of the old sinner to understand that any strong sign of interest would be the surest way to stop his confidences.

'Some poaching case, no doubt?' said I, with an indifferent manner.

'Ha, ha, my boy, a very much more important matter than that! What about the convict on the moor?'

I started. 'You don't mean that you know where he is?' said I.

'I may not know exactly where he is, but I am quite sure that I could help the police to lay their hands on him. Has it never struck you that the way to catch that man was to find out where he got his food, and so trace it to him?'

He certainly seemed to be getting uncomfortably near the truth. 'No doubt,' said I; 'but how do you know that he is anywhere upon the moor?'

'I know it because I have seen with my own eyes the messenger who takes him his food.'

My heart sank for Barrymore. It was a serious thing to be in the power of this spiteful old busybody. But his next remark took a weight from my mind.

'You'll be surprised to hear that his food is taken to him by a child. I see him every day through my telescope upon the roof. He passes along the same path at the same hour, and to whom should he be going except to the convict?'

Here was luck indeed! And yet I suppressed all appearance of interest. A child! Barrymore had said that our unknown was supplied by a boy. It was on his track, and not upon the convict's, that Frankland had stumbled. If I could get his knowledge it might save me a long and weary hunt. But incredulity and indifference were evidently my strongest cards.

'I should say that it was much more likely that it was the son of one of the moorland shepherds taking out his father's dinner.'

The least appearance of opposition struck fire out of the old autocrat. His eyes looked malignantly at me, and his grey whiskers bristled like those of an angry cat.

'Indeed, sir!' said he, pointing out over the wide-stretching moor. 'Do you see that Black Tor over yonder? Well, do you see the low hill beyond with the thorn-bush upon it? It is the stoniest part of the whole moor. Is that a place where a shepherd would be likely to take his station? Your suggestion, sir, is a most absurd one.'

I meekly answered that I had spoken without knowing all the facts. My submission pleased him and led him to further confidences.

'You may be sure, sir, that I have very good grounds before I come to an opinion. I have seen the boy again and again with his bundle. Every day, and sometimes twice a day, I have been able – but wait a moment, Dr Watson. Do my eyes deceive me, or is there at the present moment something moving upon that hillside?'

It was several miles off, but I could distinctly see a small dark dot against the dull green and grey.

'Come, sir, come!' cried Frankland, rushing upstairs. 'You will see with your own eyes and judge for yourself.'

The telescope, a formidable instrument mounted upon a tripod, stood upon the flat leads of the house. Frankland clapped his eye to it and gave a cry of satisfaction.

'Quick, Dr Watson, quick, before he passes over the hill!'

There he was, sure enough, a small urchin with a little bundle upon his shoulder, toiling slowly up the hill. When he reached the crest I saw the ragged, uncouth figure outlined for an instant against the cold blue sky. He looked round him, with a furtive and stealthy air, as one who dreads pursuit. Then he vanished over the hill.

'Well! Am I right?'

'Certainly, there is a boy who seems to have some secret errand.'

'And what the errand is even a county constable could guess. But not one word shall they have from me, and I bind you to secrecy also, Dr Watson. Not a word! You understand?'

'Just as you wish.'

'They have treated me shamefully – shamefully. When the facts come out in Frankland *v.* Regina I venture to think that a thrill of indignation will run through the country. Nothing would induce me to help the police in any way. For all they cared it might have been me, instead of my effigy, which these rascals burned at the stake. Surely you are not going! You will help me to empty the decanter in honour of this great occasion!'

But I resisted all his solicitations and succeeded in dissuading him from his announced intention of walking home with me. I kept the road as long as his eye was on me, and then I struck off across the moor and made for the stony hill over which the boy had disappeared. Everything was working in my favour, and I swore that it should not be through lack of energy or perseverance that I should miss the chance which Fortune had thrown in my way.

The sun was already sinking when I reached the summit of the hill, and the long slopes beneath me were all golden-green on one side and grey shadow on the other. A haze lay low upon the farthest sky-line, out of which jutted the fantastic shapes of Belliver and Vixen Tor.[17] Over the wide expanse there was no sound and no movement. One great grey bird, a gull or curlew, soared aloft in the blue heaven. He and I seemed to be the only living things between the huge arch of the sky and the desert beneath it. The barren scene, the sense of loneliness, and the mystery and urgency of my task all struck a chill into my heart. The boy was nowhere to be seen. But down beneath me in a cleft of the hills there was a circle of the old stone huts, and in the middle of them there was one which retained sufficient roof[18] to act as a screen against the weather. My heart leaped within me as I saw it. This must be the burrow where the stranger lurked. At last my foot was on the threshold of his hiding-place – his secret was within my grasp.

As I approached the hut, walking as warily as Stapleton would do when with poised net he drew near the settled butterfly, I satisfied myself that the place had indeed been used as a habitation. A vague pathway among the boulders led to the dilapidated opening which served as a door. All was silent within. The unknown might be lurking there, or he might be prowling on the moor. My nerves tingled with the sense of adventure. Throwing aside my cigarette, I closed my hand upon the butt of my revolver, and, walking swiftly up to the door, I looked in. The place was empty.

But there were ample signs that I had not come upon a false scent. This was certainly where the man lived. Some blankets rolled in a waterproof lay upon that very stone slab upon which neolithic man had once slumbered. The ashes of a fire were heaped in a rude grate. Beside it lay some cooking utensils and a bucket half-full of water. A litter of empty tins showed that the place had been occupied for some time, and I saw, as my eyes became accustomed to the chequered light,[19] a pannikin[20] and a half-full bottle of spirits standing in the corner. In the middle of the hut a flat stone served the purpose of a table, and upon this stood a small cloth bundle – the same, no doubt, which I had seen through the telescope upon the shoulder of the boy. It contained a loaf of bread, a tinned tongue, and two tins of preserved peaches. As I set it down again, after having examined it, my heart leaped to see that beneath it there lay a sheet of paper with writing upon it. I raised it, and this was what I read, roughly scrawled in pencil:

'Dr Watson has gone to Coombe Tracey.'

For a minute I stood there with the paper in my hands thinking out the meaning of this curt message. It was I, then, and not Sir Henry, who was being dogged by this secret man. He had not followed me himself, but he had set an agent – the boy, perhaps – upon my track, and this was his report. Possibly I had taken no step since I had been upon the moor which had not been observed and repeated. Always there was this feeling of an unseen force, a fine net drawn round us[21] with infinite skill and delicacy, holding us so lightly that it was only at some supreme moment that one realized that one was indeed entangled in its meshes.

If there was one report there might be others, so I looked round the hut in search of them. There was no trace, however, of anything of the kind, nor could I discover any sign which might indicate the character or intentions of the man who lived in this singular place, save that he must be of Spartan habits,[22] and cared little for the comforts of life. When I thought of the heavy rains and looked at the gaping roof I understood how strong and immutable must be the purpose which had kept him in that inhospitable abode. Was he our malignant enemy, or was he by chance our guardian angel? I swore that I would not leave the hut until I knew.

Outside the sun was sinking low and the west was blazing with scarlet and gold. Its reflection was shot back in ruddy patches by the distant pools which lay amid the great Grimpen Mire. There were the two towers of Baskerville Hall, and there a distant blur of smoke which marked the village of Grimpen. Between the two, behind the hill, was the house of the Stapletons. All was sweet and mellow and peaceful in the golden evening light, and yet as I looked at them my soul shared none of the peace of Nature, but quivered at the vagueness and the terror of that interview which every instant was bringing nearer.[23] With tingling nerves, but a fixed purpose, I sat in the dark recess of the hut and waited with sombre patience for the coming of its tenant.

And then at last I heard him. Far away came the sharp clink of a boot striking upon a stone. Then another and yet another, coming nearer and nearer. I shrank back into the darkest corner, and cocked the pistol in my pocket, determined not to discover myself until I had an opportunity of seeing something of the stranger. There was a long pause, which showed that he had stopped. Then once more the footsteps approached and a shadow fell across the opening of the hut.

'It is a lovely evening, my dear Watson,'[24] said a well-known voice. 'I really think that you will be more comfortable outside than in.'

Tension built and broken. And then at last.

"I heard him... nearer and nearer... it is a lovely evening, my dear Watson."

12

Death on the Moor

For a moment or two I sat breathless, hardly able to believe my ears. Then my senses and my voice came back to me, while a crushing weight of responsibility seemed in an instant to be lifted from my soul. That cold, incisive, ironical voice could belong to but one man in all the world.

'Holmes!' I cried – 'Holmes!'

'Come out,' said he, 'and please be careful with the revolver.'

I stooped under the rude lintel, and there he sat upon a stone outside, his grey eyes dancing with amusement as they fell upon my astonished features. He was thin and worn, but clear and alert, his keen face bronzed by the sun and roughened by the wind. In his tweed suit and cloth cap[1] he looked like any other tourist upon the moor, and he had contrived, with that cat-like love of personal cleanliness which was one of his characteristics, that his chin should be as smooth and his linen as perfect as if he were in Baker Street.

'I never was more glad to see anyone in my life,' said I, as I wrung him by the hand.

'Or more astonished, eh?'

'Well, I must confess to it.'

'The surprise was not all on one side, I assure you. I had no idea that you found my occasional retreat, still less that you were inside it, until I was within twenty paces of the door.'

'My footprint, I presume?'

'No, Watson; I fear that I could not undertake to recognize your footprint amid all the footprints of the world. If you seriously desire to deceive me you must change your tobacconist; for when I see the stub

of a cigarette marked Bradley, Oxford Street, I know that my friend
Watson is in the neighbourhood. You will see it there beside the path.
You threw it down, no doubt, at that supreme moment when you
charged into the empty hut.'

'Exactly.'

'I thought as much – and knowing your admirable tenacity, I was
convinced that you were sitting in ambush, a weapon within reach,
waiting for the tenant to return. So you actually thought that I was
the criminal?'

'I did not know who you were, but I was determined to find out.'

'Excellent, Watson! And how did you localize me? You saw me,
perhaps, on the night of the convict hunt, when I was so imprudent
as to allow the moon to rise behind me?'

'Yes, I saw you then.'

'And have, no doubt, searched all the huts until you came to this
one?'

'No, your boy had been observed, and that gave me a guide where
to look.'

'The old gentleman with the telescope, no doubt. I could not make
it out when first I saw the light flashing upon the lens.' He rose and
peeped into the hut. 'Ha, I see that Cartwright has brought up some
supplies. What's this paper? So you have been to Coombe Tracey,
have you?'

'Yes.'

'To see Mrs Laura Lyons?'

'Exactly.'

'Well done! Our researches have evidently been running on parallel
lines, and when we unite our results I expect we shall have a fairly full
knowledge of the case.'

'Well, I am glad from my heart that you are here, for indeed the
responsibility and the mystery were both becoming too much for my
nerves. But how in the name of wonder did you come here, and what
have you been doing? I thought that you were in Baker Street working
out that case of blackmailing.'

'That was what I wished you to think.'

'Then you use me, and yet do not trust me!'[2] I cried, with some bitterness. 'I think that I have deserved better at your hands, Holmes.'

'My dear fellow, you have been invaluable to me in this as in many other cases, and I beg that you will forgive me if I have seemed to play a trick upon you. In truth, it was partly for your own sake that I did it, and it was my appreciation of the danger which you ran which led me to come down and examine the matter for myself. Had I been with Sir Henry and you it is evident that my point of view would have been the same as yours, and my presence would have warned our very formidable opponents to be on their guard. As it is, I have been able to get about as I could not possibly have done had I been living at the Hall, and I remain an unknown factor in the business, ready to throw in all my weight at a critical moment.'[3]

'But why keep me in the dark?'

'For you to know could not have helped us, and might possibly have led to my discovery. You would have wished to tell me something, or in your kindness you would have brought me out some comfort or other, and so an unnecessary risk would be run. I brought Cartwright down with me – you remember the little chap at the Express office – and he has seen after my simple wants: a loaf of bread and a clean collar. What does a man want more? He has given me an extra pair of eyes upon a very active pair of feet, and both have been invaluable.'

'Then my reports have all been wasted!' My voice trembled as I recalled the pains and the pride with which I had composed them.

Holmes took a bundle of papers from his pocket.

'Here are your reports, my dear fellow, and very well thumbed, I assure you. I made excellent arrangements, and they are only delayed one day upon their way. I must compliment you exceedingly upon the zeal and the intelligence which you have shown over an extraordinarily difficult case.'

I was still rather raw over the deception which had been practised upon me, but the warmth of Holmes's praise drove my anger from my mind. I felt also in my heart that he was right in what he said, and that it was really best for our purpose that I should not have known that he was upon the moor.

'That's better,' said he, seeing the shadow rise from my face. 'And now tell me the result of your visit to Mrs Laura Lyons – it was not difficult for me to guess that it was to see her that you had gone, for I am already aware that she is the one person in Coombe Tracey who might be of service to us in the matter. In fact, if you had not gone today it is exceedingly probable that I should have gone tomorrow.'

The sun had set and dusk was settling over the moor. The air had turned chill, and we withdrew into the hut for warmth. There, sitting together in the twilight, I told Holmes of my conversation with the lady. So interested was he that I had to repeat some of it twice before he was satisfied.

'This is most important,' said he, when I had concluded. 'It fills up a gap which I had been unable to bridge in this most complex affair. You are aware, perhaps, that a close intimacy exists between this lady and the man Stapleton?'

'I did not know of a close intimacy.'

'There can be no doubt about the matter. They meet, they write, there is a complete understanding between them. Now, this puts a very powerful weapon into our hands. If I could use it to detach his wife –'

'His wife?'

'I am giving you some information now, in return for all that you have given me. The lady who has passed here as Miss Stapleton is in reality his wife.'

'Good heavens, Holmes! Are you sure of what you say? How could he have permitted Sir Henry to fall in love with her?'

'Sir Henry's falling in love could do no harm to anyone except Sir Henry. He took particular care that Sir Henry did not *make* love[4] to her, as you have yourself observed. I repeat that the lady is his wife and not his sister.'

'But why this elaborate deception?'

'Because he foresaw that she would be very much more useful to him in the character of a free woman.'

All my unspoken instincts, my vague suspicions, suddenly took shape and centred upon the naturalist. In that impassive, colourless man, with his straw hat and his butterfly-net, I seemed to see something terrible – a creature of infinite patience and craft, with a smiling face and a murderous heart.

Grimpen Mire

la Belle Dams Sans Merci.

'It is he, then, who is our enemy – it is he who dogged us in London?'

'So I read the riddle.'

'And the warning – it must have come from her!'

'Exactly.'

The shape of some monstrous villainy, half seen, half guessed, loomed through the darkness which had girt me so long.

'But are you sure of this, Holmes? How do you know that the woman is his wife?'

'Because he so far forgot himself as to tell you a true piece of autobiography upon the occasion when he first met you, and I dare say he has many a time regretted it since. He *was* once a schoolmaster in the North of England. Now, there is no one more easy to trace than a schoolmaster. There are scholastic agencies by which one may identify any man who has been in the profession. A little investigation showed me that a school had come to grief under atrocious circum-stances, and that the man who had owned it – the name was different – had disappeared with his wife. The description agreed. When I learned that the missing man was devoted to entomology the identifi-cation was complete.'

The darkness was rising, but much was still hidden by the shadows.

'If this woman is in truth his wife, where does Mrs Laura Lyons come in?' I asked.

'That is one of the points upon which your own researches have shed a light. Your interview with the lady has cleared the situation very much. I did not know about a projected divorce between herself and her husband. In that case, regarding Stapleton as an unmarried man, she counted no doubt upon becoming his wife.'

'And when she is undeceived?'

'Why, then we may find the lady of service. It must be our first duty to see her – both of us – tomorrow. Don't you think, Watson, that you are away from your charge rather long? Your place should be at Baskerville Hall.'

The last red streaks had faded away in the west and night had settled upon the moor. A few faint stars were gleaming in a violet sky.

'One last question, Holmes,' I said, as I rose. 'Surely there is no need of secrecy between you and me. What is the meaning of it all? What is he after?'

Holmes's voice sank as he answered – 'It is murder, Watson – refined, cold-blooded, deliberate murder.[5] Do not ask me for particulars. My nets are closing upon him, even as his are upon Sir Henry, and with your help he is already almost at my mercy. There is but one danger which can threaten us. It is that he should strike before we are ready to do so. Another day – two at the most – and I have my case complete, but until then guard your charge as closely as ever a fond mother watched her ailing child. Your mission today has justified itself, and yet I could almost wish that you had not left his side – Hark!'

A terrible scream – a prolonged yell of horror and anguish burst out of the silence of the moor. That frightful cry turned the blood to ice in my veins.

'Oh, my God!' I gasped. 'What is it? What does it mean?'

Holmes had sprung to his feet, and I saw his dark, athletic outline at the door of the hut, his shoulders stooping, his head thrust forward, his face peering into the darkness.

'Hush!' he whispered. 'Hush!'

The cry had been loud on account of its vehemence, but it had pealed out from somewhere far off on the shadowy plain. Now it burst upon our ears, nearer, louder, more urgent than before.

'Where is it?' Holmes whispered; and I knew from the thrill of his voice that he, the man of iron, was shaken to the soul. 'Where is it, Watson?'

'There, I think.' I pointed into the darkness.

'No, there!'

Again the agonized cry swept through the silent night, louder and much nearer than ever. And a new sound mingled with it, a deep, muttered rumble, musical and yet menacing, rising and falling like the low, constant murmur of the sea.

'The hound!' cried Holmes. 'Come, Watson, come! Great heavens, if we are too late!'

He had started running swiftly over the moor, and I had followed at his heels. But now from somewhere among the broken ground immediately in front of us there came one last despairing yell, and then a dull, heavy thud. We halted and listened. Not another sound broke the heavy silence of the windless night.

I saw Holmes put his hand to his forehead, like a man distracted. He stamped his feet upon the ground.

'He has beaten us, Watson. We are too late.'

'No, no, surely not!'

'Fool that I was to hold my hand.[6] And you, Watson, see what comes of abandoning your charge! But, by Heaven, if the worst has happened, we'll avenge him!'

b   aliteration.

Blindly we ran through the gloom, blundering against boulders, forcing our way through gorse bushes, panting up hills and rushing down slopes, heading always in the direction whence those dreadful sounds had come. At every rise Holmes looked eagerly round him, but the shadows were thick upon the moor and nothing moved upon its dreary face.

'Can you see anything?'

'Nothing.'

'But hark, what is that?'

A low moan had fallen upon our ears. There it was again upon our left! On that side a ridge of rocks ended in a sheer cliff, which overlooked a stone-strewn slope. On its jagged face was spreadeagled some dark, irregular object. As we ran towards it the vague outline hardened into a definite shape. It was a prostrate man face downwards upon the ground, the head doubled under him at a horrible angle, the shoulders rounded and the body hunched together as if in the act of throwing a somersault. So grotesque was the attitude that I could not for the instant realize that that moan had been the passing of his soul. Not a whisper, not a rustle, rose now from the dark figure over which we stooped. Holmes laid his hand upon him, and held it up again, with an exclamation of horror. The gleam of the match which he struck shone upon his clotted fingers and upon the ghastly pool which widened slowly from the crushed skull of the victim. And it shone upon something else which turned our hearts sick and faint within us – the body of Sir Henry Baskerville!

There was no chance of either of us forgetting that peculiar ruddy tweed suit[7] – the very one which he had worn on the first morning that we had seen him in Baker Street. We caught the one clear glimpse of it, and then the match flickered and went out, even as the hope had gone out of our souls. Holmes groaned, and his face glimmered white through the darkness.

'The brute! the brute!' I cried, with clenched hands. 'Oh, Holmes, I shall never forgive myself for having left him to his fate.'

'I am more to blame than you, Watson. In order to have my case well rounded and complete, I have thrown away the life of my client. It is the greatest blow which has befallen me in my career. But how could I know – how *could* I know – that he would risk his life alone upon the moor in the face of all my warnings?' More Concerned

'That we should have heard his screams – my God, those screams! tha – and yet have been unable to save him! Where is this brute of a dea hound which drove him to his death? It may be lurking among these rocks at this instant. And Stapleton, where is he? He shall answer for this deed.'

'He shall. I will see to that. Uncle and nephew have been murdered – the one frightened to death by the very sight of a beast, which he thought to be supernatural, the other driven to his end in his wild flight to escape from it. But now we have to prove the connection between the man and the beast. Save from what we heard, we cannot even swear to the existence of the latter, since Sir Henry has evidently died from the fall. But, by heavens, cunning as he is, the fellow shall be in my power before another day is past!'

We stood with bitter hearts on either side of the mangled body, overwhelmed by this sudden and irrevocable disaster which had brought all our long and weary labours to so piteous an end. Then, as the moon rose, we climbed to the top of the rocks over which our poor friend had fallen, and from the summit we gazed out over the shadowy moor, half silver and half gloom. Far away, miles off, in the direction of Grimpen, a single steady yellow light was shining. It could only come from the lonely abode of the Stapletons. With a bitter curse I shook my fist at it as I gazed.

'Why should we not seize him at once?'

'Our case is not complete. The fellow is wary and cunning to the last degree. It is not what we know, but what we can prove. If we make one false move the villain may escape us yet.'

'What can we do?'

'There will be plenty for us to do tomorrow. Tonight we can only perform the last offices to our poor friend.'

Together we made our way down the precipitous slope and approached the body, black and clear against the silver stones. The agony of those contorted limbs struck me with a spasm of pain and blurred my eyes with tears.

'We must send for help, Holmes! We cannot carry him all the way to the Hall. Good heavens, are you mad?'

He had uttered a cry and bent over the body. Now he was dancing and laughing and wringing my hand. Could this be my stern, self-contained friend? These were hidden fires, indeed!

'A beard! A beard! The man has a beard!'

'A beard?' *We were led to believe that Sir Henry is dead.*

'It is not the baronet – it is – why, it is my neighbour, the convict!'

With feverish haste we had turned the body over, and that dripping beard was pointing up to the cold, clear moon. There could be no doubt about the beetling forehead,[8] the sunken animal eyes. It was indeed the same face which had glared upon me in the light of the candle from over the rock – the face of Selden, the criminal.

Then in an instant it was all clear to me. I remembered how the baronet had told me that he had handed his old wardrobe to Barrymore. Barrymore had passed it on in order to help Selden in his escape. Boots, shirt, cap – it was all Sir Henry's. The tragedy was still black enough, but this man had at least deserved death[9] by the laws of his country. I told Holmes how the matter stood, my heart bubbling over with thankfulness and joy.

'Then the clothes have been the poor fellow's death,'[10] said he. 'It is clear enough that the hound has been laid on from some article of Sir Henry's – the boot which was abstracted in the hotel, in all probability – and so ran this man down. There is one very singular thing, however: How came Selden, in the darkness, to know that the hound was on his trail?'

'He heard him.'

'To hear a hound upon the moor would not work a hard man like this convict into such a paroxysm of terror that he would risk recapture by screaming wildly for help. By his cries he must have run a long way after he knew the animal was on his track. How did he know?'

'A greater mystery to me is why this hound, presuming that all our conjectures are correct –'

'I presume nothing.'

'Well, then, why this hound should be loose tonight. I suppose that it does not always run loose upon the moor. Stapleton would not let it go unless he had reason to think that Sir Henry would be there.'

'My difficulty is the more formidable of the two, for I think that we shall very shortly get an explanation of yours, while mine may remain for ever a mystery. The question now is, what shall we do with this poor wretch's body? We cannot leave it here to the foxes and the ravens.'

'I suggest that we put it in one of the huts until we can communicate with the police.'

'Exactly. I have no doubt that you and I could carry it so far. Halloa, Watson, what's this? It's the man himself, by all that's wonderful[11] and audacious! Not a word to show your suspicions – not a word, or my plans crumble to the ground.'

A figure was approaching us over the moor, and I saw the dull red glow of a cigar. The moon shone upon him, and I could distinguish the dapper shape and jaunty walk of the naturalist. He stopped when he saw us, and then came on again.

'Why, Dr Watson, that's not you, is it? You are the last man that I should have expected to see out on the moor at this time of night. But, dear me, what's this? Somebody hurt? Not – don't tell me that is our friend Sir Henry!'

He hurried past me and stooped over the dead man. I heard a sharp intake of his breath and the cigar fell from his fingers.

'Who – who's this?' he stammered.

'It is Selden, the man who escaped from Princetown.'

Stapleton turned a ghastly face upon us, but by a supreme effort he had overcome his amazement and his disappointment. He looked sharply from Holmes to me.

'Dear me! What a very shocking affair! How did he die?'

'He appears to have broken his neck by falling over these rocks. My friend and I were strolling on the moor when we heard a cry.'

'I heard a cry also. That was what brought me out. I was uneasy about Sir Henry.'

'Why about Sir Henry in particular?' I could not help asking.

'Because I had suggested that he should come over. When he did not come I was surprised, and I naturally became alarmed for his safety when I heard cries upon the moor. By the way' – his eyes darted again from my face to Holmes's – 'did you hear anything else besides a cry?'

'No,' said Holmes; 'did you?'

'No.'

'What do you mean then?'

'Oh, you know the stories that the peasants tell about a phantom hound, and so on. It is said to be heard at night upon the moor. I was wondering if there were any evidence of such a sound tonight.'

'We heard nothing of the kind,' said I.

'And what is your theory of this poor fellow's death?'

'I have no doubt that anxiety and exposure have driven him off his head. He has rushed about the moor in a crazy state and eventually fallen over here and broken his neck.'

'That seems the most reasonable theory,' said Stapleton, and he gave a sigh which I took to indicate his relief. 'What do you think about it, Mr Sherlock Holmes?'

My friend bowed his compliments.

'You are quick at identification,' said he.

'We have been expecting you in these parts since Dr Watson came down. You are in time to see a tragedy.'

'Yes, indeed. I have no doubt that my friend's explanation will cover the facts. I will take an unpleasant remembrance back to London with me tomorrow.'

'Oh, you return tomorrow?'

'That is my intention.'

'I hope your visit has cast some light upon those occurrences which have puzzled us?'

Holmes shrugged his shoulders. 'One cannot always have the success for which one hopes. An investigator needs facts, and not legends or rumours. It has not been a satisfactory case.'

My friend spoke in his frankest and most unconcerned manner. Stapleton still looked hard at him. Then he turned to me.

'I would suggest carrying this poor fellow to my house, but it would give my sister such a fright that I do not feel justified in doing it. I think that if we put something over his face he will be safe until morning.'

And so it was arranged. Resisting Stapleton's offer of hospitality, Holmes and I set off to Baskerville Hall, leaving the naturalist to return alone. Looking back we saw the figure moving slowly away over the broad moor, and behind him that one black smudge on the silvered slope which showed where the man was lying who had come so horribly to his end.

'We're at close grips at last,' said Holmes, as we walked together across the moor. 'What a nerve the fellow has! How he pulled himself together in the face of what must have been a paralysing shock when he found that the wrong man had fallen a victim to his plot. I told you in London, Watson, and I will tell you now again, that we have never had a foeman more worthy of our steel.'[12]

'I am sorry that he has seen you.'

'And so was I at first. But there was no getting out of it.'

'What effect do you think it will have upon his plans, now that he knows you are here?'

'It may cause him to be more cautious, or it may drive him to desperate measures at once. Like most clever criminals, he may be too confident in his own cleverness and imagine that he has completely deceived us.'

'Why should we not arrest him at once?'

'My dear Watson, you were born to be a man of action. Your instinct is always to do something energetic. But supposing, for argument's sake, that we had him arrested tonight, what on earth the better off should we be for that? We could prove nothing against him.

There's the devilish cunning of it! If he were acting through a human agent we could get some evidence, but if we were to drag this great dog to the light of day it would not help in putting a rope round the neck of its master.'

'Surely we have a case.'

'Not a shadow of one – only surmise and conjecture. We should be laughed out of court if we came with such a story and such evidence.'

'There is Sir Charles's death.'

'Found dead without a mark upon him. You and I know that he died of sheer fright, and we know also what frightened him; but how are we to get twelve stolid jurymen to know it? What signs are there of a hound? Where are the marks of its fangs? Of course, we know that a hound does not bite a dead body, and that Sir Charles was dead before ever the brute overtook him. But we have to *prove* all this, and we are not in a position to do it.'

'Well, then, tonight?'

'We are not much better off tonight. Again, there was no direct connection between the hound and the man's death. We never saw the hound. We heard it; but we could not prove that it was running upon this man's trail. There is a complete absence of motive. No, my dear fellow; we must reconcile ourselves to the fact that we have no case at present, and that it is worth our while to run any risk in order to establish one.'

'And how do you propose to do so?'

'I have great hopes of what Mrs Laura Lyons may do for us when the position of affairs is made clear to her. And I have my own plan as well. Sufficient for tomorrow is the evil thereof;[13] but I hope before the day is past to have the upper hand at last.'

I could draw nothing further from him, and he walked, lost in thought, as far as the Baskerville gates.

'Are you coming up?'

'Yes; I see no reason for further concealment. But one last word, Watson. Say nothing of the hound to Sir Henry. Let him think that Selden's death was as Stapleton would have us believe. He will have a better nerve for the ordeal which he will have to undergo tomorrow, when he is engaged, if I remember your report aright, to dine with these people.'

'And so am I.'

'Then you must excuse yourself, and he must go alone. That will be easily arranged. And now, if we are too late for dinner, I think that we are both ready for our suppers.'

13

Fixing the Nets[1]

Sir Henry was more pleased than surprised to see Sherlock Holmes, for he had for some days been expecting that recent events would bring him down from London. He did raise his eyebrows, however, when he found that my friend had neither any luggage nor any explanations for its absence. Between us we soon supplied his wants, and then over a belated supper we explained to the baronet as much of our experience as it seemed desirable that he should know. But first I had the unpleasant duty of breaking the news of Selden's death to Barrymore and his wife. To him it may have been an unmitigated relief, but she wept bitterly in her apron. To all the world he was the man of violence, half animal and half demon; but to her he always remained the little wilful boy of her own girlhood, the child who had clung to her hand. Evil indeed is the man who has not one woman to mourn him.

'I've been moping in the house all day since Watson went off in the morning,' said the baronet. 'I guess I should have some credit, for I have kept my promise. If I hadn't sworn not to go about alone I might have had a more lively evening, for I had a message from Stapleton asking me over there.'

'I have no doubt that you would have had a more lively evening,' said Holmes, dryly. 'By the way, I don't suppose you appreciate that we have been mourning over you as having broken your neck?'

Sir Henry opened his eyes. 'How was that?'

'This poor wretch was dressed in your clothes. I fear your servant who gave them to him may get into trouble with the police.'

'That is unlikely. There was no mark on any of them, so far as I know.'

'That's lucky for him – in fact, it's lucky for all of you, since you are all on the wrong side of the law in this matter. I am not sure that as a conscientious detective my first duty is not to arrest the whole household. Watson's reports are most incriminating documents.'

'But how about the case?' asked the baronet. 'Have you made anything out of the tangle? I don't know that Watson and I are much the wiser since we came down.'

'I think that I shall be in a position to make the situation rather more clear to you before long. It has been an exceedingly difficult and most complicated business. There are several points upon which we still want light – but it is coming, all the same.'

'We've had one experience, as Watson has no doubt told you. We heard the hound on the moor, so I can swear that it is not all empty superstition. I had something to do with dogs when I was out West, and I know one when I hear one. If you can muzzle that one and put him on a chain I'll be ready to swear you are the greatest detective of all time.'

'I think I will muzzle him and chain him all right if you will give your help.'

'Whatever you tell me to do I will do.'

'Very good; and I will ask you also to do it blindly, without always asking the reason.'

'Just as you like.'

'If you will do this I think the chances are that our little problem will soon be solved. I have no doubt –'

He stopped suddenly and stared fixedly up over my head into the air. The lamp beat upon his face, and so intent was it and so still that it might have been that of a clear-cut classical statue, a personification of alertness and expectation.

'What is it?' we both cried.

I could see as he looked down that he was repressing some internal emotion. His features were still composed, but his eyes shone with amused exultation.

'Excuse the admiration of a connoisseur,' said he, as he waved his hand towards the line of portraits which covered the opposite wall. 'Watson won't allow that I know anything of art, but that is mere jealousy, because our views upon the subject differ. Now, these are a really very fine series of portraits.'

'Well, I'm glad to hear you say so,' said Sir Henry, glancing with some surprise at my friend. 'I don't pretend to know much about these things, and I'd be a better judge of a horse or a steer[2] than of a picture. I didn't know that you found time for such things.'

'I know what is good when I see it, and I see it now. That's a Kneller,[3] I'll swear, that lady in the blue silk over yonder, and the stout gentleman with the wig ought to be a Reynolds.[4] They are all family portraits I presume?'

'Every one.'

'Do you know the names?'

'Barrymore has been coaching me in them, and I think I can say my lessons fairly well.'

'Who is the gentleman with the telescope?'

'That is Rear-Admiral Baskerville, who served under Rodney in the West Indies.[5] The man with the blue coat and the roll of paper is Sir William Baskerville, who was Chairman of Committees of the House of Commons under Pitt.'[6]

'And this Cavalier[7] opposite to me – the one with the black velvet and the lace?'

'Ah, you have a right to know about him. That is the cause of all the mischief, the wicked Hugo, who started the Hound of the Baskervilles. We're not likely to forget him.'

I gazed with interest and some surprise upon the portrait.

'Dear me!' said Holmes, 'he seems a quiet, meek-mannered man enough, but I dare say that there was a lurking devil in his eyes. I had pictured him as a more robust and ruffianly person.'

'There's no doubt about the authenticity, for the name and the date, 1647, are on the back of the canvas.'

Holmes said little more, but the picture of the old roisterer seemed to have a fascination for him, and his eyes were continually fixed upon it during supper. It was not until later, when Sir Henry had gone to his room, that I was able to follow the trend of his thoughts. He led me back into the banqueting-hall, his bedroom candle in his hand, and he held it up against the time-stained portrait on the wall.

'Do you see anything there?'

I looked at the broad plumed hat, the curling lovelocks, the white lace collar, and the straight severe face which was framed between them. It was not a brutal countenance, but it was prim, hard and stern, with a firm-set, thin-lipped mouth, and a coldly intolerant eye.

'Is it like anyone you know?'

'There is something of Sir Henry about the jaw.'

'Just a suggestion, perhaps. But wait an instant!'

He stood upon a chair, and holding up the light in his left hand, he curved his right arm over the broad hat, and round the long ringlets.

'Good heavens!' I cried, in amazement.

The face of Stapleton had sprung out of the canvas.

'Ha, you see it now. My eyes have been trained to examine faces and not their trimmings. It is the first quality of a criminal investigator that he should see through a disguise.'

'But this is marvellous. It might be his portrait.'

'Yes, it is an interesting instance of a throwback,[8] which appears to be both physical and spiritual. A study of family portraits is enough to convert a man to the doctrine of reincarnation. The fellow is a Baskerville – that is evident.'

'With designs upon the succession.'

'Exactly. This chance of the picture has supplied us with one of our most obvious missing links. We have him, Watson, we have him, and I dare swear that before tomorrow night he will be fluttering in our net as helpless as one of his own butterflies. A pin, a cork, and a card, and we add him to the Baker Street collection!'

He burst into one of his rare fits of laughter as he turned away from the picture. I have not heard him laugh often, and it has always boded ill to somebody.

I was up betimes in the morning, but Holmes was afoot earlier still, for I saw him as I dressed coming up the drive.

'Yes, we should have a full day today,' he remarked, and he rubbed his hands with the joy of action. 'The nets are all in place, and the drag is about to begin. We'll know before the day is out whether we have caught our big, lean-jawed pike, or whether he has got through the meshes.'

'Have you been on the moor already?'

'I have sent a report from Grimpen to Princetown[9] as to the death of Selden. I think I can promise that none of you will be troubled in the matter. And I have also communicated with my faithful Cartwright, who would certainly have pined away at the door of my hut as a dog does at his master's grave if I had not set his mind at rest about my safety.'

'What is the next move?'

'To see Sir Henry. Ah, here he is!'

'Good morning, Holmes,' said the baronet. 'You look like a general who is planning a battle with his chief of the staff.'

'That is the exact situation. Watson was asking for orders.'

'And so do I.'

'Very good. You are engaged, as I understand, to dine with our friends the Stapletons tonight.'

'I hope that you will come also. They are very hospitable people, and I am sure that they would be very glad to see you.'

'I fear that Watson and I must go to London.'

'To London?'

'Yes, I think that we should be more useful there at the present juncture.'

The baronet's face perceptibly lengthened. 'I hoped that you were going to see me through this business. The Hall and the moor are not very pleasant places when one is alone.'

'My dear fellow, you must trust me implicitly and do exactly what I tell you. You can tell your friends that we should have been happy to have come with you, but that urgent business required us to be in town. We hope very soon to return to Devonshire. Will you remember to give them that message?'

'If you insist upon it.'

'There is no alternative, I assure you.'

I saw by the baronet's clouded brow that he was deeply hurt by what he regarded as our desertion.

'When do you desire to go?' he asked, coldly.

'Immediately after breakfast. We will drive in to Coombe Tracey, but Watson will leave his things as a pledge that he will come back to you. Watson, you will send a note to Stapleton to tell him that you regret that you cannot come.'

'I have a good mind to go to London with you,' said the baronet. 'Why should I stay here alone?'

'Because it is your post of duty. Because you gave me your word that you would do as you were told, and I tell you to stay.'

'All right, then, I'll stay.'

'One more direction! I wish you to drive to Merripit House. Send back your trap, however, and let them know that you intend to walk home.'[10]

'To walk across the moor?'

'Yes.'

'But that is the very thing which you have so often cautioned me not to do.'

'This time you may do it with safety. If I had not every confidence in your nerve and courage I would not suggest it, but it is essential that you should do it.'

'Then I will do it.'

'And as you value your life, do not go across the moor in any direction save along the straight path which leads from Merripit House to the Grimpen Road, and is your natural way home.'

'I will do just what you say.'

'Very good. I should be glad to get away as soon after breakfast as possible, so as to reach London in the afternoon.'

I was much astounded by this programme, though I remembered that Holmes had said to Stapleton on the night before that his visit would terminate next day. It had not crossed my mind, however, that he would wish me to go with him, nor could I understand how we could both be absent at a moment which he himself declared to be critical. There was nothing for it, however, but implicit obedience; so we bade good-bye to our rueful friend, and a couple of hours afterwards we were at the station of Coombe Tracey and had dispatched the trap upon its return journey. A small boy was waiting upon the platform.

'Any orders, sir?'

'You will take this train to town, Cartwright. The moment you arrive you will send a wire to Sir Henry Baskerville, in my name, to say that if he finds the pocketbook which I have dropped he is to send it by registered post to Baker Street.'

'Yes, sir.'

'And ask at the station office if there is a message for me.'

The boy returned with a telegram, which Holmes handed to me. It ran:

Wire received. Coming down with unsigned warrant. Arrive five-forty – LESTRADE.[11]

'That is in answer to mine of this morning. He is the best of the professionals, I think, and we may need his assistance. Now, Watson, I think that we cannot employ our time better than by calling upon your acquaintance, Mrs Laura Lyons.'

His plan of campaign was beginning to be evident. He would use the baronet in order to convince the Stapletons that we were really gone, while we would actually return at the instant when we were likely to be needed. That telegram from London, if mentioned by Sir Henry to the Stapletons, must remove the last suspicions from their minds. Already I seemed to see our nets drawing close round that lean-jawed pike.

Mrs Laura Lyons was in her office, and Sherlock Holmes opened his interview with a frankness and directness which considerably amazed her.

'I am investigating the circumstances which attended the death of the late Sir Charles Baskerville,' said he. 'My friend here, Dr Watson, has informed me of what you have communicated, and also of what you have withheld in connection with that matter.'

'What have I withheld?' she asked defiantly.

'You have confessed that you asked Sir Charles to be at the gate at ten o'clock. We know that that was the place and hour of his death. You have withheld what the connection is between these events.'

'There is no connection.'

'In that case the coincidence must indeed be an extraordinary one. But I think that we shall succeed in establishing a connection after all. I wish to be perfectly frank with you, Mrs Lyons. We regard this case as one of murder, and the evidence may implicate not only your friend, Mr Stapleton, but his wife as well.'

The lady sprang from her chair. 'His wife!' she cried.

'The fact is no longer a secret. The person who has passed for his sister is really his wife.'

Mrs Lyons had resumed her seat. Her hands were grasping the arms of her chair, and I saw that the pink nails had turned white with the pressure of her grip.

'His wife!' she said, again. 'His wife! He was not a married man.'

Sherlock Holmes shrugged his shoulders.

'Prove it to me! Prove it to me! And if you can do so – !' The fierce flash of her eyes said more than any words.

'I have come prepared to do so,' said Holmes, drawing several papers from his pocket. 'Here is a photograph of the couple taken in York[12] four years ago. It is endorsed "Mr and Mrs Vandeleur", but you will have no difficulty in recognizing him, and her also, if you know her by sight. Here are three written descriptions by trustworthy witnesses of Mr and Mrs Vandeleur, who at that time kept St Oliver's private school. Read them, and see if you can doubt the identity of these people.'

She glanced at them, and then looked up at us with the set, rigid face of a desperate woman.

'Mr Holmes,' she said, 'this man had offered me marriage on condition that I could get a divorce from my husband. He has lied to me, the villain, in every conceivable way. Not one word of truth has he ever told me. And why – why? I imagined that all was for my own sake. But now I see that I was never anything but a tool in his hands. Why should I preserve faith with him who never kept any with me? Why should I try to shield him from the consequences of his own wicked acts? Ask me what you like, and there is nothing which I shall hold back. One thing I swear to you, and that is, that when I wrote the letter I never dreamed of any harm to the old gentleman, who had been my kindest friend.'

'I entirely believe you, madam,' said Sherlock Holmes. 'The recital of these events must be very painful to you, and perhaps it will make it easier if I tell you what occurred, and you can check me if I make any material mistake. The sending of this letter was suggested to you by Stapleton?'

'He dictated it.'

'I presume that the reason he gave was that you would receive help from Sir Charles for the legal expenses connected with your divorce?'[13]

'Exactly.'

'And then after you had sent the letter he dissuaded you from keeping the appointment?'

'He told me that it would hurt his self-respect that any other man should find the money for such an object, and that though he was a poor man himself he would devote his last penny to removing the obstacles which divided us.'

'He appears to be a very consistent character. And then you heard nothing until you read the reports of the death in the paper?'

'No.'

'And he made you swear to say nothing about your appointment with Sir Charles?'

'He did. He said that the death was a very mysterious one, and that I should certainly be suspected if the facts came out. He frightened me into remaining silent.'

'Quite so. But you had your suspicions?'

She hesitated and looked down. 'I knew him,' she said. 'But if he had kept faith with me I should always have done so with him.'

'I think that on the whole you have had a fortunate escape,' said Sherlock Holmes. 'You have had him in your power and he knew it, and yet you are alive. You have been walking for some months very near to the edge of a precipice. We must wish you good morning now, Mrs Lyons, and it is probable that you will very shortly hear from us again.'

'Our case becomes rounded off, and difficulty after difficulty thins away in front of us,' said Holmes as we stood waiting for the arrival of the express[14] from town. 'I shall soon be in the position of being able to put into a single connected narrative one of the most singular and sensational crimes of modern times. Students of criminology will remember the analogous incidents in Grodno, in Little Russia,[15] in the year '66, and of course there are the Anderson murders in North

Carolina, but this case possesses some features which are entirely its own. Even now we have no clear case against this very wily man. But I shall be very much surprised if it is not clear enough before we go to bed this night.'

The London express came roaring into the station, and a small, wiry bulldog of a man had sprung from a first-class carriage. We all three shook hands, and I saw at once from the reverential way in which Lestrade gazed at my companion that he had learned a good deal since the days when they had first worked together. I could well remember the scorn which the theories of the reasoner used then to excite in the practical man.

'Anything good?' he asked.

'The biggest thing for years,' said Holmes. 'We have two hours before we need think of starting. I think we might employ it in getting some dinner, and then, Lestrade, we will take the London fog out of your throat by giving you a breath of the pure night-air of Dartmoor. Never been there? Ah, well, I don't suppose you will forget your first visit.'

14

The Hound of the Baskervilles

One of Sherlock Holmes's defects – if, indeed, one may call it a defect – was that he was exceedingly loth to communicate his full plans to any other person until the instant of their fulfilment. Partly it came no doubt from his own masterful nature, which loved to dominate and surprise those who were around him. Partly also from his professional caution, which urged him never to take any chances. The result, however, was very trying for those who were acting as his agents and assistants. I had often suffered under it, but never more so than during that long drive in the darkness. The great ordeal was in front of us; at last we were about to make our final effort, and yet Holmes had said nothing, and I could only surmise what his course of action would be. My nerves thrilled with anticipation when at last the cold wind upon our faces and the dark, void spaces on either side of the narrow road told me that we were back upon the moor once again. Every stride of the horses and every turn of the wheels was taking us nearer to our supreme adventure.

Our conversation was hampered by the presence of the driver of the hired wagonette, so that we were forced to talk of trivial matters when our nerves were tense with emotion and anticipation. It was a relief to me, after that unnatural restraint, when we at last passed Frankland's house and knew that we were drawing near to the Hall and to the scene of action. We did not drive up to the door, but got down near the gate of the avenue. The wagonette was paid off and ordered to return to Coombe Tracey[1] forthwith, while we started to walk to Merripit House.

'Are you armed, Lestrade?'

The little detective smiled. 'As long as I have my trousers, I have a hip-pocket,[2] and as long as I have my hip-pocket I have something in it.'

'Good! My friend and I are also ready for emergencies.'

'You're mighty close about this affair, Mr Holmes. What's the game now?'

'A waiting game.'

'My word, it does not seem a very cheerful place,' said the detective, with a shiver, glancing round him at the gloomy slopes of the hill and at the huge <u>lake of fog</u> which lay over the Grimpen Mire. 'I see the lights of a house ahead of us.'

'That is Merripit House and the end of our journey. I must request you to walk on tiptoe and not to talk above a whisper.'

We moved cautiously along the track as if we were bound for the house, but Holmes halted us when we were about two hundred yards from it.

'This will do,' said he. 'These rocks upon the right make an admirable screen.'

'We are to wait here?'

'Yes, we shall make our little ambush here. Get into this hollow, Lestrade. You have been inside the house, have you not, Watson? Can you tell the position of the rooms? What are those latticed windows at this end?'

'I think they are the kitchen windows.'

'And the one beyond, which shines so brightly?'

'That is certainly the dining-room.'

'The blinds are up. You know the lie of the land best. Creep forward quietly and see what they are doing – but for Heaven's sake don't let them know that they are watched!'

I tiptoed down the path and stooped behind the low wall which surrounded the stunted orchard. Creeping in its shadow, I reached a point whence I could look straight through the uncurtained window.

There were only two men in the room, Sir Henry and Stapleton. They sat with their profiles towards me on either side of the round table. Both of them were smoking cigars, and coffee and wine were in front of them. Stapleton was talking with animation, but the baronet looked pale and distrait. Perhaps the thought of that lonely walk across the ill-omened moor was weighing heavily upon his mind.

As I watched them Stapleton rose and left the room, while Sir Henry filled his glass again and leaned back in his chair, puffing at his cigar. I heard the creak of a door and the crisp sound of boots upon gravel. The steps passed along the path on the other side of the wall under which I crouched. Looking over, I saw the naturalist pause at the door of an out-house in the corner of the orchard. A key turned in a lock, and as he passed in there was a curious scuffling noise from within. He was only a minute or so inside, and then I heard the key turn once more, and he passed me and re-entered the house. I saw him rejoin his guest and I crept quietly back to where my companions were waiting to tell them what I had seen.

'You say, Watson, that the lady is not there?' Holmes asked, when I had finished my report.

'No.'

'Where can she be, then, since there is no light in any other room except the kitchen?'

'I cannot think where she is.'

I have said that over the great Grimpen Mire there hung a dense, white fog. It was drifting slowly in our direction, and banked itself up like a wall on that side of us, low, but thick and well defined. The moon shone on it, and it looked like a great shimmering icefield, with the heads of the distant tors as rocks borne upon its surface. Holmes's face was turned towards it, and he muttered impatiently as he watched its sluggish drift.

'It's moving towards us, Watson.'

'Is that serious?'

'Very serious, indeed – the one thing upon earth which could have disarranged my plans. He can't be very long now. It is already ten o'clock. Our success and even his life may depend upon his coming out before the fog is over the path.' Career First

The night was clear and fine above us. The stars shone cold and bright, while a half-moon bathed the whole scene in a soft, uncertain light. Before us lay the dark bulk of the house, its serrated roof and bristling chimneys hard outlined against the silver-spangled sky. Broad bars of golden light from the lower windows stretched across the orchard and the moor. One of them was suddenly shut off. The servants had left the kitchen. There only remained the lamp in the dining-room where the two men, the murderous host and the unconscious guest, still chatted over their cigars.

Every minute that white woolly plain which covered one-half of the moor was drifting closer and closer to the house. Already the first thin wisps of it were curling across the golden square of the lighted window. The farther wall of the orchard was already invisible, and the trees were standing out of a swirl of white vapour. As we watched it the fog-wreaths came crawling round both corners of the house and rolled slowly into one dense bank, on which the upper floor and the roof floated like a strange ship upon a shadowy sea. Holmes struck his hand passionately upon the rock in front of us, and stamped his feet in his impatience.

'If he isn't out in a quarter of an hour the path will be covered. In half an hour we won't be able to see our hands in front of us.'

'Shall we move farther back upon higher ground?'

'Yes, I think it would be as well.'

So as the fog-bank flowed onwards we fell back before it until we were half a mile from the house, and still that dense white sea, with the moon silvering its upper edge, swept slowly and inexorably on.

'We are going too far,' said Holmes. 'We dare not take the chance of his being overtaken before he can reach us. At all costs we must hold our ground where we are.' He dropped on his knees and clapped his ear to the ground. 'Thank God,[3] I think that I hear him coming.'

A sound of quick steps broke the silence of the moor. Crouching among the stones, we stared intently at the silver-tipped bank in front of us. The steps grew louder, and through the fog, as through a curtain, there stepped the man whom we were awaiting. He looked round him in surprise as he emerged into the clear, starlit night. Then he came swiftly along the path, passed close to where we lay, and went on up the long slope behind us. As he walked he glanced continually over either shoulder, like a man who is ill at ease.

'Hist!' cried Holmes, and I heard the sharp click of a cocking pistol. 'Look out! It's coming!'

There was a thin, crisp, continuous patter from somewhere in the heart of that crawling bank. The cloud was within fifty yards of where we lay, and we glared at it, all three, uncertain what horror was about to break from the heart of it. I was at Holmes's elbow, and I glanced for an instant at his face. It was pale and exultant, his eyes shining brightly in the moonlight. But suddenly they started forward in a rigid, fixed stare, and his lips parted in amazement. At the same instant Lestrade gave a yell of terror[4] and threw himself face downwards upon the ground. I sprang to my feet, my inert hand grasping my pistol, my mind paralysed by the dreadful shape which had sprung out upon us from the shadows of the fog. A hound it was, an enormous coal-black hound, but not such a hound as mortal eyes have ever seen. Fire burst from its open mouth, its eyes glowed with a smouldering glare, its muzzle and hackles and dewlap[5] were outlined in flickering flame. Never in the delirious dream of a disordered brain could anything more savage, more appalling, more hellish, be conceived than that dark form and savage face which broke upon us out of the wall of fog.[6]

With long bounds the huge black creature was leaping down the track, following hard upon the footsteps of our friend. So paralysed were we by the apparition that we allowed him to pass before we had recovered our nerve. Then Holmes and I both fired together, and the creature gave a hideous howl, which showed that one at least had hit him. He did not pause, however, but bounded onwards. Far away on the path we saw Sir Henry looking back, his face white in the moonlight, his hands raised in horror, glaring helplessly at the frightful thing which was hunting him down.

But that cry of pain from the hound had blown all our fears to the winds. If he was vulnerable he was mortal, and if we could wound him we could kill him. Never have I seen a man run as Holmes ran that night. I am reckoned fleet of foot, but he outpaced me as much as I outpaced the little professional. In front of us as we flew up the track we heard scream after scream from Sir Henry and the deep roar of the hound. I was in time to see the beast spring upon its victim, hurl him to the ground and worry at his throat. But the next instant Holmes had emptied five barrels of his revolver[7] into the creature's flank. With a last howl of agony and a vicious snap in the air it rolled upon its back, four feet pawing furiously, and then fell limp upon its side. I stooped, panting, and pressed my pistol to the dreadful, shimmering head, but it was useless to press the trigger. The giant hound was dead.

Sir Henry lay insensible where he had fallen. We tore away his collar, and Holmes breathed a prayer of gratitude when we saw that there was no sign of a wound and that the rescue had been in time. Already our friend's eyelids shivered and he made a feeble effort to move. Lestrade thrust his brandy-flask between the baronet's teeth, and two frightened eyes were looking up at us.

'My God!' he whispered. 'What was it? What, in Heaven's name, was it?'

'It's dead, whatever it is,' said Holmes. 'We've laid the family ghost once and for ever.'

In mere size and strength it was a terrible creature which was lying stretched before us. It was not a pure bloodhound and it was not a pure mastiff;[8] but it appeared to be a combination of the two – gaunt, savage, and as large as a small lioness. Even now, in the stillness of death, the huge jaws seemed to be dripping with a bluish flame, and the small, deep-set, cruel eyes were ringed with fire. I placed my hand upon the glowing muzzle, and as I held them up my own fingers smouldered and gleamed in the darkness.

'Phosphorus,'[9] I said.

'A cunning preparation of it,' said Holmes, sniffing at the dead animal. 'There is no smell which might have interfered with his power of scent. We owe you a deep apology, Sir Henry, for having exposed you to this fright. I was prepared for a hound, but not for such a creature as this. And the fog gave us little time to receive him.'

'You have saved my life.'

'Having first endangered it. Are you strong enough to stand?'

'Give me another mouthful of that brandy, and I shall be ready for anything. So! Now, if you will help me up. What do you propose to do?'

'To leave you here. You are not fit for further adventures tonight. If you will wait, one or other of us will go back with you to the Hall.'

He tried to stagger to his feet; but he was still ghastly pale and trembling in every limb. We helped him to a rock, where he sat shivering with his face buried in his hands.

'We must leave you now,' said Holmes. 'The rest of our work must be done, and every moment is of importance. We have our case, and now we only want our man.

'It's a thousand to one against our finding him at the house,' he continued, as we retraced our steps swiftly down the path. 'Those shots must have told him that the game was up.'

'We were some distance off, and this fog may have deadened them.'

'He followed the hound to call him off – of that you may be certain. No, no, he's gone by this time! But we'll search the house and make sure.'

The front door was open, so we rushed in and hurried from room to room, to the amazement of a doddering old manservant, who met us in the passage. There was no light save in the dining-room, but Holmes caught up the lamp, and left no corner of the house unexplored. No sign could we see of the man whom we were chasing. On the upper floor, however, one of the bedroom doors was locked.

'There's someone in here!' cried Lestrade. 'I can hear a movement. Open this door!'

A faint moaning and rustling came from within. Holmes struck the door just over the lock with the flat of his foot, and it flew open. Pistol in hand, we all three rushed into the room.

But there was no sign within it of that desperate and defiant villain whom we expected to see. Instead we were faced by an object so strange and so unexpected that we stood for a moment staring at it in amazement.

The room had been fashioned into a small museum, and the walls were lined by a number of glass-topped cases full of that collection of butterflies and moths the formation of which had been the relaxation of this complex and dangerous man. In the centre of this room there was an upright beam, which had been placed at some period as a support for the old worm-eaten balk of timber which spanned the roof. To this post a figure was tied, so swathed and muffled in sheets which had been used to secure it that one could not for the moment tell whether it was that of a man or a woman. One towel passed round the throat, and was secured at the back of the pillar. Another covered the lower part of the face and over it two dark eyes – eyes full of grief and shame and a dreadful questioning – stared back at us. In a minute we had torn off the gag, unswathed the bonds, and Mrs Stapleton sank upon the floor in front of us. As her beautiful head fell upon her chest I saw the clear red weal of a whip-lash across her neck.

'The brute!' cried Holmes. 'Here, Lestrade, your brandy-bottle! Put her in the chair! She has fainted from ill-usage and exhaustion.'

She opened her eyes again. 'Is he safe?' she asked. 'Has he escaped?'

'He cannot escape us, madam.'

'No, no, I did not mean my husband. Sir Henry? Is he safe?'

'Yes.'

'And the hound?'

'It is dead.'

She gave a long sigh of satisfaction. 'Thank God! Thank God! Oh, this villain! See how he has treated me!' She shot her arms out from her sleeves, and we saw with horror that they were all mottled with bruises. 'But this is nothing – nothing! It is my mind and soul that he has tortured and defiled. I could endure it all, ill-usage, solitude, a life of deception, everything, as long as I could still cling to the hope that I had his love, but now I know that in this also I have been his dupe and his tool.' She broke into passionate sobbing as she spoke.

'You bear him no good will, madam,' said Holmes. 'Tell us, then, where we shall find him. If you have ever aided him in evil, help us now and so atone.'

'There is but one place where he can have fled,' she answered. 'There is an old tin mine on an island in the heart of the Mire. It was there that he kept his hound, and there also he had made preparations so that he might have a refuge. That is where he would fly.'

The fog-bank lay like white wool against the window. Holmes held the lamp towards it.

'See,' said he. 'No one could find his way into the Grimpen Mire tonight.'

She laughed and clapped her hands. Her eyes and teeth gleamed with fierce merriment.

'He may find his way in, but never out,' she cried. 'How can he see the guiding wands[10] tonight? We planted them together, he and I, to mark the pathway through the Mire. Oh, if I could only have plucked them out today! Then indeed you would have had him at your mercy.'

It was evident to us that all pursuit was in vain until the fog had lifted. Meanwhile we left Lestrade in possession of the house, while Holmes and I went back with the baronet to Baskerville Hall. The story of the Stapletons could no longer be withheld from him, but he took the blow bravely when he learned the truth about the woman whom he had loved. But the shock of the night's adventures had shattered his nerves, and before morning he lay delirious in a high fever, under the care of Dr Mortimer. The two of them were destined to travel together[11] round the world before Sir Henry had become once more the hale, hearty man that he had been before he became master of that ill-omened estate.

And now I come rapidly to the conclusion of this singular narrative, in which I have tried to make the reader share those dark fears and vague surmises which clouded our lives so long, and ended in so tragic a manner. On the morning after the death of the hound the fog had lifted and we were guided by Mrs Stapleton to the point where they had found a pathway through the bog. It helped us to realize the horror of this woman's life when we saw the eagerness and joy with which she laid us on her husband's track. We left her standing upon the thin peninsula of firm, peaty soil which tapered out into the wide-spread bog. From the end of it a small wand planted here and there showed where the path zigzagged from tuft to tuft of rushes among those green-scummed pits and foul quagmires which barred the way to the stranger. Rank reeds and lush, slimy water-plants sent an odour of decay and a heavy miasmatic vapour[12] into our faces, while a false step plunged us more than once thigh-deep into the dark, quivering mire, which shook for yards in soft undulations around our feet. Its tenacious grip plucked at our heels as we walked, and when we sank into it it was as if some malignant hand was tugging us down into those obscene depths, so grim and purposeful was the clutch in which it held us. Once only we saw a trace that someone had passed that perilous way before us. From amid a tuft of cotton-grass which

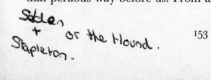

Stolen
+ of the Hound.
Stapleton.

153

bore it up out of the slime some dark thing was projecting. Holmes sank to his waist as he stepped from the path to seize it, and had we not been there to drag him out he could never have set his foot upon firm land again. He held an old black boot in the air. 'Meyers, Toronto', was printed on the leather inside.

'It is worth a mud bath,' said he. 'It is our friend Sir Henry's missing boot.'

'Thrown there by Stapleton in his flight.'

'Exactly. He retained it in his hand after using it to set the hound upon his track. He fled when he knew the game was up, still clutching it. And he hurled it away at this point of his flight. We know at least that he came so far in safety.'

But more than that we were never destined to know, though there was much which we might surmise. There was no chance of finding footsteps in the mire, for the rising mud oozed swiftly in upon them, but as we at last reached firmer ground beyond the morass we all looked eagerly for them. But no slightest sign of them ever met our eyes. If the earth told a true story, then Stapleton never reached that island of refuge towards which he struggled through the fog upon that last night. Somewhere in the heart of the great Grimpen Mire, down in the foul slime of the huge morass which had sucked him in, this cold and cruel-hearted man is for ever buried.

Many traces we found of him in the bog-girt island where he had hid his savage ally. A huge driving-wheel and a shaft[13] half-filled with rubbish showed the position of an abandoned mine. Beside it were the crumbling remains of the cottages of the miners, driven away, no doubt, by the foul reek of the surrounding swamp. In one of these a staple and chain, with a quantity of gnawed bones, showed where the animal had been confined. A skeleton with a tangle of brown hair adhering to it lay among the débris.

'A dog!' said Holmes. 'By Jove, a curly-haired spaniel.[14] Poor Mortimer will never see his pet again. Well, I do not know that this place contains any secret which we have not already fathomed. He could hide his hound, but he could not hush its voice, and hence came those cries which even in daylight were not pleasant to hear. On an emergency he could keep the hound in the out-house at Merripit, but it was always a risk, and it was only on the supreme day, which he regarded as the end of all his efforts, that he dared do it. This paste in the tin is no doubt the luminous mixture with which the creature was daubed. It was suggested, of course, by the story of the family hell-hound, and by the desire to frighten old Sir Charles to death. No wonder the poor devil of a convict ran and screamed, even as our friend did, and as we ourselves might have done, when he saw such a creature bounding through the darkness of the moor upon his track. It was a cunning device, for, apart, from the chance of driving your victim to his death, what peasant would venture to inquire too closely into such a creature should he get sight of it, as many have done, upon the moor? I said it in London, Watson, and I say it again now, that never yet have we helped to hunt down a more dangerous man than he who is lying yonder' – he swept his long arm towards the huge mottled expanse of green-splotched bog which stretched away until it merged into the russet slopes of the moor.

15

A Retrospection

It was the end of November, and Holmes and I sat, upon a raw and foggy night, on either side of a blazing fire[1] in our sitting-room in Baker Street. Since the tragic upshot[2] of our visit to Devonshire he had been engaged in two affairs of the utmost importance, in the first of which he had exposed the atrocious conduct of Colonel Upwood in connection with the famous card scandal[3] of the Nonpareil Club, while in the second he had defended the unfortunate Mme Montpensier from the charge of murder, which hung over her in connection with the death of her step-daughter, Mlle Carère, the young lady who, as it will be remembered, was found six months later alive and married in New York. My friend was in excellent spirits over the success which had attended a succession of difficult and important cases, so that I was able to induce him to discuss the details of the Baskerville mystery. I had waited patiently for the opportunity, for I was aware that he would never permit cases to overlap, and that his clear and logical mind would not be drawn from its present work to dwell upon memories of the past. Sir Henry and Dr Mortimer were, however, in London, on their way to that long voyage which had been recommended for the restoration of his shattered nerves. They had called upon us that very afternoon, so that it was natural that the subject should come up for discussion.

'The whole course of events,' said Holmes, 'from the point of view of the man who called himself Stapleton, was simple and direct, although to us, who had no means in the beginning of knowing the motives of his actions and could only learn part of the facts, it all appeared exceedingly complex. I have had the advantage of two conversations with Mrs Stapleton, and the case has now been so entirely cleared up that I am not aware that there is anything which has remained a secret to us. You will find a few notes upon the matter under the heading B in my indexed list of cases.'

'Perhaps you would kindly give me a sketch of the course of events from memory.'

'Certainly, though I cannot guarantee that I carry all the facts in my mind. Intense mental concentration has a curious way of blotting out what has passed. The barrister who has his case at his fingers' end, and is able to argue with an expert upon his own subject, finds that a week or two of the courts will drive it all out of his head once more. So each of my cases displaces the last, and Mlle Carère has blurred my recollection of Baskerville Hall. Tomorrow some other little problem may be submitted to my notice, which will in turn dispossess the fair French lady and the infamous Upwood.[4] So far as the case of the hound goes, however, I will give you the course of events as nearly as I can, and you will suggest anything which I may have forgotten.

'My inquiries show beyond all question that the family portrait did not lie, and that this fellow was indeed a Baskerville. He was a son of that Rodger Baskerville, the younger brother of Sir Charles, who fled with a sinister reputation to South America, where he was said to have died unmarried. He did, as a matter of fact, marry, and had one child, this fellow, whose real name is the same as his father. He married Beryl Garçia, one of the beauties of Costa Rica,[5] and, having purloined a considerable sum of public money, he changed his name to Vandeleur and fled to England, where he established a school in the east of Yorkshire. His reason for attempting this special line of business was that he had struck up an acquaintance with a consumptive tutor upon the voyage home,[6] and that he had used this man's ability to make the undertaking a success. Fraser, the tutor, died, however, and the school which had begun well, sank from disrepute into infamy. The Vandeleurs found it convenient to change their name to Stapleton, and he brought the remains of his fortune, his schemes for the future, and his taste for entomology to the south of England. I learn at the British Museum that he was a recognized authority upon the subject, and that the name of Vandeleur has been permanently attached to a certain moth which he had, in his Yorkshire days, been the first to describe.[7]

'We now come to that portion of his life which has proved to be of such intense interest to us. The fellow had evidently made inquiry, and found that only two lives intervened between him and a valuable estate. When he went to Devonshire his plans were, I believe, exceedingly hazy, but that he meant mischief from the first is evident from the way in which he took his wife with him in the character of his sister. The idea of using her as a decoy was clearly already in his mind, though he may not have been certain how the details of his plot were to be arranged. He meant in the end to have the estate, and he was ready to use any tool or run any risk for that end. His first act was to establish himself as near to his ancestral home as he could, and his second was to cultivate a friendship with Sir Charles Baskerville, and with the neighbours.

'The baronet himself told him about the family hound, and so prepared the way for his own death. Stapleton, as I will continue to call him, knew that the old man's heart was weak, and that a shock would kill him. So much he had learned from Dr Mortimer. He had heard also that Sir Charles was superstitious and had taken this grim legend very seriously. His ingenious mind instantly suggested a way by which the baronet could be done to death, and yet it would be hardly possible to bring home the guilt to the real murderer.

'Having conceived the idea, he proceeded to carry it out with considerable finesse. An ordinary schemer would have been content to work with a savage hound. The use of artificial means to make the creature diabolical was a flash of genius upon his part. The dog he bought in London from Ross and Mangles,[8] the dealers in Fulham Road. It was the strongest and most savage in their possession. He brought it down by the North Devon line, and walked a great distance over the moor, so as to get it home without exciting any remarks. He had already on his insect hunts learned to penetrate the Grimpen Mire, and so had found a safe hiding-place for the creature. Here he kennelled it and waited his chance.

'But it was some time coming. The old gentleman could not be decoyed outside of his grounds at night. Several times Stapleton lurked about with his hound, but without avail. It was during these fruitless quests that he, or rather his ally, was seen by peasants, and that the legend of the demon dog received a new confirmation. He had hoped that his wife might lure Sir Charles to his ruin, but here she proved unexpectedly independent. She would not endeavour to entangle the old gentleman in a sentimental attachment which might deliver him over to his enemy. Threats and even, I am sorry to say, blows failed to move her. She would have nothing to do with it, and for a time Stapleton was at a deadlock.

'He found a way out of his difficulties through the chance that Sir Charles, who had conceived a friendship with him, made him the minister of his charity in the case of this unfortunate woman, Mrs Laura Lyons. By representing himself as a single man, he acquired complete influence over her, and he gave her to understand that in the event of her obtaining a divorce from her husband he would marry her. His plans were suddenly brought to a head by his knowledge that Sir Charles was about to leave the Hall on the advice of Dr Mortimer, with whose opinion he himself pretended to coincide. He must act at once, or his victim might get beyond his power. He therefore put pressure upon Mrs Lyons to write this letter, imploring the old man to give her an interview on the evening before his departure for London. He then, by a specious argument, prevented her from going, and so had the chance for which he had waited.

'Driving back in the evening from Coombe Tracey, he was in time to get his hound, to treat it with his infernal paint, and to bring the beast round to the gate at which he had reason to expect that he would find the old gentleman waiting. The dog, incited by its master, sprang over the wicket-gate and pursued the unfortunate baronet, who fled screaming down the Yew Alley. In that gloomy tunnel it must indeed have been a dreadful sight to see that huge black creature, with its flaming jaws and blazing eyes, bounding after its victim. He fell dead at the end of the alley from heart disease and terror. The hound had kept upon the grassy border while the baronet had run down the path, so that no track but the man's was visible. On seeing him lying still the creature had probably approached to sniff at him, but, finding him dead, had turned away again. It was then that it left the print which was actually observed by Dr Mortimer. The hound was called off and hurried away to its lair in the Grimpen Mire, and a mystery was left which puzzled the authorities, alarmed the countryside, and finally brought the case within the scope of our observation.

'So much for the death of Sir Charles Baskerville. You perceive the devilish cunning of it, for really it would be almost impossible to make a case against the real murderer. His only accomplice was one who could never give him away, and the grotesque, inconceivable nature of the device only served to make it more effective. Both of the women concerned in the case, Mrs Stapleton and Mrs Laura Lyons, were left with a strong suspicion against Stapleton. Mrs Stapleton knew that he had designs upon the old man, and also of the existence of the hound. Mrs Lyons knew neither of these things, but had been impressed by the death occurring at the time of an uncancelled appointment which was only known to him. However, both of them were under his influence, and he had nothing to fear from them. The first half of his task was successfully accomplished, but the more difficult still remained.

'It is possible that Stapleton did not know of the existence of an heir in Canada. In any case he would very soon learn it from his friend Dr Mortimer, and he was told by the latter all details about the arrival of Henry Baskerville. Stapleton's first idea was that this young stranger from Canada might possibly be done to death in London without coming down to Devonshire at all. He distrusted his wife ever since she had refused to help him in laying a trap for the old man, and he dared not leave her long out of his sight for fear he should lose his influence over her. It was for this reason that he took her to London with him. They lodged, I find, at the Mexborough Private Hotel, in Craven Street,[9] which was actually one of those called upon by my agent in search of evidence. Here he kept his wife imprisoned in her room while he, disguised in a beard, followed Dr Mortimer to Baker Street, and afterwards to the station and to the Northumberland Hotel. His wife had some inkling of his plans; but she had such a fear of her husband – a fear founded upon brutal ill-treatment – that she dare not write to warn the man whom she knew to be in danger. If the letter should fall into Stapleton's hands her own life would not be safe. Eventually, as we know, she adopted the expedient of cutting out the words which would form the message, and addressing the letter in a disguised hand. It reached the baronet, and gave him the first warning of his danger.

'It was very essential for Stapleton to get some article of Sir Henry's attire, so that, in case he was driven to use the dog, he might always have the means of setting him upon his track. With characteristic promptness and audacity he set about this at once, and we cannot doubt that the boots[10] or chambermaid of the hotel was well bribed to help him in his design. By chance, however, the first boot which was procured for him was a new one, and, therefore, useless for his purpose. He then had it returned and obtained another – a most instructive incident, since it proved conclusively to my mind that we were dealing with a real hound, as no other supposition could explain this anxiety to obtain an old boot and this indifference to a new one. The more *outré*[11] and grotesque an incident is the more carefully it deserves to be examined, and the very point which appears to complicate a case is, when duly considered and scientifically handled, the one which is most likely to elucidate it.

'Then we had the visit from our friends next morning, shadowed always by Stapleton in the cab. From his knowledge of our rooms and of my appearance, as well as from his general conduct, I am inclined to think that Stapleton's career of crime has been by no means limited to this single Baskerville affair. It is suggestive that during the last three years there have been four considerable burglaries in the West Country, for none of which was any criminal ever arrested. The last of these, at Folkestone Court, in May, was remarkable for the cold-blooded pistolling of the page, who surprised the masked and solitary burglar. I cannot doubt that Stapleton[12] recruited his waning resources in this fashion, and that for years he has been a desperate and dangerous man.

'We had an example of his readiness of resource that morning when he got away from us so successfully, and also of his audacity in sending back my own name to me through the cabman. From that moment he understood that I had taken over the case in London, and that therefore there was no chance for him there. He returned to Dartmoor and awaited the arrival of the baronet.'

'One moment!' said I. 'You have, no doubt, described the sequence of events correctly, but there is one point which you have left unexplained. What became of the hound when its master was in London?'

'I have given some attention to this matter, and it is undoubtedly of importance. There can be no question that Stapleton had a confidant, though it is unlikely that he ever placed himself in his power by sharing all his plans with him. There was an old manservant at Merripit House, whose name was Anthony. His connection with the Stapletons can be traced for several years, as far back as the schoolmastering days, so that he must have been aware that his master and mistress were really husband and wife. This man has disappeared and has escaped from the country. It is suggestive that Anthony is not a common name in England, while Antonio is so in all Spanish or Spanish-American countries. The man, like Mrs Stapleton herself, spoke good English, but with a curious lisping accent. I have myself seen this old man cross the Grimpen Mire by the path which Stapleton had marked out. It is very probable, therefore, that in the absence of his master it was he who cared for the hound, though he may never have known the purpose for which the beast was used.

'The Stapletons then went down to Devonshire, whither they were soon followed by Sir Henry and you. One word now as to how I stood myself at that time. It may possibly recur to your memory that when I examined the paper upon which the printed words were fastened I made a close inspection for the watermark. In doing so I held it within a few inches of my eyes, and was conscious of a faint smell of the scent known as white jessamine.[13] There are seventy-five perfumes, which it is very necessary that the criminal expert should be able to distinguish from each other, and cases have more than once within my own experience depended upon their prompt recognition. The scene suggested the presence of a lady, and already my thoughts began to turn towards the Stapletons. Thus I had made certain of the hound, and had guessed at the criminal[14] before ever we went to the West Country.

'It was my game to watch Stapleton. It was evident, however, that I could not do this if I were with you, since he would be keenly on his guard. I deceived everybody, therefore, yourself included, and I came down secretly when I was supposed to be in London. My hardships were not so great as you imagine, though such trifling details must never interfere with the investigation of a case. I stayed for the most part at Coombe Tracey, and only used the hut upon the moor when it was necessary to be near the scene of action. Cartwright had come down with me, and in his disguise as a country boy he was of great assistance to me. I was dependent upon him for food and clean linen. When I was watching Stapleton, Cartwright was frequently watching you, so that I was able to keep my hands upon all the strings.

'I have already told you that your reports reached me rapidly, being forwarded instantly from Baker Street[15] to Coombe Tracey. They were of great service to me, and especially that one incidentally truthful piece of biography of Stapleton's. I was able to establish the identity of the man and the woman, and knew at last exactly how I stood. The case had been considerably complicated through the incident of the escaped convict and the relations between him and the Barrymores. This also you cleared up in a very effective way, though I had already come to the same conclusions from my own observations.

'By the time that you discovered me upon the moor I had a complete knowledge of the whole business, but I had not a case which could go to a jury. Even Stapleton's attempt upon Sir Henry that night, which ended in the death of the unfortunate convict, did not help us much in proving murder against our man. There seemed to be no alternative but to catch him red-handed, and to do so we had to use Sir Henry, alone and apparently unprotected, as a bait. We did so, and at the cost of a severe shock to our client we succeeded in completing our case and driving Stapleton to his destruction. That Sir Henry should have been exposed to this is, I must confess, a reproach to my management of the case, but we had no means of foreseeing the terrible and paralysing spectacle which the beast presented, nor could we predict the fog which enabled him to burst upon us at short notice. We succeeded in our object at a cost which both the specialist and Dr Mortimer assure me will be a temporary one. A long journey may enable our friend to recover not only from his shattered nerves but also from his wounded feelings. His love for the lady was deep and sincere,[16] and to him the saddest part of all this black business was that he should have been deceived by her.

'It only remains now to indicate the part which she had played throughout. There can be no doubt that Stapleton exercised an influence over her which may have been love or may have been fear, or very possibly both, since they are by no means incompatible emotions. It was, at least, absolutely effective. At his command she consented to pass as his sister, though he found the limits of his power over her when he endeavoured to make her the direct accessory to murder. She was ready to warn Sir Henry so far as she could without implicating her husband, and again and again she tried to do so. Stapleton himself seems to have been capable of jealousy, and when he saw the baronet paying court to the lady, even though it was part of his own plan, still he could not help interrupting with a passionate outburst which revealed the fiery soul which his self-contained manner so cleverly concealed. By encouraging the intimacy he made it certain that Sir Henry would frequently come to Merripit House, and that he would sooner or later get the opportunity which he desired. On the day of the crisis, however, his wife turned suddenly against him. She had learned something of the death of the convict, and she knew that the hound was being kept in the out-house on the evening that Sir Henry was coming to dinner. She taxed her husband with his intended crime and a furious scene followed, in which he showed her for the first time that she had a rival in his love. Her fidelity turned in an instant to bitter hatred, and he saw that she would betray him. He tied her up, therefore, that she might have no chance of warning Sir Henry, and he hoped, no doubt, that when the whole countryside put down the baronet's death to the curse of his family, as they certainly would do, he could win his wife back to accept an accomplished fact, and to keep silent upon what she knew. In this I fancy that in any case he made a miscalculation, and that, if we had not been there, his doom would none the less have been sealed. A woman of Spanish blood does not condone such an injury so lightly. And now, my dear Watson, without referring to my notes, I cannot give you a more detailed account of this curious case. I do not know that anything essential has been left unexplained.'

'He could not hope to frighten Sir Henry to death, as he had done the old uncle, with his bogy hound.'

'The beast was savage and half-starved. If its appearance did not frighten its victim to death, at least it would paralyse the resistance which might be offered.'

'No doubt. There only remains one difficulty. If Stapleton came into the succession, how could he explain the fact that he, the heir, had been living unannounced under another name so close to the property? How could he claim it without causing suspicion and inquiry?'

'It is a formidable difficulty, and I fear that you ask too much when you expect me to solve it. The past and the present are within the field of my inquiry, but what a man may do in the future is a hard question to answer. Mrs Stapleton has heard her husband discuss the problem on several occasions. There were three possible courses. He might claim the property from South America, establish his identity before the British authorities there, and so obtain the fortune without ever coming to England at all; or he might adopt an elaborate disguise during the short time that he need be in London; or, again, he might furnish an accomplice with the proofs and papers, putting him in as heir, and retaining a claim upon some proportion of his income. We cannot doubt, from what we know of him, that he would have found some way out of the difficulty. And now, my dear Watson, we have had some weeks of severe work, and for one evening, I think, we may turn our thoughts into more pleasant channels. I have a box for *Les Huguenots*. Have you heard the De Reszkes?[17] Might I trouble you then to be ready in half an hour, and we can stop at Marcini's for a little dinner on the way?'

NOTES

INTRODUCTION

1. *baying at the gates of the bourgeoisie*: See Jerry Palmer, 'Satan Baying at the Gates', *Time Out* (5 April 1974), p. 21.

2. *Theo Brown*: Author of *The Black Dog in Devon* (1959) and *The Fate of the Dead* (1979).

3. *at a suitable distance*: See Michael Pointer, *The Sherlock Holmes File* (1976), pp. 80–81.

4. *as a filing is drawn to its magnet*: See Ronald Pearsall, *Conan Doyle* (1989), pp. 135–6, and Richard Lancelyn Green, *The Uncollected Sherlock Holmes* (1983), pp. 91–2.

5. *He would write in a train or anywhere . . .*: See Pierre Nordon, *Conan Doyle* (1966).

6. *with lantern slides on the topography of the Great Grimpen*: See Catherine Cooke, 'Cats, a Gentleman and a Saint', *Sherlock Holmes Gazette*, 18 (1997), p. 18.

7. *the plot which eventuated in* The Hound of the Baskervilles: Robinson later made the claim to his close friend Archibald Marshall, who recalled it in *Out and About – Random Reminiscences* (1933), pp. 4–5. The Robinson quote is from his *Associated Sunday Magazines* article.

8. *enriched English literature*: See Dorothy L. Sayers, *Studies in Sherlock Holmes*, (privately printed for The Sherlock Holmes Society of London, 1996; first published 1946).

9. *would do well to consider Holmes . . .*: See T. S. Eliot, 'Sherlock Holmes and His Times', *The Criterion* (April 1929), pp. 551–6.

10. *the one that heads Chapter 3*: See John Fowles, *Afterword to The Hound of the Baskervilles* (1974), p. 190.

CHAPTER I
Mr Sherlock Holmes

1. *Mr Sherlock Holmes*: The major film adaptations of *The Hound of the Baskervilles* have all begun the story either at Baskerville Hall, or with the manuscript 'Curse of the Baskervilles'. The 1939 Hollywood version opens with Sir Charles Baskerville's death, and Selden the escaped prisoner trying to steal his watch; it then moves to the coroner's court. The 1959 Hammer Films version opens with the curse – 'Know, then, the legend of the hound of the Baskervilles' – and then moves to Baker Street, where Holmes observes: 'This, I think, is a two pipe problem.' The 1973 Universal television film begins with the shadow of Holmes in his deerstalker, then introduces the 'most blood-curdling and awesome [adventure] of all' – the curse of the Baskervilles. Both *Sir Arthur Conan Doyle's The Hound of the Baskervilles* (1983) and Granada Television's *The Hound of the Baskervilles* (1988) open with Sir Charles Baskerville having an after-dinner smoke, outside the Hall, and hearing the baleful howl of the hound. The 1983 film then shows Holmes's reaction, back at Baker Street: 'The game's afoot, Watson.' The BBC television film *The Hound of the Baskervilles* (2002) begins with an inquest on Sir Charles, continues with the convict Selden being chased by prison guards across the moor, then introduces Holmes and Watson in a Turkish Bath: 'hot enough for you, Watson?' The opening of the novel is less spectacular but, to readers of the short stories, reassuringly traditional.

2. *when he stayed up all night*: The *Strand* version has 'when he was up all night'.

3. *which our visitor had left behind him the night before*: As numerous commentators have pointed out, many of Holmes's stunning feats of deduction depend on his clients leaving items of property behind in Baker Street, only to return for them and in the process confirm the validity of Holmes's methods. Dorothy L. Sayers called this 'one of Holmes's favourite tricks'.

4. *a 'Penang lawyer'*: Walking stick made, according to William S. Baring-Gould, 'from the stem of a small palm (*Licuala acutifida*) that grows in Penang, an island in the straits of Malacca'. In 'Silver Blaze', Holmes's other Dartmoor adventure (from *The Memoirs*), another 'Penang lawyer' – a heavy, bulbous-headed cane weighted with lead – is thought to be the murder weapon.

5. *MRCS, from his friends of the CCH*: MRCS means Member of the Royal College of Surgeons; Charing Cross Hospital was founded in 1818 as the 'Royal West London Infirmary and Lying-in Institute'; the Regency building where Dr Mortimer was a house-surgeon from 1882 to 1884 was opened in 1829.

6. *a well-polished, silver-plated coffee-pot*: Holmes's observation of Watson's behaviour shows how his methods, so often parodied since, were a touch parodic in the first place.

7. *the thick iron ferrule*: The metal ring encasing the base of the stick, to prevent the wood splitting when in use.

8. *all accounts which you have been so good as to give*: This links *The Hound of the Baskervilles* with Holmes's earlier stories, and confirms the subtitle, *Another Adventure of Sherlock Holmes*; later, Stapleton will mention 'the records of your detective [which] have reached us here [on Dartmoor]', which links *The Hound* with the fame of Sherlock Holmes as well.

9. *you are not yourself luminous, but you are a conductor of light*: Something like William Shakespeare's Falstaff, who says in I.ii of *Henry IV, Part II*, 'I am not only witty in myself, but the cause that wit is in other men.'

10. *he laid down his cigarette*: In the popular imagination, Holmes is always smoking a meerschaum pipe with a curved stem – never once mentioned in the stories; his preferred pipes are in fact a 'cherry wood', an 'amber stem', a 'brier', a 'before-breakfast pipe', and a 'clay pipe'; but when he smokes (as he does in forty-nine of the stories), he just as often smokes a cigarette.

11. *interesting, though elementary*: The famous phrase 'elementary, my dear Watson' never in fact occurs in the sixty Holmes narratives; this comes close to it, though.

12. *several deductions*: Holmes's method was rarely based on deductions; more commonly, it combined some logical (mainly deductive) and some empirical (mainly inductive) elements, plus a measure of inspired guesswork; most of Holmes's conclusions from the evidence before him do not stand up to strictly logical analysis. On the whole, Holmes arrives at correct conclusions largely because the author wants him to, rather than because of any systematic method.

13. *he could not have been on the* staff *of the hospital*: He could not have had an established, or permanent, contract with the institution he left five years ago; there has been much debate about the year in which *The Hound* was supposed to be set – suggestions range from 1886 to 1900; five years after 1884 would mean the year 1889. Conan Doyle does not seem to have been very concerned about exact dates.

14. *Reversion ... Corresponding member ... Atavism*: Dr Mortimer's essay was evidently about whether disease is evidence of inherited/ancestral characteristics; his article in the prestigious *Lancet*, a weekly medical journal founded earlier in the century, was about unusual examples of resemblances to ancestors; these linked themes play an important part in the plot of *The Hound*. A 'Corresponding member' of the Society is one who lives some way away, and thus corresponds by letter.

15. *a picker-up of shells on the shores of the great unknown ocean*: A reference to Sir

Isaac Newton's famous admission (as repeated in D. Brewster's *Memoirs of Newton*, vol. ii, Ch. 27) '. . . to myself I seem to have been only like a little boy playing on the sea-shore, and diverting myself in now and then finding a smoother pebble or prettier shell than ordinary, whilst the great ocean of truth lay all undiscovered before me'; also compare William Blake's 'To see the world in a grain of sand' (from 'Auguries of Innocence').

16. *so dolichocephalic a skull or such well-marked supra-orbital development . . . parietal fissure*: So 'long-headed' or 'elongated' a skull; so much of the skull above the orbit of the eye; the fissure or division between the right and left parietal bones, along the top of the skull. 'Our scientific friend' Dr, or Mr, Mortimer is rather overplaying his hand here. Dr Watson will later write of him 'never was there such a single-minded enthusiast as he!'

17. *I observe from your forefinger that you make your own cigarettes*: Holmes may have been an authority on the ashes produced by cigar, cigarette and pipe tobacco – he had, early on in his career, written a monograph 'Upon the Distinction between the Ashes of the Various Tobaccos' – but even he couldn't possibly deduce from a forefinger whether a client rolled his own cigarettes or purchased them from a tobacconist; he could, of course, tell from nicotine stains whether the client was a *smoker*, but that is a very different conclusion and a much more mundane one.

18. *the work of Monsieur Bertillon*: Alphonse Bertillon (1853–1914), French anthropologist who had recently invented the science of 'anthropometry' which involved measuring and recording physical characteristics – including scars – and then classifying them according to the length of the individual's head; this data was thought to be especially valuable for identifying criminals and what were known as 'criminal types'. Holmes was an early advocate through his practice of the importance of the Bertillon system, fingerprinting and ballistics – in short, of the *science* of detection. But Bertillon's system, when used crudely, was also used to distinguish 'racial types' and to generalize about criminal tendencies from facial characteristics.

CHAPTER 2
The Curse of the Baskervilles

1. *the alternative use of the long s and the short*: Holmes is not exactly correct about this; the long *s* was never used at the end of a word, or as the first letter of a word if it was supposed to begin with a capital *S* – so the use was not, strictly speaking, 'alternative'.

2. *1742*: Sidney Paget's illustration of the legend for the *Strand* magazine has Sir Hugo Baskerville and followers in eighteenth-century costume; the

Hammer Films version of *The Hound* (1959) also presents the legend in an eighteenth-century, Hell Fire Club, setting. Yet in the novel it takes place 'in the time of the Great Rebellion' – i.e. in the mid-1640s. Interestingly, according to folklorist Theo Brown, legendary black dogs tended to be associated with supporters of the Royalist cause rather than the Parliamentarians – the old way of life, before the world was turned upside down.

3. *the learned Lord Clarendon*: Edward Hyde, first Earl of Clarendon (1609–74), Royalist politician and historian, whose monumental *History of the Great Rebellion* was published posthumously in 1702–4. The style of the Baskerville manuscript shows Conan Doyle in his historical novel mode: it bears very little resemblance to the sentence structure and vocabulary of real eighteenth-century documents. The manuscript may owe something to the legend associated with a house belonging to the Battishill family of Dartmoor recounted in Sabine Baring-Gould's *A Book of Dartmoor* (1900): it told of the wicked Richard Weekes who, in 1660, terrorized his brother's widow Katherine by driving her out of the house and across the moor, shouting as he did so, 'I have come to do the devil's work and my own.'

4. *Michaelmas*: St Michael's Day, 29 September.

5. *flagons and trenchers*: Wine-containers and wooden plates.

6. *he swung them to the line*: He drove the hounds towards the direction in which the girl had escaped.

7. *a sound of galloping*: The *Strand* version just has 'there came a galloping across the moor'.

8. *which is threatened in Holy Writ*: A reference to Exodus 20:5 in the Authorized Version, part of the Ten Commandments, 'I the Lord thy God am a jealous God, visiting the iniquity of the fathers upon the children unto the third and fourth generation of them that hate me'; Conan Doyle had written a short story called 'The Third Generation' (published 1894).

9. *the* Devon County Chronicle *of June 14th*: The newspaper did not really exist; the date, in the *Strand* version, was 'May 14th'.

10. *In these days of* nouveaux riches: The reporter does not seem to approve of new money; it is much better, apparently, for old money to keep the estate going – even if Sir Charles's fortune came from speculation in the gold mines of South Africa (where gold was first found in 1869), a relatively recent source of wealth.

11. *On the 4th of June*: The *Strand* version has 'On the 4th of May'.

12. *in cases of dyspnoea*: Cases of laboured breathing, due to weakness of the heart and lack of oxygen in the blood.

13. *a tenant for Baskerville Hall*: Meaning someone who was prepared to live in the Hall, rather than a paying tenant; W. W. Robson suggests that this phrase is a conscious echo by Conan Doyle of the title of Anne Brontë's novel *The Tenant of Wildfell Hall* (1848).

14. *the Pope*: The reigning pope was Leo XIII (1810–1903; as Pope, 1878–1903); in the later story 'Black Peter' (from *The Return of Sherlock Holmes*), the detective investigates the death of a cardinal at this same Pope's request.

15. *Lafter Hall*: A fictitious name, though there was and is a Laughter Hole Farm and a Lafter Tor on the moor – which is where Conan Doyle may have come across the name.

16. *the comparative anatomy of the Bushman and the Hottentot*: Another memory, perhaps, of Conan Doyle's South African experiences; these were the Victorian names for two types of native South African, names which were also embedded as racial stereotypes in British popular culture.

17. *my gig*: Not a rock concert (the modern usage), but a light one-horse two-wheeled carriage.

18. *Mr Holmes, they were the footprints of a gigantic hound!*: One of the greatest lines in all crime fiction, which like a lot of good lines does not bear too much scrutiny; it is not, in fact, possible to identify the breed of a large dog just by his footprints; Dr Mortimer assumed it *would* be a hound, therefore he read the prints as those of a hound. The footprints could have been those of a Great Dane, a St Bernard, a large Alsatian or even a big mongrel. In the 1951 Festival of Britain 'Sherlock Holmes' exhibition, there was a plaster cast 'prepared by Scotland Yard' of the footprint of a gigantic hound – and next to it the footprint of an ordinary hound, for comparison.

CHAPTER 3

The Problem

1. *wicket-gate*: In this case, a four-foot-high white wooden gate with a latch.

2. *defaced by the clogs of curious peasants*: It is unlikely that the locals would really have been wearing clogs; Holmes is expressing his characteristically condescending attitude towards country folk. In the Hammer Films version of 1959, Holmes at one point says to Sir Henry Baskerville (about the Stapletons), 'You musn't be late for your peasant friends . . . I hope you enjoy your rabbit pie.'

3. *a farrier*: A blacksmith.

4. *Waterloo Station*: Then, as now, an important London railway terminus connecting with Southampton – where Sir Henry Baskerville had just docked.

5. *trustee and executor of Sir Charles's will*: Person appointed by Sir Charles to execute the provisions of his last will and testament.

6. *yellow fever*: A tropical disease, in this case caught in Central America.

7. *depends upon his presence*: Conan Doyle did not personally approve of absentee landlords; for him, the role of landlord seems to have brought with it obligations of an almost feudal kind to 'the whole poor, bleak countryside'.

8. *like a parish vestry*: Like a meeting of members of a local parish.

9. *You put the matter more flippantly, Mr Holmes* . . .: It is noticeable that when the detective actually visits Dartmoor, his sarcastic tone disappears.

10. *Bradley's*: A fictitious tobacconist in Oxford Street; the shop supplies Dr Watson's cigarettes, a fact which later enables Holmes to identify one of them from the tobacconist's name printed on the stub; it also supplies Holmes with his strong, coarsely cut pipe tobacco. We do not learn where Holmes buys his cigarettes, though. One of the first things he asks Dr Watson, on learning that the doctor seeks someone to share rooms in *A Study in Scarlet*, is, 'You don't mind the smell of strong tobacco, do you?'

11. *I sent down to Stanford's for the Ordnance map* . . .: The *Strand* version and the first American edition have 'Stamford's'. Edward Stanford of 26 Cockspur Street, Charing Cross, was the sole agent for Ordnance Survey maps of England and Wales – very detailed maps prepared under the aegis of the military.

12. *the hamlet of Grimpen*: A fictitious village although there was and is a Grimspound on the moor – the Bronze Age circle which Conan Doyle and Fletcher Robinson visited at the beginning of June 1901. Some have suggested that the model for Grimpen was the village of Widecombe-in-the-Moor, made famous by the ballad 'Widecombe Fair' which was popularized in print (a cleaned-up version) by the Revd Sabine Baring-Gould.

13. *High Tor and Foulmire*: These two moorland farmhouses do not exist, though there is a Higher Tor and a Higher White Tor, and Foulmire may be a version of the real-life Fox Tor Mire – the 'mighty bog' which Conan Doyle visited with Fletcher Robinson at the beginning of June 1901. A 'tor' is a tower-like rounded hill on the moor, with a granite rock formation at its summit. Baring-Gould's *A Book of Dartmoor* observes that many tors 'have been weathered into forms resembling the heads of dogs peering over the natural battlements'.

14. *fourteen miles away the great convict prison of Princetown*: Conan Doyle and Fletcher Robinson stayed at Rowe's Duchy Hotel, Princetown, just down the road from Dartmoor prison, at the end of May/beginning of June 1901; by the late nineteenth century Dartmoor had become a maximum-security prison for inmates serving long sentences – originally, it had been built to house French prisoners during the Napoleonic Wars. If the prison was *fourteen* miles away from Baskerville Hall, though, it would not be on the moor at all! This could well be an uncorrected printer's error for *four* miles, or one of Conan Doyle's slips of the pen.

15. *This, then, is the stage upon which tragedy has been played*: Holmes maps out the scene for Act Two of the narrative, for which Chs. 1–3 have been the curtain-raiser.

16. *a concentrated atmosphere*: Like the room 'full of dense tobacco haze' in the Holmes's story 'The Man with the Twisted Lip' (from *The Adventures*); Dr Watson had been warned about the detective's habit.

17. *getting into a box to think*: Possibly a satirical reference to some of the fictional detectives, more like thinking machines than human beings, who had appeared in short story magazines as literary rivals of Sherlock Holmes.

CHAPTER 4
Sir Henry Baskerville

1. *the young baronet*: The young hereditary knight, who has inherited his title from his uncle, Sir Charles Baskerville.

2. *Northumberland Hotel*: It has been suggested, by William S. Baring-Gould among others, that this was at 10–11 Northumberland Street, off Northumberland Avenue (and opposite Old Scotland Yard) – part of which would later become the Sherlock Holmes pub, which still houses relics of the 1951 Festival of Britain 'Sherlock Holmes' exhibition including the footprint of the hound. But more likely candidates, all in Northumberland Avenue proper, include the three large hotels of the day: the Grand (400 rooms), the Metropole (600 rooms) and the Victoria (400 rooms). The Northumberland Arms, at 10–11 Northumberland Street, was little more than a pub.

3. *yesterday's* Times: Founded in the late eighteenth century as the *Daily Universal Register*, *The Times* – published in London – was known at that time as *the* English newspaper and the journal of official historical record.

4. *Capital article this on Free Trade*: Some commentators have suggested that a leading article on free trade was not likely to have appeared in *The Times* until the turn of the century, so this is an anachronism; but free trade as an economic principle (and as distinct from protectionism) had been high on the political agenda of mercantile nations since the Napoleonic Wars. *The Times* article is in favour of free trade, and against 'a protective tariff': this policy was fashionable in the late 1880s.

5. *you could tell the skull of a Negro from that of an Esquimaux?*: Two racial 'types' of the Victorian period; Esquimaux was the contemporary spelling of Eskimo (today, more properly, 'Inuit').

6. *The supra-orbital crest . . . the maxillary curve*: The ridge above the orbit of the eye . . . the curve of the upper jaw.

7. *leaded bourgeois type*: Bourgeois is a trade term for a size of type-face; 'leaded type' means that the lines of type were separated by metal strips and hence more straight and crisp than 'the slovenly print of an evening halfpenny paper'. *The Times* was set in small Bourgeois, 9 point, 2 point leaded, a type-face known as 'the modern face'.

8. *I confused the* Leeds Mercury *with the* Western Morning News: They actually had very different type-faces at the time of Holmes's youth; the *Leeds Mercury* was to become the *Yorkshire Post* (still published); the *Western Morning News* (also still published), based in Plymouth, would have been well known to Conan Doyle when he was starting out on his medical career in Southsea.

9. *someone cut out this message with a scissors*: In the regular 'Curiosities' slot of the *Strand* magazine for July 1898 (a slot which Conan Doyle enjoyed reading, for its puzzles), there was a story – with illustration – about a letter written by an inmate of H.M. Convict Prison Millbank to her aunt, where each character had been 'cut separately out of a Bible, and then the requisite words are made up with much patience and perseverance'. Conan Doyle may well have read this 'delightfully ingenious puzzle'. The scissors-and-paste message in *The Hound* is from a woman, too, as we discover. In the Holmes stories, the detective often refers to the 'agony column' of newspapers, is intrigued by their 'cipher messages' and sometimes places a message of his own to flush out suspects.

10. *We are coming now rather into the region of guesswork*: We certainly are, though Holmes prefers to see it as balancing probabilities and selecting 'the most likely' – imagination applied methodically.

11. *watermark*: The mark of the paper-maker, sometimes visible through quality papers when they are held up to the light. In the Granada Television version of *The Hound* (1988), with Jeremy Brett as Holmes, there *is* a watermark which leads the detective to observe 'you will find that paper in a hundred middle-grade hotels'.

12. *dime novel*: The American equivalent of the Victorian 'penny dreadful' or 'shilling shocker' – a cheap, sensational story, usually featuring detectives or cowboys and costing ten cents.

13. *I only bought the pair last night in the Strand*: A famous bootmaker of the time was G. H. Harris, 418 Strand, which was founded in 1865.

14. *from the languid dreamer to the man of action*: The two sides of Sherlock Holmes's personality; his mind rebels at stagnation, and when he is not intellectually challenged – or when the pieces of the puzzle fit together too easily – he retreats into moody lethargy; in later post-*Hound* stories, the languid *fin de siècle* side was to become less and less pronounced. Dr Watson's diagnosis is that the 'extreme exactness' is a reaction against the 'poetic and contemplative side'.

15. *There's our man, Watson!*: Sidney Paget's illustration of Holmes and Watson walking down Regent Street, in top hats and frock-coats, was published full page in the *Strand* (introducing the second instalment, September 1901) in reverse: Holmes and Watson are looking at the hansom cab from left to right, and Paget's name is back to front. This mistake was continued in the first English edition. In the *Strand*, the illustration may have been deliberately reversed for design reasons to make Holmes and Watson face the text of Ch. 3. The illustration was the correct way round in the first American edition.

16. *the district messenger offices*: Essential at a time when there were few telephones in private hands – messages would be left, or parcels deposited, for despatch by a small army of district messenger boys such as Cartwright; the offices (which were privately run) sometimes also offered access to telephones and telegrams, the Victorian equivalent of today's internet centres.

17. *the Bond Street picture-galleries*: The best-known art gallery in New Bond Street at the time was the Grosvenor Gallery; lampooned by Gilbert and Sullivan as the 'greenery, yallery Grosvenor Gallery', it had specialized since the late 1870s in modern British artists and, notoriously, Whistler – the avant-garde of its day, with picture titles such as 'A Study in . . .' rather than narrative or descriptive labels. There was, and is, also a cluster of galleries at the Royal Academy end of Bond Street. Reviewing the inaugural exhibition of the Grosvenor Gallery, Oscar Wilde wrote 'we see that this dull land of England with its short summer, its dreary rains and fogs . . . has yet produced very great masters of art . . .' Lord Henry Wotton, in *The Picture of Dorian Gray*, says, 'The Grosvenor is really the only place.'

CHAPTER 5
Three Broken Threads

1. *Three Broken Threads*: In the original *Strand* version, this third instalment was introduced with a full-page illustration by Sidney Paget of a wagonette – with Doctors Watson and Mortimer, and Sir Henry Baskerville, sitting inside it – travelling through the wilderness of Dartmoor: the caption read 'The driver pointed with his whip – "Baskerville Hall," said he'. Readers were immediately alerted to the change of scene which would happen in Ch. 6.

2. *the pictures of the modern Belgian masters*: Probably a reference to the Symbolist, visionary work of the 'Groupe des Vingt', which included such artists as Félicien Rops and James Ensor. Rops specialized in lithographs and etchings of fantastic and macabre subjects – often with erotic and occult elements – while Ensor specialized in paintings of carnival masks, grotesque figures and skeletons. Like the artist Odilon Redon in France (whose first successes were in Belgium), the 'xx' were proto-surrealists – just right for the atmosphere of

The Hound. Holmes may have had 'the crudest ideas' about art (as Dr Watson claimed), but he was certainly not put off by the cutting-edge work of his contemporaries.

3. *Newcastle*: Industrial city in the northeast of England, on the River Tyne, in the county of Northumberland; famous at that time for the shipping of coal – hence 'Mr Johnson the coal-owner'.

4. *Alton*: Leafy market town in Hampshire.

5. *Gloucester*: Cathedral city in the west of England, on the River Severn.

6. *more Western dialect*: In his agitation, Sir Henry starts talking like Conan Doyle's idea of a cowboy – 'seems they are playing me for a sucker', 'by thunder', etc. Later, Sir Henry will reminisce about 'when I was out West'. The popularity of Sherlock Holmes on the American market had been one reason why Conan Doyle decided to turn *The Hound* into a Holmes story.

7. *the five hundred cases of capital importance*: In the short story 'The Final Problem', the most recently published Holmes case before *The Hound*, the detective says to Watson, 'The air of London is the sweeter for my presence. In over a thousand cases I am not aware that I have ever used my powers upon the wrong side.' Clearly, Holmes – much given to melodramatic statements of this kind – considered that more than half of the cases in which he was involved were 'of capital importance'. And Dr Watson had only narrated a small fraction of them.

8. *Barrymore, Sir Charles's butler*: In the Hollywood film version of *The Hound* (1939), the butler's name was changed to Barryman – presumably to avoid confusion with the American theatrical dynasty of the Barrymores; John Barrymore had, in fact, played the great detective himself in *Sherlock Holmes* (1922) for Goldwyn Pictures.

9. *securities*: Share certificates.

10. *Westmorland*: A bleak and mountainous region in the north of England; the Revd Desmond evidently associates the 'saintly life' with geographical remoteness from the hustle and bustle of modern life.

11. *one of the most revered names in England*: Adrian Conan Doyle was to write a pastiche of this intriguing case, 'The Adventure of the Two Women', in *The Exploits of Sherlock Holmes*; but – as later becomes clear – Holmes is not telling the whole truth; the case succeeds in removing the detective from the story for the entire central section of *The Hound*.

12. *the 10.30 train from Paddington*: At that time the terminus of the Great Western Railway; the station was and is the starting-point for train journeys to the West Country; the huge complex – with platforms 700 feet long – was constructed in the early 1850s. Agatha Christie was to write a famous Miss Marple mystery called *The 4.50 from Paddington* (1957). In 1901, there was in fact a 10.30 train from Paddington to Plymouth, but it only ran on Sundays.

13. *to frame some scheme*: Once Holmes had worked out that the old black boot had been stolen to provide a scent for the hound – and that the new brown boot had been useless for the purpose – the supernatural explanation could be discarded, and the case was reduced to sifting through the suspects. One reason, perhaps, why Holmes had to disappear from the story.

14. *the Borough*: District of London just southeast of London Bridge, which includes Guy's Hospital; Clayton does not have to cross the river to pick up his cab from the yard near Waterloo Station.

15. *A touch, Watson – an undeniable touch!*: These metaphors from the world of fencing include references to Shakespeare's *Hamlet* (the final duel), V.ii, where Laertes says 'a touch, a touch I do confess' and Osric 'a hit, a very palpable hit'. Sherlock Holmes is not as a rule a fan of team sports in the stories, but is drawn to more solitary ones like fencing and fishing. In the BBC television film (2002), Holmes – stepping out of character – takes solitary sports further than usual by having a fight with the hapless cab driver and extracting information from him with brute force and a cane.

16. *two or three inches shorter than you*: The black beard may be false, but the man's stature will become a definite clue when the action shifts to Dartmoor.

17. *dressed like a toff*: Dressed like an upper-class sort of person.

18. *a foeman who is worthy of our steel*: A reference to Walter Scott's poem *The Lady of the Lake* (1810) which includes the couplet, 'And the stern joy which warriors feel/In foemen worthy of their steel!'; also perhaps to Gilbert and Sullivan's parody of the line in Act II of *The Pirates of Penzance* (1880), where the Sergeant of Police says, 'When the foeman bares his steel/Tarantara, Tarantara!/We uncomfortable feel.'

19. *I've been checkmated in London*: Conan Doyle sometimes liked to use chess imagery in the Sherlock Holmes stories – especially references to 'check' or 'a provoking check' – but there is no evidence that the detective actually played the game. Our first glimpse of Sherlock Holmes in Baker Street, though, in the Hammer Films version of *The Hound* (1959), is of him playing chess.

CHAPTER 6

Baskerville Hall

1. *to get rid of this Barrymore couple*: An unusually callous suggestion by Dr Watson; there is no sustainable evidence to link them with the case, and certainly no grounds on which to sack them; their family has been looking after the Hall for four generations – since the beginning of the nineteenth century.

2. *there is his wife, of whom we know nothing*: And we never, in fact, discover anything more about Mrs Mortimer – except that her existence provides an excuse for Dr Mortimer to travel the four miles to Grimpen rather than stay all the time with the others at Baskerville Hall; in the 1939 Hollywood version of *The Hound*, this gap is filled by turning Mrs Mortimer into a spiritualist medium who is used to communicate with the deceased Sir Charles Baskerville. 'My wife,' says Dr Mortimer at dinner with the Stapletons, 'has agreed to a seance.' Before she can make contact with the other side, the distant howl of a hound puts a stop to the proceedings. This was probably a reference to Conan Doyle's own much-publicized interest, a little later in his life, in spiritualism. The Hollywood idea of Mrs Mortimer as a medium was revived in the 2002 BBC film, only instead of just howling, the hound actually puts in a personal appearance during the seance – his giant paw pressing against the window. In the novel, we also hear nothing more about the inhabitants of the 'two moorland farmhouses, High Tor and Foulmire', mentioned by Holmes in Ch. 3.

3. *Museum of the College of Surgeons*: Located on the south side of Lincoln's Inn Fields, and built in 1835, the Museum was apparently 'intended to illustrate . . . the whole subject of life, by preparations of the bodies in which its phenomena are represented' (cited by William S. Baring-Gould, in his *Annotated Sherlock Holmes*, vol. 2, p. 36); among its sometimes macabre specimens, it included the skeleton of an outsized elephant called Chunee – a strange form of 'pure amusement' for Dr Mortimer.

4. *the rounded head of the Celt . . . half Gaelic, half Ivernian*: Half-Scottish, half-Irish – like Conan Doyle's own family, in fact.

5. *like some fantastic landscape in a dream*: From the comprehensible world of the big city – Sherlock Holmes prides himself on his 'exact knowledge of London' and its streets – we are entering the impressionistic, sometimes Gothic, sometimes surreal, landscape of the moor. In the 1939 film version, Dr Mortimer enhances the surrealism by pointing to a studio mock-up of Stonehenge (actually on Salisbury Plain) shortly after this, and saying, 'You see those rocks over there – actually they're stone houses built by neolithic man.'

6. *how true a descendant he was*: The theme of ancestral influences, and of age-old traditions challenged by upstarts and throwbacks, runs right through *The Hound* like a fine tweed. Sir Henry may be from the new world, full of Yankee know-how, but he is still 'of that long line of high-blooded, fiery, and masterful men' which goes back to the 1400s. This theme, and the attraction Sir Henry feels for his ancestral duties, has been absent from all the major film adaptations of *The Hound*.

7. *a small wayside station*: Not the same station as the one into which the London express later comes roaring; if Conan Doyle had a real country railway station in mind, the candidates include Ashburton, Bovey Tracey, Buckfastleigh, and Brent or Ivy Bridge to the south.

8. *a wagonette with a pair of cobs*: A four-wheeled open carriage, with benches attached to the insides; the cobs were sturdy, short-legged horses used for heavy work – though Sidney Paget illustrated them for the *Strand* as more elegant animals.

9. *a hard-faced, gnarled little fellow*: If this *was* a description of Fletcher Robinson's coachman Harry Baskerville, he can't have been amused by it.

10. *fleshy hart's-tongue ferns*: Ferns with undivided leaves, thought to resemble the tongues of deer in their soothing effects; in folklore, they were sometimes called 'pillows for the Son of Man' and were used as a cure for burns; but they do *not*, in fact, have fleshy leaves.

11. *At every turning Baskerville gave an exclamation of delight*: Parts of this could well be a first-hand description of Conan Doyle's trip around the moor with Fletcher Robinson on 1 June 1901.

12. *There's a convict escaped from Princetown, sir*: Baring-Gould's *A Book of Dartmoor* (1900) has several anecdotes about escaped convicts; one of them 'was last seen making a bee-line for Fox Tor Mire', another paid a visit to his wife in a remote moorland cottage only to be told 'not likely; you don't come in here'; Conan Doyle would also, no doubt, have heard such stories from the prison governor and party who chatted with him about 'general subjects' in the smoking room of Rowe's Duchy Hotel (see Introduction). In the 1973 television film, *three* prisoners escape: following a gun-battle on the moor, one is shot, one caught, and the third gets away.

13. *Selden, the Notting Hill murderer*: It has been suggested that Selden was based by Conan Doyle on a particularly nasty real-life prison warder; Notting Hill – a region of west London just north of Kensington Gardens and west of Paddington – was soon to be immortalized in G.K. Chesterton's first novel, *The Napoleon of Notting Hill* (1904), in which war is declared in the name of Notting Hill.

14. *cairns*: Stone mounds built as memorials to the dead in ancient times.

15. *the darkling sky*: The darkening sky.

16. *We had left the fertile country*: The greenery of the moor (moss, bracken, bramble, scrub oak, fir, heath, woodlands) makes way for a waste-land of stunted trees and giant boulders.

17. *Baskerville Hall*: If Conan Doyle *was* describing a real house on the moor – the twin ancient towers, the Yew Valley, the porch, the high mullioned windows, the minstrels' gallery overlooking the huge panelled dining-room, are more likely to be stock features of remote and spooky mansions in literature and melodrama – the candidates include the Jacobean stone mansion house at Lew-trenchard (which had a fine collection of portraits of a 'line of ancestors in every variety of dress' including a Kneller and a Reynolds), the mullioned home of the Revd Sabine Baring-Gould; Heatree House near Manaton, with its long drive and imposing porch, which Harry Baskerville claimed was once the property of the Dartmoor Baskervilles and which he further claimed to have shown Conan Doyle on an outing from Ipplepen; and Brook Manor in the parish of Buckfastleigh, home of the wicked seventeenth-century squire and staunch Royalist Richard Cabell (or Capel) who had a 'wisht hound' legend associated with him. When Sir Henry says 'it's just as I imagined it', though, he is suggesting that the house was archetypal. In the two-part BBC television version of *The Hound* (1968), the stained-glass windows of Baskerville Hall include the motto '*Cave Canem Nocte*' ('Beware of the dog in the night-time') – a witty addition.

18. *the boars' heads of the Baskervilles*: The main branch of the real-life Baskerville family, which was descended from an ancient Norman line and was based near Clyro on the borders of England and Wales, had a family crest which included a wolf's head (or a wolfhound's head) with a broken spear pointing upwards through its mouth. The boar's head was more usually associated with Shakespeare's *Richard III* and the tavern in Eastcheap where Shakespeare's Falstaff, Doll Tearsheet and friends liked to drink.

19. *a thousand-candle-power Swan and Edison*: Sir Joseph Swan was the English inventor of an incandescent lamp which was named after him; Thomas Alva Edison also invented an incandescent lamp in 1879. Their two companies were linked in England, as 'Swan and Edison'. At this stage in the story, the gung-ho Sir Henry reckons that the latest Anglo-American technology will be enough to lighten the darkness surrounding Baskerville Hall.

20. *Welcome, Sir Henry!*: By the time Sidney Paget had prepared his illustration of this moment for the *Strand*, he had evidently seen Conan Doyle's description of Barrymore which appeared on the next page – unlike his illustration of Barrymore discovering Sir Charles's body in Ch. 2; but he had evidently yet to see Conan Doyle's description of Mrs Barrymore, which appears at the beginning of Ch. 7. In the 1973 American television film of *The Hound*, Mrs Barrymore offers the guests some refreshment: 'Cream and sugar, sir?'

CHAPTER 7
The Stapletons of Merripit House

1. *the first to dog the new heir*: The novelist John Fowles has written that 'far more . . . could have been made of the hound symbolism [in the book] – for Holmes also is houndlike in his cunning, his pertinacity, his secretive patience, his ability to dog, his ferocious concentration once the scent is warm. Baker Street is his kennel . . .' (*Afterword to The Hound of the Baskervilles*, 1974, p. 195). Actually, later in the story (Chs. 10–12), there is a series of references to the stranger who 'dogged us in London' and to the other stranger on the tor who 'is still dogging us'.

2. *He was a small . . . prim-faced man*: After the heavy and foreboding symbolism of the moor, and the hound, Stapleton immediately seems a pale, lightweight inhabitant.

3. *our mutual friend*: Possibly an arch reference to Charles Dickens's novel, and Stapleton's way of implying that he is much more sophisticated than the 'credulous . . . peasants'.

4. *Merripit House*: There was in fact a farmhouse on the moor near Postbridge called Higher Merripit House, a hill called Merripit and a hamlet called Merrivale just northwest of Princetown.

5. *The records of your detective have reached us here*: A reference to the national fame of Sherlock Holmes – almost an in-joke – spread by the 'records' written by Dr Watson.

6. *the great Grimpen Mire*: A 'mire' is an expanse of swampy ground, in this case one where ponies and riders can be sucked beneath the surface; the bright green spots are the soggiest. The model for this – though it is considerably less dramatic in real life – was 'the mighty bog' at Fox Tor Mire with its nearby shallow tin mine of Whiteworks which Conan Doyle visited with Fletcher Robinson. There is also a Grimspound Bog, northwest of Widecombe-in-the-Moor, a photograph of which was included in Baring-Gould's *A Book of Dartmoor*: the book also contained descriptions of horses falling into the 'vivid green pillow of moss' covering the quaking bog; because the horses instinctively struggled, they sank deeper.

7. *the cry of the last of the bitterns*: The bittern is a long-legged marsh and reed bird (rather than a moor bird); it is rarely seen but its 'boom', or mating-call which sounds like the lowing of cattle, can be heard in the spring (rather than the autumn); in Conan Doyle's time, the bird was nearly extinct. The boom of the bittern provides a suitably eerie sound for the author's purposes, but from the naturalist's point of view is very far-fetched indeed: Dr Watson later refers to the bittern as 'a strange bird'. In the Granada Television version of *The Hound* (1988), Stapleton describes the 'boom' as 'something between a foghorn and a soul in torment'. Baring-Gould's *A Book of Dartmoor* also refers to strange sounds heard on the moor – 'howls as of a spirit in torment' – but these are 'doubtless caused by a swirl of wind' in old mine shafts filled with water.

8. *Neolithic man – no date*: The neolithic was the last period of the Stone Age, *c.* 6000–3000 BC; this 'town' is based on Conan Doyle's visit to the four-acre circular stone enclosure of Grimspound which he described on 2 June 1901 as 'very sad and wild, dotted with dwellings of prehistoric man, strange monoliths and huts and graves'. Baring-Gould's *A Book of Dartmoor* included a lot of historical detail about Grimspound – two chapters including detailed diagrams and plans – which had been excavated by archaeologists in the 1890s. The 'highly educated' Stapleton's guided tour of the moor may be a reminiscence of Fletcher Robinson's style: Robinson recalled that Conan Doyle 'listened eagerly to my stories of . . . the devils that lurk in the hollows – legends upon which I had been reared, for my home lay on the borders of the moor'; Robinson had been away – to Cambridge, the Inns of Court and Fleet Street – but had retained his boyish enthusiasm. It is unlikely, though, that he would have made as many mistakes as Stapleton.

9. *Cyclopides*: Butterfly now known as the 'Chequered Skipper', which resembles a moth; Stapleton says 'he is very rare and seldom found in the late autumn', which is something of an understatement on both counts; apparently, a sighting of this butterfly on Dartmoor would have been the first and only recorded sighting in this location. The eco-system of the moor, as presented by Conan Doyle, is rich and strange indeed – more like *The Lost World*, a never-never land kept in suspended animation, than the real thing. Or are these perhaps esoteric clues, hinting at Stapleton's lack of credibility?

10. *this was the Miss Stapleton*: An incongruity well captured in the Hammer Films version (1959), the first Holmes feature in colour, where the glamorous and sultry 'Cecile' – dressed garishly – is discovered posing on a Dartmoor rock, much to Dr Watson's excitement.

11. *mare's-tails*: Plant that grows in marshlands, but not apparently on Dartmoor; perhaps Miss Stapleton was thinking of the marsh horsetail which does grow there.

12. *We are very rich in orchids on the moor, though, of course, you are rather late . . .*: In fact, very few wild orchids grow on Dartmoor, and when they do – such as the Marsh Spotted Orchid – they never flourish in mid-October. It has been suggested that the 'tropical and exotic' Miss Stapleton may perhaps have been thinking about her native Costa Rica rather than the moor. When she later says 'it cannot much matter . . . whether it is early or late for the orchids', she is perhaps echoing Conan Doyle's own sentiments.

13. *Only a humble commoner*: So, to be precise, was Sir Henry Baskerville who was a knight rather than a lord.

14. *my collection of* Lepidoptera: My collection of dead butterflies and moths.

15. *Life has become like that great Grimpen Mire . . . with no guide to point the track*: Again, Dr Watson treats Dartmoor as a symbolic landscape – a sense picked up by T. S. Eliot in part II of *East Coker* (1944) when he wrote of 'a grimpen, where there is no secure foothold, And menaced by monsters . . .'

CHAPTER 8
First Report of Dr Watson

1. *First Report of Dr Watson*: Watson changes role from narrator to correspondent; the convention of presenting horror stories in the form of collections of documents such as letters, diaries and reports – *Frankenstein*, *Dr Jekyll and Mr Hyde*, most recently *Dracula* – was well established as a way of dividing the authorial voice into different registers. The claim that 'one page is missing' was presumably intended to add authenticity; in fact, to judge by the letters as printed, no page seems to be missing.

2. *monoliths*: Large stone pillars.

3. *whether the sun moved round the earth . . .*: In the first Holmes story, *A Study in Scarlet* (Ch. 2), Dr Watson expresses astonishment that 'any civilized human being should not be aware that the earth travelled round the sun', to which the detective replies, 'If we went round the moon it would not make a pennyworth of difference to me or my work.'

4. *the spot where the legend of the wicked Hugo is supposed to have had its origin*: In Sidney Paget's illustration to the first instalment in the *Strand* (to go with the Baskerville manuscript), the two great stones have blunt ends rather than sharpened ones; the Hammer Films version (1959) added a ruined abbey and sacrificial slab used in 'some diabolical ceremony', for good measure.

5. *He told us of similar cases where families had suffered from some evil influence*: The origin of *The Hound* in folklore could have come from various sources – among them, families on Dartmoor, in Norfolk and in the Welsh border country (see Introduction).

6. *Mr Frankland*: For the possible origins of Frankland's name, see Introduction; in the 1939 Hollywood version, he became a caricature Scotsman; in the 1959 Hammer version an eccentric bishop 'of the outer isles' who collects rare spiders and rides a tricycle. The 1988 Granada Television version included Mr Frankland but added an elderly, shy vicar who doesn't 'think local hysteria is an adequate explanation [of the hound], myself'. In the 1973 American television film, Frankland at one point warns Dr Watson, 'Mind you stay clear of the creek.'

7. *the villagers of Fernworthy*: There was a village of Fernworthy, midway between Postbridge and Moretonhampstead, but it no longer exists.

8. *the barrow*: The ancient burial mound; there is no Long Down on the moor.

9. *on the escaped convict*: The *Strand* version has 'in the escaped convict'.

CHAPTER 9
The Light upon the Moor

1. *quite a budget*: A week's events gathered into a single instalment; some daily newspapers of the day printed a weekly 'Budget'.

2. *decorators and furnishers up from Plymouth*: Sir Henry, like his uncle, wants to modernize the Hall and bring it into the contemporary world; unlike Dr Mortimer, he is far from an antiquarian; Plymouth, to the southwest, was and is the nearest big city.

3. *that prairie . . . by thunder*: Sir Henry in his excitement again becomes a cowboy.

4. *the tangled skein*: Conan Doyle's original title for *A Study in Scarlet*, early in 1886, was *A Tangled Skein*.

5. *was of the same blood*: Again the popular view of the influence of heredity on criminal behaviour.

6. *he was always the little curly-headed boy*: In the Granada Television version of *The Hound* (1988), Selden is the victim in prison of a lobotomy operation – he has a livid scar across the top of his head to prove it, and Mrs Barrymore explains 'they done surgery on him' – so he literally behaves like a child; this plot-twist makes Mrs Barrymore's behaviour less risky than in the novel, and the subsequent decision of Watson and Sir Henry to let him escape to South America less culpable. Later in the novel, Selden will be described as 'the little wilful boy of her [Mrs Barrymore's] own girlhood'.

7. *Cleft Tor*: There is no Cleft Tor on Dartmoor, but there is a Cleft Rock near Holne Chase – a photograph of which was in Baring-Gould's *A Book of Dartmoor*.

8. *hunting-crop*: A stiff, pliable hunting whip.

9. *The folk on the countryside*: In the *Strand* version 'country-side'; modern printings sometimes have 'of' rather than 'on'.

10. *it was one thing to laugh about it in London*: Holmes's sarcastic response to the legend in Chs. 2 and 3 – 'To a collector of fairy-tales'; 'And you, a trained man of science, believe it to be supernatural?'; '. . . to take on the Father of Evil himself would, perhaps, be too ambitious a task' – is here confronted with the grim reality of the moor. Even in cosy Baker Street Dr Mortimer had observed of Holmes's attitude, 'You put the matter more flippantly, Mr Holmes, than you would probably do if you were brought into personal contact with these things.'

11. *an evil yellow face, a terrible animal face . . . old savages . . . small, cunning eyes . . . short, squat*: Adjectives and physical characteristics associated at the time with criminal 'types', and 'primitive' peoples; some of Sherlock Holmes's observations, reading people's appearance as if in a book, depended on one-to-one associations of this kind. In the Holmes story 'The Yellow Face' (from *The Memoirs*), the face in question – 'of a livid dead yellow, and with something set and rigid about it' – stares out of the window of a deserted cottage on a country lane in Norbury. It turns out to be a mask, hiding the face of a little black girl.

12. *come down to us*: In American editions of *The Hound*, an extra sentence reads: 'In any case you will hear from me again in the course of the next few days.'

CHAPTER 10
Extract from the Diary of Dr Watson

1. *Extract from the Diary . . .*: The only time in the Sherlock Holmes stories when Conan Doyle opted for the immediacy of the first-person 'diary' format. In the *Strand* version, Sidney Paget's full-page illustration, facing the text, showed Watson on one knee inside a neolithic hut, and half a man's shadow in the doorway: the giveaway caption 'The Shadow of Sherlock Holmes' revealed to the reader the mystery of the man upon the tor two chapters too early. The illustration also showed Holmes in a soft hat with a brim rather than the 'cloth cap' of the text.

2. *there are the repeated reports*: The *Strand* version has 'there is the repeated reports . . .'

3. *a mere fiend-dog*: The manuscript of this page, from the words 'may fall in' to 'I must now . . .', now in the Rare Books and Manuscripts Division of New York Public Library, has 'a mere spectral hound'; it is the only substantive correction on the page, presumably made to avoid repetition of 'spectral hound'.

4. *And he will never trouble*: The *Strand* version has 'But he will never trouble . . .' which suggests a missing sentence.

5. *Coombe Tracey*: A fictitious village, perhaps an amalgam of the real Combe, near Holne, and Bovey Tracey.

6. *my report of the morning's conversation for Holmes*: Maybe *this* was meant to be the missing page referred to by Dr Watson at the beginning of Ch. 8.

7. *I found the Black Tor*: There are, in fact, four Black Tors on Dartmoor; the one nearest to Princetown was illustrated in Baring-Gould's *A Book of Dartmoor*.

8. *dog-cart*: A small one-horse carriage.

9. *écarté*: French card game played by two people.

10. *he had some lay of his own*: Some personal occupation.

CHAPTER 11
The Man on the Tor

1. *The Man on the Tor*: This is the only complete manuscript chapter of *The Hound* to have survived (in the Berg Collection at New York Public Library, 16pp.); the original manuscript of the novel was dispersed by S. S. McClure around America in 1902 and distributed as individual pages in frames for shop-window display in bookstores. Fifteen single pages have surfaced so far, of which five are in universities or libraries and the remainder in private hands. They do not contain many variations from the final text.

2. *Coombe Tracey*: The manuscript originally had 'Newton Abbot' throughout; Conan Doyle then crossed the name out – perhaps because it was a real place – and substituted 'Coombe Tracey'.

3. *a Remington typewriter*: The first mass-market typewriter, manufactured since the mid-1870s in the state of New York. In 'A Case of Identity' (from *The Adventures of Sherlock Holmes*), Miss Mary Sutherland – a plumber's daughter – supplements her income by 'the machine': this earns her 'twopence a sheet, and I can often do from fifteen to twenty sheets in a day'. Like Mina Harker in Bram Stoker's *Dracula* (1897), she is one of the first generation of women for whom typewriting was both a career option and a useful social skill.

4. *Her face fell*: Clearly Mrs Lyons does not receive many visitors, and expects her usual guest, Mr Stapleton.

5. *the sulphur rose*: A double yellow rose with a pinkish centre.

6. *a passage of your letter*: The manuscript originally had 'a postscript of your letter'.

7. *you wrote it*: The manuscript originally had 'you read it', a slip of the pen.

8. *a husband whom I abhor*: In the 1983 film version of *The Hound of the Baskervilles*, with Ian Richardson as Sherlock Holmes, the larger-than-life character of Geoffrey Lyons (Brian Blessed) – a short-fused, disappointed and alcoholic painter, whose vision is greater than his talent – plays a key part in the story: he is bearded (therefore a suspect), he threateningly bends a poker in half ('you can look forward to *this*') – only to watch Holmes coolly bend it back again – and he is falsely imprisoned for strangling his wife Laura. Only with the solution to the mystery is he released. In the novel, he never appears.

9. *if certain expenses could be met*: The manuscript originally had 'if a certain sum of money could be found for his expenses my husband was willing to leave the country'.

10. *had I not seen his death in the paper next morning*: But Sir Charles's body was not discovered until midnight . . .

11. *a trap*: A small, two-wheeled, horse-drawn carriage.

12. *that other clue which was to be sought for among the stone huts upon the moor*: On the manuscript, Conan Doyle stopped writing at this point – sixteen lines down the page – and there is a fresh page with a different version of the questions Watson asks himself between the words 'disheartened' and 'For the moment'. This version of the intervening paragraph (which was to follow the words 'I came away baffled and disheartened') was subsequently, or had already been, deleted: '. . . disheartened. Either she was an accomplished actor and a deep conspirator, or Barrymore had misread the letter, or the letter was a forgery – unless indeed there could by some extraordinary coincidence be a second lady writing from Newton Abbot whose initials were L.L. For the time my clue had come to nothing and I could only turn back to that other one which lay among the stone huts upon the moor.' Conan Doyle crossed out the passage 'Either . . . LL', then continued with the chapter. The passage suggests that the discussion about the letter to Sir Charles between Dr Watson and Laura Lyons was at one stage to be very different: Mrs Lyons had originally denied all knowledge of it.

13. *red-faced*: The manuscript originally had 'choleric'.

14. *they can swarm where they like with their papers and their bottles*: Mr Frankland's attitude to trippers on the moor is similar to the Revd Sabine Baring-Gould's in *A Book of Dartmoor*.

15. *Sir John Morland*: The manuscript originally had 'the Mayor of Plymouth', which Conan Doyle crossed out – again presumably because the reference was too specific.

16. *The county constabulary is in a scandalous state*: One of the mysteries surrounding *The Hound* is why the local constabulary is never once consulted about the case, and why an Inspector from Scotland Yard has to stray so far from his usual patch. Holmes and Lestrade behave as if Dartmoor is so remote that it is beyond the reach of any official police jurisdiction. And Mr Frankland is suing the government (Frankland *v.* Regina) for the lack of adequate police protection.

17. *Belliver and Vixen Tor*: Both real tors on the moor – though Conan Doyle changed the spelling of 'Bellever Tor', which could just be seen from a hill behind Rowe's Duchy Hotel; a photograph of Vixen Tor was included in Baring-Gould's *A Book of Dartmoor*.

18. *a circle of the old stone huts, and . . . there was one which retained sufficient roof*: Probably another reference to Grimspound; if so, although the enclosure had recently been excavated and restored (including a four-foot-high 'show house' protected by a railing in the middle of the site), none of the huts in fact had 'sufficient roof' to act as a screen against the weather; even the 'show house' had only the bare outline of a shell.

19. *to the chequered light*: The manuscript originally had 'the dim light'.

20. *a pannikin*: A small cup.

21. *a fine net drawn round us*: Again, like Stapleton approaching a hapless butterfly.

22. *Spartan habits*: Frugal, simple habits.

23. *and yet as I looked at them . . . which every instant was bringing nearer*: The manuscript originally had 'and yet here was I waiting for some crisis, waiting with my nerves in a quiver, knowing that . . .', which is much less strong than the final draft.

24. *It is a lovely evening, my dear Watson*: All the well-known film versions of *The Hound* have indicated Holmes's presence on the moor throughout much of the period Dr Watson thinks he is on his own – revealing that the detective's blackmailing case was pure invention; in the 1939 Hollywood version and the 1983 Douglas Hickox version, Holmes disguises himself as a pedlar or fortune-teller and puts on a mummerset accent; in the 1988 Granada version, there is a recurring shot of Holmes's black sleeve and glove and a sequence of him returning by train to Baker Street and the Royal Observatory in Greenwich; in the 1973 American television movie, with Stewart Granger as Holmes, the detective accompanies Watson to the moor from the word go; and in the 1959 Hammer version, he appears as himself much earlier in the story – before the signal to Selden on the moor. It is as if the screenwriters cannot trust Watson to sustain the narrative by himself, or rather without the star to guide him. The absence of Holmes works much better on the page, as does Dr Watson's mounting sense of panic that the detective has not arrived yet.

CHAPTER 12
Death on the Moor

1. *cloth cap*: Holmes's headgear, when in the countryside, is always thought in the public imagination to be a tweed deerstalker; actually, the deerstalker is never once explicitly mentioned by Conan Doyle. In 'The Boscombe Valley Mystery' (from *The Adventures*) when Holmes and Watson travel to 'the West of England', the detective wears a 'close-fitting cloth cap'; in 'Silver Blaze' (from *The Memoirs*), when they both travel to Dartmoor, he wears 'his ear-flapped travelling cap'. To go with both descriptions, Sidney Paget supplied very similar illustrations for the *Strand* of Holmes sitting opposite Watson in a first-class railway carriage, a smoker, wearing a deerstalker and tweed cape. But to go with the 'cloth cap' mentioned in *The Hound*, Paget depicted a soft hat with a brim, and on one occasion in Ch. 13 – 'The lady sprang from her chair' – a flat cloth cap. According to Paget's daughter Winifred, the artist himself liked wearing a deerstalker in the country – not to stalk deer but as an eccentric leisure garment – which 'inspired him to depict Holmes wearing it' and to use the idea for *Strand* stories by other writers. Like the pipe with the curved stem, this hat has since become part of Holmes's 'corporate image' and is an example of the media, and the public, projecting on to the detective a life beyond the text. He would *never* have worn that hat in town. Weaker film versions of *The Hound*, such as the 1973 television film with Stewart Granger, show him doing just that.

2. *Then you use me, and yet do not trust me!*: The subtlety of the relationship between Holmes and Watson – Watson takes offence, Holmes reassures him, the 'warmth of Holmes's praise drove my anger from my mind', Holmes says 'That's better' – is brilliantly encapsulated here.

3. *ready to throw in all my weight at a critical moment*: A comment on the construction of the novel as well.

4. make *love*: Not in the sense of having sex, of course, but in the Victorian sense of courting or wooing.

5. *refined, cold-blooded, deliberate murder*: Holmes's 'flippant' tone in Baker Street has gone completely, to make way for melodramatic statements such as this.

6. *Fool that I was to hold my hand*: This is the first occasion – of two – when Holmes has to admit he has risked his client's life 'in order to have my case well rounded and complete'.

7. *that peculiar ruddy tweed suit*: When Conan Doyle (see Introduction) made his late change to the beginning of Ch. 4 – 'I should like to convey that Sir Henry Baskerville wore a "ruddy-tinted tweed suit"' – he was presumably making the clothing Sir Henry wore in Baker Street consistent with this.

8. *the beetling forehead*: The overhanging or projecting forehead; in *Barnaby Rudge*, Ch. xxxvi, Charles Dickens wrote, 'His beetling brow almost obscured his eyes' – which is perhaps where Conan Doyle encountered the image.

9. *this man had at least deserved death*: But Selden was sentenced to life imprisonment in Princetown, and Dr Watson had earlier agreed to turn a blind eye to his escape abroad.

10. *the poor fellow's death*: In *The Sign of the Four*, Ch. 7, the 'ugly, long-haired, lop-eared' dog Toby follows the scent of a handkerchief dipped in creosote halfway across south London – only to reach a barrel of creosote in Nine Elms; he, too, has followed the correct scent but with the wrong result; on this occasion, Holmes and Watson roar with laughter about the dog's mistake. In *The Hound*, it is 'a tragedy'.

11. *by all that's wonderful*: A reference to the discovery of Lady Teazle by Charles Surface during the famous screen scene of Sheridan's *The School for Scandal* (1777) – 'Lady Teazle, by all that's wonderful!'

12. *we have never had a foeman more worthy of our steel*: Compare the end of Ch. 5 and also n. 18, Ch. 5; *The Hound* was intended by Conan Doyle to predate the short story 'The Final Problem', in which Holmes confronts Professor Moriarty and both fall to their deaths into the Reichenbach Falls.

13. *Sufficient for tomorrow is the evil thereof*: A stylish misquotation of the New Testament (Matthew 6:34), 'Sufficient unto the day is the evil thereof.' At this point in the 2002 BBC film, Sir Henry throws an elaborate Christmas Eve party at the Hall, which includes a folkloric pageant in rhyme involving Father Christmas, a hobby-horse and a giant black dog. Holmes uses the party as cover, while he searches Stapleton's house for evidence.

CHAPTER 13
Fixing the Nets

1. *Fixing the Nets*: This, the eighth instalment in the *Strand* magazine, was introduced with a full-page Sidney Paget illustration – the most famous of all *Hound* images – of the glowing, spectral dog running past Holmes and Watson on the moor at night; again, this was introducing visual information too early for readers, in the interests of drama, since the creature did not appear until the end of Ch. 14.

2. *a horse or a steer*: Sir Henry becomes a cowboy again; if he had known of the Wild West paintings of Frederic Remington, he might have encountered pictures *of* horses and steers.

3. *a Kneller*: Sir Godfrey Kneller (1646 or 1649–1723), who succeeded Sir Peter Lely as Principal Painter at the Royal Court, and who was the first artist in England to be made a baronet. In his heyday, the 1680s, he produced literally hundreds of portraits – some of which are in London's National Portrait Gallery.

4. *a Reynolds*: Sir Joshua Reynolds (1723–92), very prolific portrait painter of the Georgian era, first President of the Royal Academy, and in the words of Peter and Linda Murray in *The Penguin Dictionary of Art and Artists*, 'historically the most important figure in British painting'; his subjects included just about every man or woman in English 'high society' of the second half of the eighteenth century. Some nineteenth-century critics reacted against his style – flattering likenesses with classical references – and dubbed him 'Sir Sloshua'. Most major museums in Britain and America have at least one Reynolds. He was born and raised in Plympton, just south of Dartmoor.

5. *Rodney in the West Indies*: Admiral George Rodney (1719–92), first Baron Rodney, who defeated the French fleet in the West Indies in 1782.

6. *under Pitt*: During the administration of the younger William Pitt

(1759–1806), who was Prime Minister from 1783 to 1801 – a record number of re-elections – and again in 1804–6.

7. *this Cavalier*. This supporter of the Royalist cause during the English Civil War; since Conan Doyle spelt the word with a capital C and since the Baskervilles evidently liked to commission the best-known portraitists of their day, the most likely artist is Frans Hals (1581/5–1666, born in Antwerp of Flemish parents), who painted *The Laughing Cavalier* (1624), now in London's Wallace Collection – in England, one of the best-known paintings of the seventeenth century. In the 1640s, Hals specialized in military portraits.

8. *it is an interesting instance of a throwback*: Strange that Dr Mortimer, an authority on skulls, faces and heredity, should never have noticed the resemblance. In Sabine Baring-Gould's *Old Country Life* (1890), in the chapter on 'Family Portraits', the idea that facial 'throwbacks' can be detected through a collection of family paintings is examined in some detail. In particular, Baring-Gould writes of the portrait of a haughty-looking dandy in 'long flowing curls', dated *c*. 1672 and found in an old manor house, which so strongly resembles the current descendant that 'he might have been the same man' – if the Restoration curls, ribbons and velvet jacket were covered up. The facial characteristics had apparently lain dormant for six or seven generations. And yet the current descendant came from the *brother's* line. 'Consider what misery,' concludes Baring-Gould, 'a strain of tainted blood brings into a family – a strain of blood that carries vicious propensities with it . . .' Whether or not Conan Doyle had read this chapter, he was certainly drawn to its central thesis: the real villains of *The Hound* – the 'throwback' Stapleton and the 'savage hound' – both represent biology run wild, at a time when classification of 'the normal' had become intellectually fashionable. In the 1959 Hammer Films version of *The Hound*, the giveaway is not, for some reason, Sir Hugo's face but the webbed fingers of his right hand.

9. *I have sent a report from Grimpen to Princetown*: Holmes reports Selden's death to the prison, rather than to the local Devonshire police; and yet Dr Watson's first reaction was to suggest 'we . . . communicate with the police'.

10. *let them know that you intend to walk home*: Holmes is placing his client in very considerable danger, by using him as bait.

11. *Coming down with unsigned warrant . . . LESTRADE*: The police inspector from London is summoned by Holmes because 'we may need his assistance', but what – again – of the local force; and why has the inspector been asked to bring an unsigned warrant? If it is for the arrest of Stapleton, then why is it unsigned? And why did Holmes require a warrant from London at all? If Lestrade is indeed 'the best of the professionals', he would surely know these things.

12. *York*: Cathedral city in North Yorkshire, the 'north country' of England mentioned by Stapleton.

13. *legal expenses connected with your divorce?*: Not money to persuade Mr Lyons to leave the country, as Conan Doyle originally intended, but money for legal expenses.

14. *we stood waiting for the arrival of the express*: Conan Doyle probably had Newton Abbot Station in mind. In most film versions of *The Hound*, Lestrade does not make an appearance. An exception is the 1983 version, with Ian Richardson as Holmes, where the inspector (Ronald Lacey) is already on the moor when Dr Watson arrives: he is on a 'special assignment' to catch Selden. Watson cannot resist asking him, 'Has Scotland Yard demoted you to the provinces?'

15. *Grodno, in Little Russia*: Grodno is, in fact, in Belorussia rather than Little Russia (another name for the Ukraine).

CHAPTER 14
The Hound of the Baskervilles

1. *ordered to return to Coombe Tracey*: The *Strand* version has 'Temple Coombe', which was presumably a slip of Conan Doyle's pen; Temple Coombe was a railway junction miles away in Somerset.

2. *I have a hip-pocket*: A little later in the chapter, Lestrade produces a brandy flask from it rather than a pistol; unlike Holmes and Watson, he doesn't use a gun out on the moor, but produces one at Merripit House.

3. *Thank God*: The *Strand* version has the less extreme 'Thank Heaven'.

4. *Lestrade gave a yell of terror*: The inspector may be 'the best of the professionals', but he proves to be worse than useless in a crisis; he throws himself face downward to the ground and is then outrun by Dr Watson.

5. *dewlap*: Loose fold of skin beneath the dog's throat.

6. *out of the wall of fog*: At this cliff-hanging moment, the eighth instalment of the *Strand*'s serialization ended.

7. *five barrels of his revolver*: Conan Doyle must have meant five chambers, unless Holmes was armed with a pepperpot revolver with five separate barrels (very unlikely); Dr Watson is usually armed in the stories with his service revolver, Holmes with a short-barrelled Metropolitan Police Model which he keeps in his dressing-gown pocket in 'The Final Problem'.

8. *bloodhound . . . mastiff*: If the creature was a combination of the two, where did its giant size come from? Film versions have given the hound extra charisma in various ways (see Introduction) – including enhanced teeth (1939), a mask 'to make it look more terrifying' (1959) and slow-motion (1973).

9. *Phosphorus . . . A cunning preparation of it*: Very cunning indeed, since phosphorus is extremely poisonous to both man and beast as well as causing severe burns; barium sulphide has been suggested as a substitute; the 1983 film version adds the helpful line 'a phosphorescent – barium sulphide, I should imagine'.

10. *guiding wands*: Presumably marker-sticks.

11. *The two of them were destined to travel together*: No mention of Mrs Mortimer, who seems to have completely disappeared from the story by this stage.

12. *miasmatic vapour*: Like the vapour of poison gas.

13. *A huge driving-wheel and a shaft*: Perhaps a reminiscence of Whiteworks tin mine, which Conan Doyle would have seen on his recce with Fletcher Robinson; 'everywhere there are gutted tin mines', he wrote to his mother. Some were working, most were not. In the 1959 Hammer Films version of *The Hound*, Holmes (Peter Cushing) ventures into a disused mine with Mortimer and Stapleton, and the roof timbers collapse on to him.

14. *By Jove, a curly-haired spaniel*: Another great line which does not bear close scrutiny; like the footprints of a gigantic hound, the skeleton of a little dog could not possibly tell Holmes about the exact breed; in the 1983 film version of *The Hound*, a version which places unusual emphasis on animals in distress (a hunting horse struggling in the mire, as Sir Hugo rapes the young country maiden, etc.), we hear the spaniel being chewed up, squealing, by the hound.

CHAPTER 15
A Retrospection

1. *a blazing fire*: Back to the cosiness of Baker Street, where it may be foggy, but the London fog is much less sinister than the Dartmoor fog.

2. *Since the tragic upshot . . . married in New York*: These lines were omitted from the original *Strand* version.

3. *Colonel Upwood . . . the famous card scandal*: Possibly a reference to the real-life 'Baccarat Case' of 1891, in which Sir William Gordon Cumming of the Scots Guards was accused of cheating at cards and, partly thanks to the Prince of Wales's evidence, was found guilty. (However, the lines between *Since the tragic upshot* to *married in New York* were omitted from the original *Strand* version.)

4. *The barrister . . . infamous Upwood*: These lines were also omitted from the original *Strand* version.

5. *Costa Rica*: A republic of Central America, between Nicaragua and Panama; its capital city is San José.

6. *he had struck up an acquaintance . . . upon the voyage home*: Like Conan Doyle and Fletcher Robinson, on the way back from South Africa.

7. *a certain moth which he had . . . been the first to describe*: In the 1988 Granada Television version, it is this scrap of information – rather than Stapleton's 'true piece of autobiography' about being a schoolmaster in Yorkshire – which sets Holmes on the murderer's trail.

8. *Ross and Mangles*: Fictitious pet shop in southwest London.

9. *Craven Street*: Street leading from Victoria Embankment to the Strand, where there were numerous small hotels.

10. *the boots*: Servant who cleaned guests' boots.

11. outré: Odd, outrageous; one of the classic statements of Holmes's method.

12. *I cannot doubt that Stapleton*: Holmes has no hard evidence on which to base this assertion.

13. *white jessamine*: Usually called white jasmine, a shrub with sweet-smelling flowers.

14. *I had made certain of the hound, and had guessed at the criminal*: One reason why Holmes had to be removed from the story, from the beginning of Ch. 6 to the end of Ch. 11.

15. *being forwarded instantly from Baker Street*: In some of the well-known film versions, the postmistress at Grimpen secretly puts Watson's reports aside for Holmes or Cartwright to collect, rather than forwarding them to London.

16. *His love for the lady was deep and sincere*: There is no question of Sir Henry *marrying* Beryl Stapleton, now that he knows she was once Stapleton's wife; some of the well-known film versions, dating from a less puritanical age, have Sir Henry and Beryl Garçia walking off hand in hand. In the Hammer version (1959), on the other hand, Cecile Stapleton reveals, 'I too am a Baskerville, descended from Sir Hugo – descended from those who died in poverty while you scum ruled the moor!', before she sinks into the mire.

17. Les Huguenots . . . *the De Reszkes*: A French grand opera (1836) in five acts by Giacomo Meyerbeer (1791–1864); it is set just before the Massacre of St Bartholomew in 1572 when feelings between Catholics and Huguenots in France and especially Paris were on the boil, and it involves an arranged marriage which will bring both sides together. It is also very long, and seldom performed complete. The De Reszke brothers were Polish opera singers – Jean a tenor, Edouard a bass – who played leading roles at the Metropolitan Opera, New York, between 1891 and the early 1900s (including, on several occasions, in *Les Huguenots*). They also toured Europe. Writing of the increasing 'period charm' of *The Hound of the Baskervilles*, John Fowles asks 'is anything more redolent of their era than the three sentences that close this book?' (*Afterword to The Hound of the Baskervilles*, 1974, p. 196). And yet, of the best-known film versions only the Granada Television film (1988) finishes with Holmes offering Watson a visit to *Les Huguenots* at Covent Garden and 'a little dinner at Marcini's on the way'. The others opt for much more sensational endings. The 1939 Hollywood version concludes with Dr Mortimer's brink-of-war speech 'knowing that there is in England such a man as you gives us all a sense of safety and security': as Holmes (Basil Rathbone) makes his exit from Baskerville Hall, he says, 'Oh, Watson – the needle.' The 1959 Hammer version finishes at tea-time in Baker Street. 'Elementary, my dear Watson, elementary,' says Holmes (Peter Cushing). 'A muffin?' 'Oh, thank you,' says Watson. The 1973 Universal Television film has Holmes (Stewart Granger) conducting an experiment with nitroglycerine back in his Baker Street rooms, with Watson's nervous assistance, and promising future adventures. The 1977 Paul Morrissey comedy has the hound established as the true heir to the estate, leaving Baskerville Hall attached to a family portrait: 'And So . . . the Dog Stole the Picture' is the caption, written as if on the last page of the book. The 1983 Douglas Hickox version has Watson saying to Holmes, still at Baskerville Hall, that the legend was 'a figment of the imagination': Holmes (Ian Richardson) turns to the camera and says with a slight smile, 'But without the imagination, Watson, there would be no horror.' The 2002 BBC film has Holmes and Watson returning by train from Christmas at Baskerville Hall, examining a photograph of the two of them standing beside the carcass of the dead hound – strung up like a hunting trophy – and Holmes saying as he reads *The Times*, 'I have a box for *Les Huguenots* tonight – I thought a little dinner at Marcini's on the way' – to which Watson replies, 'The answer to your question is "no", no I don't trust you. But Marcini's would be nice'. Where all these alternative endings are concerned, Conan Doyle's novel still remains more subtle, and much more fun.